Candace and Jameson

BY DESIGN

Episodes One through Four

J.A. Armstrong

Text © Copyright 2015 J.A. Armstrong Books

All Rights Reserved. This book, or parts thereof, may not be reproduced without permission.

ISBN 10: 1514385007

ISBN 13: 978-1514385005

BY DESIGN

Chapter One

"I don't care," Candace Fletcher said to the man in front of her desk. "I don't care if the president himself told you that. That was not our agreement, and you know it."

"Now, Candy…be reasonable," Bob Miller said cautiously.

"What is it…exactly…Bob, that you find unreasonable in my position?"

"The president needs you on this."

"The president is not my boss. The people of New York are. You want me to endorse something that will further cut spending on infrastructure in a state that houses one the largest cities in the world." Bob opened his mouth to speak, and Candace ran right over him. "A city that depends on public transportation to function. Might I remind you of the cost to the city of New York, the cost to business, and the cost to the federal government when New Yorkers can't get to work?"

"You're being a bit dramatic, don't you think?" he said. Candace smiled so sweetly at Bob Miller he thought she might give him a cavity. That spelled trouble.

"Dramatic? Well, I do like the theater. No, Bob. I am thinking ahead. So, when the subways are stopped, or the George Washington Bridge is forced to close down, or the Lincoln Tunnel suddenly springs a leak, you can tell President Wallace that he can explain why we allowed that to happen to millions of people. People wo will be angry, inconvenienced and losing pay. And, he can justify that to the companies losing profit."

"Candy…"

"Don't you dare Candy me. Get me a proposal that is reasonable and I will be agreeable."

Bob Miller sighed. "This job sucks," he groaned.

Candace laughed heartily and came around her desk. "Well, Mr. Vice President, welcome to The White House," she laughed some more.

"Oh yeah, it's a joy," he returned.

"You wanted the job," she reminded him.

"Well, if you had shown any interest," he began earnestly.

Candace laughed harder. "Oh, yes, a fifty-five-year-old, divorced mother of three who happens to be a lesbian, that's always the first choice on a presidential ballot."

"Senator Fletcher?" a woman's voice called through the door.

"Come in Susan," Candace said. "The vice president was just leaving."

"Still having that Christmas party?" the vice president asked.

"Me? Turn down the chance to throw a party? Should I expect your regrets?" she asked her old friend.

"Not even a Republican landslide could prevent me from making that party."

"Bite your tongue," Candace said. "The election is only two weeks away. No way are we losing that much ground."

"I'll talk to our people," he assured her.

"I know you will. I can't endorse it, Bob," she said almost apologetically.

The vice president nodded. "I'll be in touch."

Candace watched him leave and chuckled. "Poor thing," she said before turning to her personal assistant. "I have no idea why he wanted that job."

Susan shrugged. "Why wouldn't he? Wouldn't you?"

"Hell no!" Candace answered with another laugh. "No way. I am happy where I am until I retire or get my ass handed to me."

"When do you think that might be?" Susan asked jokingly.

"Depends on which way it happens," Candace answered. She took a seat in a large leather chair and stretched.

"Well, from where I sit you do most of the 'quote' ass handing," Susan observed. Candace raised an amused brow at her assistant. "And, as for retirement? They'll be wheeling your ass in here while you hand them theirs at the same time, oxygen tank and all I am sure."

Candace smirked. "So? What do you have for me?" she asked.

"Just the usual. Dana dropped off your press schedule, and Brian said he would get you the revised budget request from the Department of Transportation."

"Great. That's timely," Candace mumbled.

"Not a great meeting, I take it?" Susan surmised.

"It was fine." Senator Candace Fletcher was the chairman of the Transportation, Housing, and Urban Development Subcommittee. Appropriations. The job always came down to appropriations. How much money who could have to spend and where they would be spending it. That was the name of the game. Candace groaned. "I have no idea where they are going to pull more money from," she said. "All I do know is that we have a lot to repair before we end up in a situation we can't fix so easily."

"Speaking of," Susan said as she handed the senator a folder.

"What's this?"

"Dana dropped it off with your press schedule. Said to tell you it's Steven's college friend that she mentioned," Susan explained.

"Oh, the illustrious architect he had such glowing praise for," Candy commented.

Candy loved her staff. Susan had been with her since her days in the New York State Senate. Dana Russo was Candy's press secretary. Dana's husband, Steven owned a large law firm in Maryland. He and Candace were kindred spirits. Both graduated from Cornell University, both studied political science and international law, and both had a secret passion for National League Baseball. Dana often joked that the only reason Senator Fletcher wanted her on staff was so she could drink beer with Steven, talk about Cornell, and watch the Mets.

"Well, interesting," Candy mused as she studied the contents of the folder. "J.D. Reid Architectural Design. Jameson Reid. Summa Cum Laude from Cornell University 2002," Candy read from the file. "And then again in 2005. Huh? Wonder if Jameson likes the Mets," Candy laughed.

"Still thinking of having the house restored?" Susan asked.

Candy smiled. She loved her home in upstate New York. She'd bought it from her brother shortly after her father's death. For years, she had thought of restoring it to its original grandeur, and building an addition to expand the kitchen. "Oh, well…I am thinking about it," she said.

"You've been thinking about it for the last fifteen years. Why not just do it?" Susan asked.

"The kids aren't interested in the house," Candy replied. Susan could detect a note of sadness in the senator's voice. "You know, they think I was crazy to have even bought it from David. If they had their way, I would sell it now and downsize," Candy snickered sarcastically. "I swear they think after fifty you are just planning for the nursing home," she laughed.

Susan nodded. The senator had three grown children, Marianne, Michelle, and Jonah. Susan had known them since they were small. They adored their mother, but they did not always understand her choices. Not the least of which was her coming out at forty-three as a lesbian after her divorce from their father. "They probably all want you to move closer to them so you can babysit."

Candy snorted. "Well, last I checked the senator from New York did not keep residence in Massachusetts, California, or heaven forbid, Texas. No, I am a Yankee through and through," she said. "They think smaller. Buy a condo. Buy a townhouse," she laughed again. "Not my style."

"So…call Mr. Reid," Susan suggested.

"Maybe I will," Candy said.

"Did I miss something?" Steven Russo asked his friend.

Jameson laughed. "No, you didn't miss anything."

"I thought this was your one true passion," he joked. "So, what's the problem?" he wondered.

"God, I hope that's not my only passion," Jameson laughed. "Steve, you know how I feel about politics."

"Yeah, well you aren't going there to debate her. You're going there to look at her house," he pointed out.

Jameson looked at the photograph of the Georgian-style colonial home. The house had been built in 1798. This picture was dated 1998. Moderate changes were evident. The windows were custom, far more modern than the period that they were meant to reflect. The old clapboards at some point had been replaced with what appeared to be synthetic siding. The landscaping was pristine, certainly not the type that would have adorned this building in its youth. Jameson sighed. It was true. This was her passion. It was not the kind of work that made her millions. It was the kind of project that was, simply put, fun. This was a project she could dig into, research, design, and that would allow her to get her hands dirty.

"Come on J.D., just go talk to her," Steven urged his friend.

Jameson puckered her lips and arched her eyebrow. "Fine."

Steven flashed a sly grin at his friend. "You won't regret it."

Jameson had to snicker at the hop in her friend's step as he left the room, phone in hand. She shook her head ruefully. "Why do I have a very bad feeling about this?" she muttered.

🐴 🐴 🐴

Candace stretched and rubbed her tired eyes. The weekend had been exhausting. Tuesday was Election Day, and that meant the last week had been full of stumping for local candidates and the district congressman. Typically, she thrived on this season. Campaigning could be tiresome, but Candace had spent her life around politics. It was in her blood. Her father had been a congressman for twenty years before his unexpected death, and her grandfather had served as Governor of New York for two terms. Candace's brothers had both served locally, but neither seemed to have caught the "bug" as her father called it. She enjoyed meeting people, pressing the flesh as the like to call it, and rallying a crowd. This year, however, she was struggling with fatigue.

There were multiple issues weighing on the senator's mind. Her children, while she adored all three, were increasing the pressure on her to consider stepping back a bit from the fast lane. Candace found their concern amusing most days. Marianne was twenty-eight and had just had her first baby. She lived in Austin with her tech-savvy husband, Rick. Candace was still not sure exactly what her son-in-law did. He was a southern boy through and through, and her daughter's move to Texas seemed inevitable once she was engaged. Marianne seemed to think that Candace should start considering retirement. She pointed out that her mother's considerable wealth meant that Candace would never have to work again. And, why wouldn't she want to be closer to her family? Candace had tried numerous times to explain gently that she had three children that qualified as family, and that she enjoyed her work. Marianne was much more like her Candace's ex-husband. She had been daddy's girl from day one. Candace finally suggested her eldest child might have more success in an attempt to entice her ex-husband to the Lone-Star State.

Michelle was Candace's middle child, and by all accounts the most like her mother. She had chosen to stay closer to home after graduating college and was teaching high school outside of Boston. Candace was eternally grateful for Michelle. They frequently visited and Michelle seemed to understand Candace's life more than her other children. When Candace and her husband Don split, it was Michelle who had remained her mother's stalwart supporter.

Candace's youngest child, It wasn't twenty-two and was

pursuing his graduate studies at Caltech. Jonah tended to stay out of the family mix as much as possible. He had little interest in the political landscape, and Candace was aware that her public persona sometimes caused her son a degree of discomfort. She was unsure if that had more to do with her political positions or her sexuality. She suspected it was a bit of both. Many of Jonah's friends came from conservative backgrounds. Candace was satisfied that he had made his peace with her life, but she was often in the press. She suspected Jonah took a fair amount of ribbing over the years from his peers about his mother's relationship.

Personal issues and stresses aside, there were several pieces of controversial legislation set to be addressed in the new session. It was never comfortable to depart from one's party platform. Candace had done it before, but never on a major piece of legislation. The president had a new education bill that he was set to propose. The House had made its revisions, and the issue was expected to come before the Senate early in the new legislative session. Candace sighed as her thoughts ran over the finer points that concerned her. It wasn't the spirit or intention of the legislation that bothered her. The devil, as they say, was in the details. There were too many loopholes, too many obscure expenditures that she did not feel had any business in an education bill. If she decided to vote against the bill, others would likely follow. It was a decision she would need to weigh carefully, and just thinking about it was bringing on a formidable headache. She was ready to pour herself a stiff drink when she was startled by the doorbell. Candace looked at the large grandfather clock and furrowed her brow. "Who the hell could that be?"

Jameson made her way up the narrow brick pathway to the front door of Candace Fletcher's home. She studied the building in front of her as she walked. It had been well preserved, but clearly updated throughout the years. She wondered what the senator envisioned. Jameson could see the structure in her mind's eye as it would have appeared just over two hundred years ago. It brought a brief smile to her lips, and she took a moment to imagine the area with no driveways, roads, or street lights. "Must have been magnificent," she mused. Jameson took a deep breath and reached out to ring the doorbell. "This ought to be interesting," she chuckled.

🫏 🫏 🫏

"Pearl?" Candace called out. She was making her way toward the door when the older woman met her. "Are we expecting someone?"

Pearl's eyes crinkled in amusement. She had worked for Candace's family for years and considered the senator one of her children. "You mentioned someone coming about the house," she winked at Candace.

"Oh my God, that's right! How did I forget that? Damn good thing I'm not in my robe already."

Pearl shook her head. It was only four o'clock and Candace was never that comfortable before the clock struck nine or ten. "You want me to send him away?" Pearl joked.

Candace waved the older woman off. "Go home, already," she scolded. "I'll take care of Mr. Reid," she assured. She was still busy shooing the older woman away when she pulled the door open. "Go on, go home," she waved Pearl off.

"I just got here," Jameson offered lightly.

Candace caught the amused expression on Pearl's face and turned to the figure in her doorway. It took her a moment to register the sight. "I'm sorry? Can I help you?"

"I think the question is—can I help you?" Jameson replied. Candace stood bewildered. "J.D. Reid," Jameson said as she extended her hand.

"The architect?"

"That's what the degree claims," Jameson countered.

Candace finally smiled. "I'm sorry. I was expecting…"

"Let me guess, someone slightly taller with more facial

hair." Jameson winked playfully. "Guess Steven left a few details out."

"Yes, he did," Candace admitted. "Come in." She watched as Jameson walked through the door and shook her head. "I am sorry," Candace apologized.

"No need to apologize Senator Fletcher. Steven has a unique sense of humor sometimes."

Candace nodded. "That he does," she agreed. "And, please, just Candace." Jameson nodded. "So, Ms. Reid…"

Jameson stopped the senator's thoughts. "J.D."

"I'm sorry?"

"J.D., that's my name, Candace."

Candace laughed. "Touché. So, J.D., what do you think of the house?"

"From the outside?" J.D. asked lightly. Candace nodded. "It's beautiful."

"But?"

"No but."

Candace frowned playfully. "Ah, J.D. I've made a career out of my ability to read people. There is definitely a but."

"It would be even grander without the modernization."

"Which is why I called you," Candace returned. "Would you like to see the inside?" she offered. Jameson nodded.

Candace spent the better part of the next hour ushering Jameson through her home. She explained the history of ownership and reveled in the attentiveness of the architect. Jameson remained quiet, listening to each detail and every anecdote with fascination. Candace watched Jameson's eyes study each room methodically. It was clear that the architect was noting even the finest details. Jameson's eyes seemed to twinkle when Candace would offer a short story about some historical moment in the home, or some treasured memory that had been passed down.

"So, this house has been in your family for a while," Jameson commented as the senator led her toward the kitchen.

"Five generations, so yes. Can I offer you something?" Candace asked as they entered the kitchen. "Wine, coffee? Water?" she asked as she set about starting a pot of coffee. "I know. It's late. It's my addiction."

"It's never too late for coffee in my book," Jameson replied. "I'd love a cup."

"Well then, I suppose we have at least two things in common."

"Two?" Jameson asked.

"We share a love of old houses, history, and coffee."

"Three," Jameson said.

"What?" Candace asked as she pulled the cream from the refrigerator.

"That's three things we have in common unless I counted wrong."

"Ah, I suppose so. So, tell me, J.D., I've seen your portfolio. You've designed some impressive buildings. Why an interest in this old place? And interior design?"

Jameson smiled. The truth was that Jameson had not had an opportunity to work on any historical projects in a long time. Her time and efforts had been consumed with building her firm. She had deliberately taken on larger projects for the last few years, designing corporate buildings and industrial complexes. Her success allowed her to bring on four additional architects and a robust support staff. Now, she was ready to take a small step back and return to her roots. This project had come about at the perfect time.

"Well, it's true. The last seven years have been full of larger projects. And, those are always challenging, but not nearly as exciting as something like this," Jameson said. She noted the curious glint in the senator's eye. "I have a secret passion for American History," she explained. "My mother was a teacher. My father worked in construction. I guess the two were destined to meet in me," she shrugged. "As far as design, I don't know how you dismiss one from the other. A home is the sum of all its parts. It's what makes projects like this so much more interesting than designing office buildings. There is history. Memories. The buildings I design have yet to tell their story."

"A soft spot for history, I see."

"Like I said, it was destined," Jameson answered. "I spent years with my father traveling to jobs. I loved to watch him work. Every house he worked on, he would remind me that it was someone's treasure. It was their home, never a structure, always a story," Jameson explained. "Crazy?"

"Hardly," Candace said before shifting gears. "What do you think about it? The house, I mean," Candace clarified as she placed a steaming cup of coffee in front of Jameson. "Is it doable?"

"Doable? Anything is doable, Senator," Jameson quipped.

Candace nearly spit out her coffee. Jameson had a dry humor and a quick wit. "You sure you aren't a politician?"

"Nope. No politics here. Safer that way," Jameson answered. She was surprised to see Candace's cheerful expression dim slightly. "I'm sorry. I didn't mean that the way it sounded." Candace smiled. "To answer your question, I think the house could be restored very closely to its original look. And, yes, I am confident we can design an addition off of this room that will appear seamless. Of course, with all the modern conveniences. We'll look to blend the old and the new eloquently. Assuming that is what you are hoping for."

"It is. What about cost?"

Jameson took a sip of her coffee. "That depends a great deal on materials, and on what might be discovered underneath all the layers. I can get you a ballpark figure on the exterior and the addition. Interior costs will depend on what you choose for materials. I'll send you some samples and ideas. I have the photos you sent. Any photos you have through the years will be helpful. I'll try to find similar options wherever possible. You see what strikes you. We can go from there. That is, assuming you think my proposal is *doable?*"

Candace narrowed her gaze at the architect. "Why don't you get me that information and I will make my assessment of its 'doability,' shall we say?"

"Is that a political term?" Jameson asked. Candace's reply was a simple wink. "This could be very interesting," Jameson thought silently. "Very."

Chapter Two

"You left a few details out," Senator Fletcher pointed to her press secretary.

"Mwah?" Dana feigned her innocence. Candace arched a fair eyebrow at her friend. "What did you think of J.D.?" Dana asked, barely concealing a sly smirk.

"Intelligent, charming, witty," Candace said a bit whimsically.

"And?" Dana urged knowingly.

"Oh, no, you don't! I know where this is heading."

"Come on now, Senator, admit it. She's not hard to look at," Dana said.

"She's young enough to be my daughter," Candace said flatly.

"She's thirty-five, Candy."

"Are you trying to help me remodel my home or are you trying to reconstruct my love life?" Candace asked.

"Well, they are both a bit dusty, so they could both use a little attention if you ask me."

"I didn't ask you," Candace replied a bit harshly.

Dana sighed and shook her head. "Are you going to hire her?"

Candace sipped her coffee and took a seat across from her friend. "Yes….to work on the house, not to remodel my love life."

"Mm-hm."

"Dana," Candace called in her best warning tone.

"Why not? Because she's younger than you? Come on, don't tell me you don't find her attractive."

Candace kneaded her temples. She had been thinking about Jameson more frequently than she ever planned to admit to her friend. It wasn't J.D.'s looks that had engaged Candace the most, not that she hadn't noticed how attractive the architect was. J.D. Reid possessed a quality that Candace did not often find in others. She carried herself with a quiet confidence that enhanced her natural good looks. That was the only way Candace could think to describe the younger woman—natural. Jameson had long, chestnut hair that fell in natural waves just below her shoulders. If the architect had been wearing any makeup, it had not been easily detectable. The feature that captured Candace's attention the most were Jameson Reid's eyes. They were a soft brown that Candace had noticed seemed to lighten to a faint golden tone when Jameson was amused or intrigued, something that seemed to occur quite often in their short time together.

Candace had enjoyed Jameson's company. Their conversation had wound its way into late evening. Jameson had shared a bit about her family and reluctantly admitted that she knew very little about baseball. Candace had even found herself opening up about her life far more than was customary to a virtual stranger.

Dana tried not to laugh at the expression on the senator's face. She'd met Candace Fletcher when she was interning for another senator during college, and immediately decided that someday she would work for Senator Fletcher. She admired the older woman. Dana valued the senator both as a friend and as a mentor. Those who were closest to Candace Fletcher understood that her life had become lonely in the last few years. A year after Candace's divorce, the senator had become involved with Jessica Stearns. Jessica had been a prominent New York lawyer. The relationship had lasted seven years. In that time, Dana had seen Candace happier than ever before. The ending of the relationship, however, proved painful and bitter.

Jessica had been caught in an affair with another lawyer in her firm. It had been splashed across the news media, made its way onto nearly every magazine cover and tainted Candace's political clout for nearly a year. Worse, it had devastated the senator personally. Trust was a precious commodity in political life. The senator had risked a great deal to follow her heart. Her political career had been tested with her decision to come out as a lesbian at all. The announcement of her relationship with the attorney and the ensuing personal appearances as a couple drew a bevy of critics with harsh and hurtful words. Candace's children had struggled with the demise of their parents' marriage, and then with their mother's new reality. Jessica's betrayal was heartbreaking for Candace. She poured herself into her work after that. And, she kept her distance from potential romantic entanglements. It had been more than a few years since Dana had witnessed the sparkle in Candace's eye that just mentioning Jameson prompted.

"Senator?" Candace heard Dana calling to her and suddenly realized that she had drifted off in thought. "Is that it?"

"What?" Candace asked.

"The age difference. Is that what bothers you about J.D.?"

Candace sighed heavily. "Dana, I barely know her. And, I have no interest in a relationship with anyone. You know that."

"If you say so."

"I do say so, so let's just change the subject," Candace replied abruptly.

"When are you seeing her again?" Dana persisted.

"What?"

"Well, you said you were hiring her. I would assume that means you will be seeing her again," Dana pointed out.

"I don't know," Candace said. "We've exchanged a few emails. Pearl will take care of whatever she needs while I am away," Candace attempted to end the conversation. "Now, what is on today's agenda?"

Dana sighed inwardly and proceeded to hand the senator the day's press schedule. Candace continually kneaded at her temples as she reviewed it and played with the glasses resting on the bridge of her nose. Dana was certain that the senator's behavior was driven by something other than the day's schedule. It might not have been obvious to most people, Dana was sure that J.D. Reid had piqued Candace Fletcher's curiosity. "I wonder what J.D. thought of you," she mused silently.

"No, Melanie. I am headed back upstate today," Jameson said.

"The project with the senator, or are you just heading toward home?" Melanie McKenna asked.

"Both," Jameson replied without looking up from her desk.

"So, what's she like?" Melanie asked her boss. Jameson was focused on the sketches Melanie had brought in for her to review and did not respond to the question. "Hello! Earth to J.D.!" she called again.

"What?"

"I asked what she is like."

"Who?" Jameson asked as he studied the papers before her.

"Senator Fletcher. What's she like?"

Jameson pushed the plans aside and looked up at her friend. "She's nice enough."

"She's nice enough? Oh, come on, J.D.! Is she a dragon lady or is she all prim and proper?"

"What is your fascination with Candace?"

"Candace? Hum, that's pretty informal. What happened to Senator Fletcher?"

Jameson rolled her eyes. "Since when are you so interested in a politician?"

"Candace Fletcher is not just a politician, J.D. She's one of the most respected women in Washington."

Jameson chuckled. "Do you have a crush on my client?"

Melanie shrugged. "You do! You have a crush on Candace Fletcher!" Jameson laughed.

"So what if I do?"

"Mel, might I remind you that you and the good senator bat for different teams," Jameson said.

"Well, I can be flexible."

Jameson shook her head in amusement. Melanie was the newest and youngest architect in Jameson's firm. She was bright, energetic, and talented. Jameson had to admit that the main reason she brought Melanie on, however, was her humor. "Uh-huh," Jameson raised an eyebrow. "Older women and younger men, huh?"

"Whatever works. Besides, Candace Fletcher is gorgeous," Melanie commented. Jameson looked back at the papers on her desk and gave a slight nod. "She is. Isn't she? Huh? Come on, J.D.! Is it all camera tricks or is she as stunning in person?"

"She's attractive," Jameson said quietly.

Melanie grinned slyly. "She's single, you know?"

"Mm-hm."

"And, she is a lesbian."

"Yes, I think I might have heard that," Jameson replied.

"So, maybe you...."

"Enough matchmaking. She's a client, Mel. But, if you are interested...."

"Yeah, yeah," Melanie laughed.

Jameson smiled. "Plans look good," she complimented the younger woman's work. "Be ready to present it next week," she instructed as she made her way to retrieve her jacket. "Bryan will lead the meeting."

"You're not going to be here?" Melanie asked in disbelief. "J.D. this is a huge account."

"Yes, I know. You've done a fantastic job. Branmore will be thrilled with your proposal. Bryan will keep you steady."

"Where are you going to be?"

Jameson winked. "I have my own client to take care of. Remember?"

Melanie narrowed her gaze at her boss as Jameson strutted out of the office. "Oh, you think you're fooling me, huh?" she whispered as Jameson walked out the door. "Not fooling me. You like the senator. Hah! I knew it!"

Pearl opened the door and greeted Jameson with a warm smile. "Well, I guess she didn't scare you away," she winked.

"Oh, it would take more than an ornery old senator to scare me away from all this," Jameson gestured to the home.

"Well, that's good to know, Ms. Reid. Cause between you and me? My little Candy can be a handful."

Jameson returned the older woman's smile. "Known the senator a long time, I take it?"

"You could say that," Pearl replied as she led Jameson through the house. "Her granddad hired me in nineteen sixty-eight. Candy was eight," the woman explained. Jameson tried to picture an eight-year-old Candace. She snickered. Pearl led Jameson through the house into the kitchen and directed her to take a seat. "Hard to imagine her that way. I know."

Jameson smiled. "Not really," she said.

Pearl nodded. She had kept quiet with the senator about her suspicions. After Jameson Reid's first visit she had noticed a lift in Candace's spirits, and a measurable bounce in the senator's step. At first, Pearl had chalked up the change to Candace's excitement over finally remodeling the house. It was a project she had talked about for years. This house, Pearl understood, meant a great deal to Candace Fletcher. As a child, Candace found any excuse she could to visit her grandparents. When her father inherited the house, he had immediately passed it on to her brother David. Candace's disappointment had been evident. As soon as David expressed an interest in selling the home, Candace swept in.

It was also evident to the older woman that there was more to Candace's sudden shift in moods. Candace was like a daughter to Pearl. It had always been impossible for Candace to hide the truth from the older woman about anything. Pearl began to suspect that the young woman now seated in front of her might be the cause of Candace's vitalized spirit. Pearl had entered the kitchen the morning after Jameson's first visit to find the senator engrossed in her computer. That was not unusual. What struck the older woman as strange was the grin that kept edging its way onto Candace's expression. She watched curiously as Candace would shake her head, type furiously, and then chuckle.

She finally asked what had the senator so amused at six-thirty on a chilly November morning.

"One second," Candace had replied. "No parakeets in the living room," Candace muttered. Pearl wrinkled her nose in confusion as Candace hit the enter button on her keyboard dramatically. "What did you ask me?" Candace turned her attention briefly to the older woman.

"I asked what has you so amused this early in the morning," Pearl repeated her question.

Candace started to answer and then looked at the computer screen. "Orinthophobe! Ha! She probably thinks I need to look that up."

Pearl shook her head. "You dealing with another health care bill?" Pearl guessed.

"What?" Candace asked. "Oh, no," she said as she typed. "Smart ass. No, no, Pearl, I am dealing with a snarky architect."

"Is there a cure?" Pearl asked cheekily.

Candace was gloating over something she had written. "A cure for the snarky or for the architect?" Candace quipped. Pearl turned away to conceal her smirk. She heard Candace let forth a caustic chuckle. "Yeah, I know. I know what a hip roof is. No, I don't think they had them at Woodstock, you lunatic! And, no I wasn't there. I was nine."

Pearl listened for the next twenty minutes while the senator typed away, making comments as she went, occasionally groaning, only to start laughing in another instant. "You know, you're going to miss your flight if you don't get moving," Pearl reminded the senator.

"Oh, shit!" Candace chastised herself. "Crap! It's almost seven. Why didn't you say something?"

"You seemed intent on solving your snarky artifact problem," Pearl said.

Candace finished typing something and closed her computer. "Architect, Pearl. It's a snarky architect, a snarky, expensive architect."

"Well, I'm sure you'll find a remedy," Pearl responded.

"I always do," Candace said with a kiss to the older woman's cheek. "I will see you next Tuesday."

"I'll be here."

Pearl pulled herself from her musings and noted that Jameson was watching her attentively. "So, what does my Candy have in store for you?" she asked the architect.

Jameson laughed. "Something tells me that I should be the one asking you that question," Jameson replied.

"You'll do just fine," Pearl said. "You want some coffee, Ms. Reid?"

Jameson looked around the large kitchen. "J.D." Pearl gave the architect an odd look. "My name is J.D. or Jameson, whichever. And, coffee would be great."

"So, Jameson," Pearl began. "What are your plans for this old place?"

Jameson pulled out her laptop. "Would you like to see some of them?" she asked excitedly. Pearl nodded and took a seat beside the young woman. "It all really depends on Candace,"

Jameson said earnestly as she booted up her computer. She pointed to the screen. "I've discovered she has a bird aversion."

"A bird aversion?"

"Yeah," Jameson said pointing to the screen again. "In the eighteenth-century wall coverings were block printed. See, here? I suggested parakeets. She didn't like that concept," Jameson smiled.

Pearl tried not to laugh as she gained a new understanding of the senator's musings earlier in the week. "I see."

"Um. So, I suggested pigeons," Jameson showed the older woman a different design.

"Pigeons?"

"Um. She didn't like that either. Bird aversion."

Pearl laughed heartily. "You're not too far off there," she said.

"Really? Candace is afraid of birds?" Jameson asked. "Oh shit," she whispered. "I've been sending her bird designs all week," she said.

Pearl watched the color drain from Jameson's face and chuckled. She put a comforting hand on the architect's shoulder. "No, no. She's not afraid of them," she said. Jameson looked up hopefully. "She had a pet canary when she was small. Her older brother let it out of the cage one day and," Pearl stopped.

"And?"

"Jinx ate it."

"Jinx?"

"Her brother's cat."

"Oh, no," Jameson said, trying to contain her laugh.

"Oh, yes. She cried for days. So sensitive, that one," Pearl said affectionately.

Jameson listened and couldn't help but smile. "She loves this house," Jameson said softly.

"Yes, she does," Pearl agreed. "Candy was her

granddaddy's baby. She was the apple of his eye. She followed him everywhere. He loved this old place. Had a story for every nook and cranny, he did. He was a good man," Pearl said wistfully. "She told you a bit about him?"

"She did," Jameson said. "Actually, she told me a great deal about spending time here as a little girl. How she always hoped she'd raise her children here."

Pearl was surprised as she listened to Jameson recap some of the highlights of her conversations with Candace. Candace was an adept communicator, and she loved people, but she had become gradually more reserved in allowing people to get close to her over the years. Pearl wondered what it was about the architect that opened the senator up so quickly. Pearl set a cup of coffee in front of Jameson. "She would have loved to have this house for the kids. It has never meant to them what it does to her," she stated a bit sadly. "For them, home is just a house. They don't have those memories," she continued. Pearl sighed. "They moved time and again. That was Jonathan. Bigger and bigger," she said with a shake of her head. "Candace used to have to fight just to cook their dinners."

"Candace's ex?" Jameson asked softly.

"Indeed," Pearl said. Jameson looked up at the older woman inquisitively. "They both came from prominent families," Pearl said. "Jonathan's employed a rather large staff. He was raised by nannies and housekeepers," she explained. She winked at the unspoken question in Jameson's eyes and laughed. "Governor Stratton had only two people in his employ, myself and Mr. Bridges, his driver. Honestly, neither of us did much," she laughed. "Mrs. Stratton seldom allowed me to cook a meal by myself, and all of her children were expected to contribute to the household duties. I was only seventeen when I started with the Strattons," she reminisced. "I could barely boil water." Pearl smiled at Jameson. "That's why Candy loved it here," Pearl said. "There was always something to do, always something to explore.

Candy's father married a woman much like her husband turned out to be. That was never Candy's way," she explained. "She wanted to learn everything about everything. When her father was away, you could always find her here with her Granddad and Gram. I think it about killed her when they both left this world. And, then she lost her father. David had this house," Pearl sighed deeply. "He didn't require my services."

"He fired you?"

Pearl chuckled. "Gracious no. David may be a bit spoiled, but he would never have dismissed his Pearlie," she said. "Candy needed me more at that time. The kids were small, she was running for office. It made more sense for me to be there for her," she said. "I was never so glad when David sold this house to her. I remember she walked through the house for hours that first day as if she needed to recall every moment." Pearl winked at the architect. "Well, I'll leave you to it."

"Pearl?" Jameson called after the older woman. Pearl turned inquisitively. "What is her favorite room?"

Pearl smiled. "That's easy, her Granddad's study."

"Do you remember?" Jameson asked. "What it looked like then?"

Pearl's expression softened. "Governor Stratton never touched that room. It stayed the same until David changed it. The wallpaper was tattered from age. The Governor could never bring himself to change it. It reminded him of his father." Pearl slipped into a memory. "She is so much like him," she said softly. She sighed again as she recalled the older man. "Yes. It was ornate even in its disrepair. Orange and reds as I recall."

"Thank you, Pearl. I may be wandering around the house on and off," Jameson said.

Pearl nodded. She began to make her way out of the kitchen and turned back to see Jameson focused intently on her computer screen. The expression reminded her of Candy's. She shook her head. "I wonder if either of them even see it," she chuckled.

Chapter Three

"Everything is open to negotiation except birds and cats. No birds. No cats." Jameson read the email and laughed. She snickered slightly and sent off a singular picture in response. Jameson waited for the reply. None came.

"You did say anything was open to negotiation," she fired off a short quip. Jameson loved toying with the senator. Their banter had lightened her days these last two weeks. In truth, she was keeping her promise to adhere as closely to the original style of the house as possible. She was certain that Candace knew that, but it seemed they both took great pleasure in this game. She was surprised that there was still no response from the senator. Normally, Candace had a quick retort. Senator Fletcher was a busy woman, and Jameson shrugged it off. There was certainly more pressing matters for Candace to address than Jameson's antics.

Jameson returned to her task of mapping out the kitchen so that she could design the addition off the back of the house. She found herself musing that she was grateful that winter was upon them. It meant that any construction would have to wait. Secretly, that gave her an excuse to draw out this project longer than she needed to. Candace Fletcher intrigued her. The sound of the phone in the distance and Pearls' voice interrupted her pondering.

"Why are you calling the house phone? Don't you have her number? Um-hum. Jameson!" Pearl's voice rang through the house. Jameson walked sheepishly into the large living room. She pointed to herself as if to question Pearl's need for her presence. Pearl shook her head and handed the phone to the architect. "It's for you," she said. "I don't know what you did to get her to call home," she chuckled.

"Hello?" Jameson said tentatively.

"Ms. Reid," a stern voice came over the line.

"Yes?"

"You apparently did not pay much attention in American History class, did you?" Candace questioned as if cross-examining a witness.

"I would beg to differ."

"Well, the evidence would suggest otherwise," Candace replied.

"You have evidence? I wasn't aware that I was on trial."

"In which part of history did you find naked marble men the most prominent?" Jameson tried not to laugh at Candace's attempt to drill her. "Ms. Reid?"

"I suppose Ancient. That would be Roman or Greek."

"Does my home look Roman or Greek to you?"

"Actually, Senator, it does," Jameson replied.

"My Colonial American home appears Greek to you?"

"Roman," Jameson returned.

"I'm sorry?"

"No need to be sorry, Senator. You apparently skipped architecture as an elective," Jameson snickered. "James Gibbs is credited with much of the English style your home reflects, as well as most notable buildings of the period."

"And he was Roman?"

"No, he was Scottish, but he studied in Rome in the early eighteenth century and his designs reflect that Roman influence," Jameson explained. "So, you see, as a point of fact, Roman statuary is actually a well-placed addition, particularly for one with as much reverence for history as you have, Senator Fletcher," Jameson gloated. The continuing silence began to unnerve her slightly. "Senator?"

"Well, aren't you just the cat that ate the canary," Candace replied.

"No, as I understand it his name was Jinx."

Another moment of silence was finally broken by Candace's roar of laughter. "You are a complete lunatic. Just how many skeletons have you discovered in my home?"

"Only the ones Pearl is willing to unearth," Jameson replied.

"That does not bode well for me," Candace sobered.

"Actually, it bodes quite well for you," Jameson replied sincerely. She and Candace had only had a few phone conversations over the last two weeks, but each had been enjoyable. Each time they had found a reason to speak, the conversation had naturally turned to discussing their days. And, each time they spoke, Jameson had found she would become spellbound by the senator's stories and her voice. Jameson found Pearl's nuggets about the senator endearing. The older woman had great affection for Candace. It was a sentiment that Jameson was beginning to understand intimately.

Candace felt Jameson's compliment lodge itself in her chest. She closed her eyes for a moment to quiet an unexpected rise of emotion. What was it about Jameson Reid that captivated her? She looked forward to Jameson's emails. She realized as the silence lingered on the line, that when more than a few hours passed without any contact from the architect, she felt disappointed. She cleared her throat. "Don't believe a word she says," Candace said lightly.

"I believe every word," Jameson said. "So, no statuary, no birds, and no felines. Any specific requests?"

"Chinese," Candace replied.

"You want me to decorate this house with an Asian influence?" Jameson asked skeptically.

"No, I want Chinese food."

Jameson laughed. "I'm afraid I am a little far to deliver on that request."

"How long are you going to be occupying my kitchen?"

"What?"

"It's a simple question, Jameson. How long can I expect you to be in my kitchen?"

"Probably another few hours. Why?"

"Do you have any specific requests?"

Jameson was lost. "I don't…."

"For Chinese food," Candace clarified. She started laughing. "I am sitting in the airport right now," she explained. "I should be home in about two hours. I thought perhaps you could show me what you've been working on over dinner."

"I would love to."

"So, any requests?"

"Surprise me," Jameson said in challenge.

Candace felt her face flush at the intended flirtation she detected. "Be careful what you wish for, Jameson."

"Sweet or spicy, Senator. I can handle it."

Candace chuckled. "Noted. I will see you in a couple of hours."

Jameson disconnected the call and stood staring at the phone in her hands. "Did I just flirt with Candace Fletcher? Oh my God, did she just flirt with me?" Jameson put the phone back in its cradle and wandered into the kitchen.

Pearl looked up and saw the architect's dazed expression. "You all right? She didn't fire you, did she?" Pearl asked half-kidding, half-worried over the expression on Jameson's face.

"What? No, she's bringing home Chinese."

Pearl pursed her lips in amusement. "Do you not like Chinese food?"

"What? No. I….I need to put this all together to show her. She already thinks I'm crazy."

Pearl shook her head watching Jameson focus on her new task. "Oh, you're crazy all right," she thought. "Crazy about my Candy."

Jameson heard Candace's voice as the front door opened and felt her heart pick up its pace. Suddenly, she felt like a high school girl waiting to be picked up for her first date. She hadn't seen Candace since their first meeting. The prospect of being in the same room with the affable senator made her stomach flutter.

Candace smiled at Pearl. "She's in the kitchen," Pearl said with a smirk.

"You've been telling my secrets, Pearlie," Candace mock scolded the older woman.

"Only the good ones," Pearl promised.

"I'm sure," Candace groaned playfully. "Jinx?" she asked. Pearl shrugged. "What other skeletons did you unearth for her?" Candace whispered.

"Why? You trying to impress her?" Pearl returned.

Candace pretended not to hear the older woman and headed for the kitchen. "Ms. Reid," Candace greeted the architect formally.

"Senator," Jameson replied, unsuccessful in concealing an automatic grin.

Candace momentarily thought her feet might have become rooted in the floor. Jameson's smile lit her from within, and Candace was helpless not to react with a broad smile of her own. "Looking for more bird motifs to torture me with?" she asked.

Jameson laughed. "No. I wouldn't do anything to jeopardize dinner."

"I see. So, the way to keep you focused is to feed you Chinese take-out?"

"No, I'm not that picky," Jameson answered.

"I guess that explains your affinity for my kitchen," Candace replied as she set the bag on the table.

"You need anything from me?" Pearl asked from the doorway.

"Not at all," Candace said. "Don't you want to join us? I

got chicken wings," she attempted to entice the older woman with a carton. "And fortune cookies."

Pearl shook her head. "No, thanks. I will leave you two to your evening," she said. "Go easy on that," she warned Candace.

"Worried about my girlish figure?" Candace asked, pulling a bottle of white wine from the refrigerator.

"No," Pearl pointed to the bottle in Candace's hand. "Worried Jameson will have to carry your girlish figure upstairs when you finish that bottle," she winked.

Candace pursed her lips. "Don't listen to her," she said to Jameson. "A glass of wine and she thinks I'm an alcoholic."

"Ha!" Pearl waved off the younger woman as Jameson listened on. "Hardly. Watch her with that, Jameson. She can hold her liquor just fine. Wine…."

"Enough of you," Candace laughed. "That was one time and I was seventeen."

"Oh? What about that time at your Christmas party when Rach…."

Candace made her way swiftly to her friend and covered Pearl's mouth with her hand. "Don't you have some place you need to be?" she asked.

Pearl shook her head when Candace removed her hand. "So eager for me to leave? I thought you wanted me to stay and share your fortune cookies," Pearl quipped. Candace just chuckled. "Just watch her," Pearl called back to Jameson as Candace gently nudged her from the room. Pearl turned to Candace and kissed her on the cheek. "Have a good night," she said with a wink.

Candace rolled her eyes as Pearl headed out the door. "Incorrigible," she mumbled as she made her way back to Jameson. "So? Chinese food and Early American décor…Would you like some wine with that?" she asked the architect.

"Depends," Jameson answered.

"On?"

"How heavy are you?"

Candace looked at Jameson in disbelief for a moment and then laughed. "I promise you, Jameson, it will take more than a couple of glasses of wine for me to get carried off to the bedroom."

Jameson smiled. "I'll make a note."

"What do you think?" Jameson asked. Candace looked at the pictures on Jameson's laptop screen in amazement. Her inability to answer began to alarm Jameson. "If you don't like something…"

"What?" Candace jumped. "Jameson….it's….I'm just amazed that you were able to put this much together in such a short time."

"It's what I do," Jameson said humbly. "You gave me a lot to work with and Pearl has been immensely helpful." Candace nodded silently. Jameson watched a myriad of emotions flicker in the senator's expression. "Candace?" she asked softly in concern. Candace sighed. "Hey, what's wrong?"

Candace released another small sigh and then looked at Jameson. The genuine concern that reflected in the architect's eyes touched her. Jameson held the senator's gaze firmly but compassionately, and Candace finally smiled. "Nothing is wrong," she said. "Pearl loves this old place as much as I do," she said.

"I know," Jameson replied. "She loves you more."

"Yes, she does," Candace agreed. "She's always been like my mother. I think if I were to be honest," Candace closed her eyes to compose herself. She felt Jameson's hand on top of hers and took a deep breath. "If I were to be honest, she might not have given birth to me, but she really is the only mother I have ever known."

Jameson listened attentively. She could feel the emotional burst emanating from Candace. The declaration did not surprise her. Jameson had spent enough time with Pearl to have gained an understanding of the unique relationship she shared with Senator Candace Fletcher. She was certain that there were a great many details about both women that she had yet to learn. Jameson tightened her grip on Candace's hand gently as the senator continued. "My mother was a debutante in every sense of that word. She's eighty, and even without dementia, she still thinks she is a sixteen-year-old at some ball," Candace said with a chuckle. "Don't get me wrong, she is my mother. I love her, but Pearl is…"

"I think I understand," Jameson interjected. Candace looked at Jameson hopefully. Jameson was certain she could detect a moniker of both guilt and fear in the older woman's eyes. She could not remove her gaze from Candace. She felt her thumb begin to stroke Candace's hand in reassurance. She was positive she noticed a slight hitch in the senator's breathing. "I don't think biology defines family," Jameson said. "It certainly doesn't define love."

"No, it doesn't," Candace replied in a whisper. She stayed locked in Jameson's gaze for a moment. Candace's head felt the urge pull away, but her heart desperately wanted to move closer to the architect. She smiled weakly and pulled her hand away to retrieve their plates. "I should pick this up," she said.

Jameson closed her eyes. She was positive that Candace had felt the gravity of the connection between them. She wasn't at all certain how to bridge the gap that she was afraid may have just widened. Composing herself, she made her way to the sink to help. "Let me help," she offered. Candace nodded with an appreciative smile. Jameson began to assist in cleaning up from their dinner. They worked silently but efficiently in tandem. Jameson was surprised as the last container was thrown away that she felt content in their continued silent companionship. She closed her computer and stowed it in its bag. "I should let you get some rest," Jameson said a bit reluctantly.

Candace nodded her affirmation. She walked with Jameson to the front door. "What are your plans for

Thanksgiving?" Candace asked curiously. "All this talk about my house and my family, I haven't even asked you."

"Same as every year," Jameson answered. "I'll head down to my folks' for the weekend." She was surprised to detect a hint of disappointment in the senator's eyes. "You?" she asked.

"Oh, well, Michelle and Jonah will be here tomorrow night," Candace explained. "Spencer, my grandson, he's still small so Marianne won't come up this year. I'll see them in Texas next month."

"How old is he?"

"Six months," Candace beamed.

Jameson smiled. "Nothing quite like a baby, is there?"

"Not really, but I did my time in that realm. I'm happy to be Nana and not Mom this round."

"I think I can understand that."

"Travel safely," Candace said.

"You worried about me, Senator Fletcher?"

Candace was surprised at the answer that flew from her lips. "Let's just say I would like to see you again."

Jameson instinctively knew the required response. She leaned in and placed a chaste kiss on Candace's cheek. "I will be sure to obey all the rules of the road," she promised. "I'll talk to you soon."

Candace nodded as Jameson walked to her car. She watched Jameson pull away and closed the door slowly, feeling an unexplainable sense of loss. "Wine," she mumbled. "I think I'll have another glass of wine."

Chapter Four

"You've been quiet all weekend," Jameson's mother observed.

"I'm sorry."

Maureen Reid took a seat next to her daughter at the kitchen table. "J.D.?"

"What?"

"Everything okay with the firm?" Maureen asked.

"Yeah, why?"

"Why? Clearly, something has you preoccupied. New project?"

Jameson chuckled uncomfortably. "You could say that." Maureen implored her daughter with her eyes. Jameson groaned. "It's not exactly the project that's the problem."

"Difficult client?" her mother inquired.

"No," Jameson answered. "I don't think I'd call Candace difficult. Puzzling, maybe—difficult no."

"Candace, huh? Would I be right in guessing this is someone you are interested in?"

Jameson took a deep breath and held it for a few moments before releasing it. "She is definitely interesting," Jameson answered with a smirk.

"So? Engineer?" Maureen guessed.

"What?"

"Well, you usually are working with engineers. Is she an engineer?"

"Not exactly."

"J.D.?"

Jameson sighed heavily. "Senator."

"I don't think I follow."

"She's a senator."

"Oooo! Moving on up, J.D.! She spends a lot of time in Albany then?"

"No, Washington," Jameson deadpanned.

"Washington County?"

"Washington D.C.," Jameson returned.

Maureen was puzzled for a moment until the realization

hit her. "J.D.?" she questioned. Jameson offered her mother a lopsided grin. "Are you telling me you are seeing Candace Fletcher?"

"Seeing? Yes. Dating? No."

Maureen regarded her daughter suspiciously. "Explain." Before Jameson could speak, her mother continued. "How on earth do you know Candace Fletcher?" she asked. Jameson was about to answer the question when her mother got up from her seat, wandered toward the sink, and then continued. "What's she like? I'll bet she's fascinating. Is she friendly? I'll bet she is demanding. Does…"

"Mom!" Jameson stopped her mother's ramblings. Maureen snapped to attention, and Jameson snickered at her mother's excitement. "Thank you," Jameson said. She rubbed her forehead in thought and sighed. "I'm working on her house. Designing an addition and planning a historically relevant remodel," she said. "That's how I know her."

"How did you…"

"Steve, Mom. Remember Steven Russo?" she asked.

"Yes…"

Jameson laughed. "Steven Russo, Mom. He married Dana."

"Yes?"

Jameson laughed again. "Dana Marelli," Jameson said. She rolled her eyes at her mother's confusion. "Now she is Dana Russo," she said. She waited for her mother to catch up. "She's Senator Fletcher's press secretary." Maureen nodded but still was not completely following her daughter's train of thought. "That's how I met Candace. She's been thinking about this remodel for a number of years. Steven and Dana gave her my name," Jameson explained.

"Oh. So, you are working on her house?"

"Yes."

"You are not dating her?"

"No."

Maureen studied her daughter's expression. "But?" she

asked. Jameson shifted uncomfortably. Maureen nodded and sat back down. "What does she think about this?" she wondered. Jameson just stared at her hands as they rested on the table. "She doesn't know?"

"That I am working on her house?" Jameson tried to be funny. "Of course, she knows."

"Very funny, J.D. She doesn't know that you are interested in her?"

"I don't know."

"You don't know if you are interested in her?" Maureen asked.

"No," Jameson answered quietly.

"No, you don't know…or no, she doesn't know? Help me out here."

Jameson intertwined her fingers nervously. "I don't know…I don't know if she knows that I am interested in her," Jameson finally managed.

"I see," Maureen replied. She gave Jameson a moment to explain before continuing. "Jameson," she called across the table. Jameson looked up. "This isn't a passing fancy, is it?" Jameson's reflective smile was the only answer her mother needed. "Are you in love with her?"

"I don't know her well enough to say that," Jameson said honestly.

"No?"

"No. I like her."

Maureen shook her head. "So, you would like to…what? Take her to the movies?" she asked with a giggle.

"Mom!"

"Oh, please, J.D.! I wish you could see the look on your face. You look like a little lost puppy," Maureen giggled.

"I do not."

"Yes, you do. It's actually quite adorable."

"Mom, come on. This is not funny. She's a client and I…."

"And, you what? Jameson Reid," her mother said

seriously. "I gave birth to you. I've seen you survive every crush and every crushed heart. I have not once seen that look in your eyes."

"What look?" Jameson asked.

Maureen took her daughter's hands. "You think love has a timetable?"

"I think love takes time."

"Relationships take time, J.D.," her mother answered. "Love happens in an instant." Jameson hung her head and swallowed hard. "What are you so afraid of?"

"I don't know," Jameson answered truthfully. "I never worried about someone…I mean about what might…."

"You've never been in love before," her mother said plainly. "Give it some time."

"You just said there is no timetable," Jameson reminded her mother.

"And, you just admitted you're at the very least, falling in love her without even knowing it," Maureen said. Jameson shook her head. "I also said that relationships take time. So, give her some. Give yourself some."

"What if she doesn't…"

"Then you will cry the tears you need to cry and pick yourself up," Maureen told Jameson. "But, I'm not convinced that is what has you the most worried."

"What do you mean?" Jameson asked.

"I think you know," her mother said. "You've waited a long time to even consider wanting a relationship with someone. Maybe you had just resigned yourself to the idea that you never would."

"I've had relationships."

"You know what I mean. Two months of weekend wantonness and a few romps in the backseat of your old Mustang in high school are not what I was referring to," her mother said.

Jameson laughed and then grew serious. "She's out of my league."

"Hardly." Jameson looked up to a pair of motherly eyes

that shone with pride. "She'd be lucky to have you, any woman would."

"You're bias."

"No, I'm not. But, if she's the one who has finally captured your heart….Well, I'd imagine she must be an extraordinary woman," Maureen observed.

"She is," Jameson said.

Maureen put her hand on her daughter's cheek and smiled. "Take your time, J.D." She pulled out her chair and reached her feet, stopping to place a kiss on Jameson's head. "And, I wouldn't be in a hurry to tell your father."

Jameson was confused. Her father had never had an issue with her sexuality or any of the girlfriends she had brought home. She combed her thoughts for the reason behind her mother's statement. "Why?" she asked. "You think he will have an issue with the age difference?"

Maureen laughed. "Nope, I think he'll have an issue with the Democrat," she winked.

Jameson laughed. "He married you," she pointed out.

"Ah, yes, he did," Maureen agreed. "And, I have never let him live it down," she winked. Jameson nodded. "Imagine another Democrat at the dinner table. One that has opinions, I mean."

Jameson laughed. "I don't think you need to worry," she said.

"Don't be so sure," Maureen told her daughter. "Stranger things have happened."

"You mean like Dad falling in love with you?"

"Nah, who wouldn't love me?" Maureen gloated. "But, I fell in love with him. I'd lay odds you can catch Senator Fletcher."

"I guess time will tell," Jameson mumbled.

Maureen made her way out of the kitchen and stopped for a moment to look back at her daughter. She just smiled. "Guess I know who we'll be voting for in the next election," she mused.

"Mom?" Michelle called to Candace.

"Hum?"

"You know Marianne doesn't mean to be such a..."

"Bitch?" Candace finished her daughter's statement. Michelle sniggered. "Yes, I know."

"She just wishes we were all closer, I think," Michelle offered. Candace just smiled. Michelle was the typical middle child. She had always been the peacemaker. They had just returned from taking Jonah to the airport for his flight home. Candace had enjoyed the weekend with her two younger children, although they were no longer children. Pearl had joined them on Saturday afternoon for a late lunch and some old movies. They had all agreed to an internet chat with Marianne in the late afternoon that day. It had started out well. The kids were catching up and cooing over little Spencer. Then it turned ugly.

Pearl mentioned the remodel of the house and she and Candace began to talk about Jameson and her plans. Marianne's reaction was less than accommodating, and far below interested. She had scolded her mother that it was a waste of time and money. None of the children wanted to live in that house. Why on earth was she so adamant about investing in something like an old house? After all, Candace was in Washington the majority of the year. And, Marianne wondered what kind of accomplished architect would accept such a project.

Candace had grown used to Marianne's harsh criticisms regarding her choice of living arrangements, and her desire to continue working until she deemed retirement was necessary or wanted. Candace did not appreciate her daughter's freely given assessments about her life, but it was not a battle she felt was worthy of her energy. She had no intention of changing her home, nor any inclination to change her career. Sooner or later, she was positive Marianne would give up the ghost and learn to live with it all. Marianne's comments and unsolicited assumptions about Jameson had touched a nerve in Candace. No one anticipated Candace's reaction.

"An architect? Mother, are you sure this woman is an architect and not some scam artist?"

Candace held her temper in check. "I do know how to check references, Marianne."

"Yes, well, you also give everyone the benefit of the doubt."

"She's a good friend of Dana and Steve's, if you must know. And, she is quite accomplished," Candace said. She mentally pictured Jameson and smiled.

"Why on earth would a successful person such as you have described want to wander around some old house in the boonies? Are you sure she isn't after something else?"

Pearl was watching Candace from across the room and immediately caught the senator's change of expression. "Uh oh," she whispered to Michelle.

"And, just what do you think she might be after?" Candace asked her daughter.

"Mom, please. You are a powerful, wealthy woman. How is it that someone as educated and intelligent as you are—cannot see the handwriting on the wall?"

"I see all the writing very clearly, Marianne. Perhaps, you are reading in a different language than me."

"I am simply trying to protect you."

Candace took a deep breath and steadied herself. She prided herself on maintaining control when arguments arose. She had always guided her children with a firm yet gentle hand. Few times in the past had Candace ever raised her voice to one of her children, even when she had been furious about one of their actions or decisions. Marianne had just entered treacherous waters with her mother. Candace was about to tell her daughter to tread lightly.

"I appreciate your concern. I am more than capable of judging a person's character and motives for myself," Candace said.

"Oh, like Jessica?"

"Jameson is not Jessica," Candace answered harshly.

"Because you are not sleeping with her? Or, are you? There is more than one way to cheat, Mom."

Pearl put her face in her hands and braced herself for the response she anticipated. Michelle and Jonah looked at the older woman and then to their mother. "My life is just that, Marianne, my life. I certainly do not need your guidance on dishonesty."

"Quick to defend this woman, aren't you?"

"Jameson does not need me to defend her," Candace said. She watched the screen in front of her and recognized her daughter's mounting protest. She effectively ended it before it could begin. "She doesn't need me to, but she certainly deserves at least that much from me." Candace saw Marianne bristle and heard her begin to speak. She held up a finger in warning. "You are entitled to whatever opinions you wish about my life, my home, and my career. It's a free country. I should know. I will thank you to keep your uninformed and rude judgments about the people in my life to yourself. I raised you better than that."

"I am simply…"

"I am simply telling you that this conversation is over," Candace said sternly.

"Mom…"

"I'll give you to your sister," Candace said. "Kiss Spencer for me."

"Mom! This woman could be…"

"Marianne!" Candace finally yelled. "I have had enough. Jameson has done nothing to warrant your scrutiny and skepticism. Now, enjoy the rest of your weekend. I will talk you to you next week." Candace got up from her seat. "Michelle," she called over to her younger daughter. Michelle looked like a deer caught in the headlights. "You and Jonah come and visit with your sister." She forced a small smile and headed toward the kitchen.

Pearl followed a few moments later and found Candace holding onto the sink to steady the shaking in her body. "Candy," she said gently.

"She has no right to attack Jameson," Candace said angrily.

"No, she doesn't."

Michelle had noted the uncharacteristic trembling in her mother's hands as she left the room. She left Jonah to chat with

Marianne, making the excuse that she needed to quickly use the bathroom so that she could check on her mother. The sound of voices stopped her just shy of her destination. She lingered outside the kitchen, listening to the two women who had instructed her the most in life.

"Candy?" Pearl called again. "You know, you are right, Jameson is not Jessica."

"I know."

"I hope you do know."

Candace turned to Pearl. Pearl wiped a tear from the corner of Candace's eye. "Give it time, my love. Give it some time."

"She could be my daughter."

"And, you could be mine," Pearl said with a wink.

"You know what I mean."

"I do know what you mean. She'll keep you on your toes," Pearl chuckled.

Candace smiled. "I don't think she sees me…"

"Oh, love, she sees you."

"You know what I mean," Candace said.

"Yes, I do. Maybe it's you who is afraid to see her," Pearl suggested. Candace sighed. "Give it time, Candy," she said. She kissed the senator's forehead as Candy began to cry and wrapped the woman in her motherly embrace. "Life is strange sometimes. It tends to take us where we need to go, if we let it, that is," she comforted the woman in her arms. "I love you, Candy."

"I love you too Mama Pearl."

"I know you do, so trust me."

Michelle stood completely still as the conversation beyond the wall turned silent. She'd only heard her mother cry a few times in her life, and she'd never heard her mother refer to Pearl as Mama before. She wondered who this Jameson person was that she could have affected her mother so deeply. "Oh, Marianne, I think you are in for a surprise."

Michelle looked back at her mother and took a deep breath for courage. She didn't want her mother to think that she had been deliberately eavesdropping on a private conversation.

She had intended to check on her mother, but the tender exchange between the two women she loved most in her life had stopped her in her tracks. Something in Pearl's words to her mother had struck a chord within Michelle. She felt the need to reach out somehow. "I'm sorry, Mom," she said.

"Sorry? What are you sorry for?" Candace wondered. Michelle just hung her head. "Shell?"

"I'm sorry Marianne upset you so much."

Candace nodded. "I'm all right."

"Mom?"

"Yes?"

"Is…Jameson is important to you," Michelle said quietly.

Candace was surprised at the observation. "She's a friend."

Michelle let the response linger for a while. She returned her focus to the book in her lap. She thought a different approach might be more successful. After she had felt a sufficient amount of time had passed to lower her mother's guard, she spoke. "Is she pretty?" Michelle asked a bit playfully.

"She's beautiful," Candace replied as if the question had come from within. Realizing that it had come from Michelle, she flushed with embarrassment. "I…"

"I figured," Michelle commented with a smile.

"It's not what," Candace began to stammer. Michelle arched an eyebrow at her mother. "Shell, it's not like that. She's a friend, that's all."

Michelle smiled at her mother. "I look forward to meeting her."

"You want to meet Jameson?" Candace suddenly felt a wave of nausea hit her.

"Some reason that you wouldn't want me to?"

"No, of course, not."

Michelle giggled. "Don't worry Mom, I prefer them short and blonde, or maybe redhead. I guess I could…"

"What?" Candace interrupted.

"What do you mean, what?" Michelle laughed. "And, I

prefer them under thirty." Candace's jaw fell slack. "Mom? You did know that I like girls? I mean, you met Donna. You met Rebecca."

Candace started to laugh. "Your sister will definitely blame me."

"I didn't think I needed to spell it out for you," Michelle laughed. "And, don't let Marianne fool you."

"Excuse me?"

"She kissed more than one cheerleader under a bleacher," Michelle winked.

"Stop!"

"Okay, I made that up," Michelle admitted.

"Why didn't you tell me before now?" Candace asked.

"You mean you really didn't know?"

"No, I knew," Candace admitted.

"I guess I just was waiting for the right time."

"Why now?"

Michelle went to sit beside her mother. "Maybe I just thought you should know that I love you no matter what, just like I know you love me no matter what."

"I know that," Candace said.

"So?"

"What?" Candace chuckled.

"Come on, Mom, the architect? Beautiful?"

"Do you have any idea how odd this conversation is?" Candace asked.

"What? A lesbian mom and her lesbian daughter talking about hot chics?"

"Shell, I think I am past the hot chics phase."

"So, Jameson isn't hot?"

Candace threw a pillow at her daughter. "Are you sure you two haven't already met?"

"Why? Think she'd like me?"

"Lunatics," Candace laughed. "I am certain she will."

"Good! Let's call her!" Michelle ran for the phone. Candace just laughed. "Chicken!" Michelle taunted her mother.

"You can argue with heads of state and you're afraid to call one little lesbian?"

"No, smart ass. She's away for the weekend."

"What? She has no phone? Is she impaired somehow? Technically? How old is this woman?" Michelle narrowed her gaze.

"No, she's not impaired, technically or otherwise," Candace replied. Michelle waited for her mother to continue with a growing smirk. "All right! She's thirty-five!" Candace exclaimed in exasperation.

"Oh my God, my mother is a cougar! Senator Candace Cougar!"

"What part of she is a friend did you not understand?" Candace laughed at her daughter's theatrics.

"A young, smart, hot, happens to be a lesbian friend," Michelle pointed out. Candace rolled her eyes. "So, why are you lying on that couch? Don't you have her number?"

"Of course."

"Hello!"

"Shell!" Candace couldn't help but laugh. Michelle was, in many ways, her best friend. They had always been kindred spirits. Candace thought most people would find it unbelievable, but she had felt the bond between them from the moment Michelle was born. Much like the felt a bond with Pearl the first day she sat with her in her granddad's kitchen, and much like she felt the moment she saw Jameson Reid standing in her doorway. She shook her head. "She's a friend. A friend who happens to be twenty years my junior," she reminded her daughter.

Michelle retrieved her mother's cell phone from the side table and put it in Candace's hand. "Senator Fletcher, meet the twenty-first century," she said. Candace sighed. "We can watch the news on phones we carry on our pockets and open car doors without a key. A woman can marry anyone she chooses, even another woman, even if she is…Wait for it twenty years younger, oh, and the entire world now knows Rock Hudson was, in fact, gay," Michelle declared.

"I'm not getting married," Candace said flatly.

"Won't be getting much of anything if you can't even make a call," Michelle said with a wide grin before starting to run away.

Candace threw another pillow at her daughter. "Lunatic!"

"Call her!"

Candace looked at the phone in her hands and sighed. "Call her, huh?"

"Might help!"

With a deep breath, Candace closed her eyes and pressed the name on the screen.

Chapter Five

"Hello?" Jameson answered the call in disbelief. Candace found herself tongue-tied for a moment, wondering what excuse she could use for the call. "Candace?" Jameson began. "You there?"

"Sorry, yes, I'm here."

"Did you butt dial me?"

"Excuse me?"

"Well, you called me, but you sound surprised to hear my voice," Jameson observed with a chuckle.

Candace laughed softly. "I'm not sure my butt, as you put it, is quite that talented," she said in reply.

"That's a good thing, trust me. Dana dialed me once at about one in the morning. Let's just say I got an earful of more than I ever needed to hear," Jameson said. "So, what can I do for you?"

"Nothing, unless you would like to bring over some Chinese food to go with this bottle of wine I opened."

"Craving Chinese food? Really? Too much home cooking?" Jameson asked.

"Let's just say I could use a fortune cookie about now," Candace said. "How's your visit home?"

"Fine. Always interesting here. Lots of unsolicited motherly advice. You know how it goes."

"Mm. I do, except in my case it seems to be lots of unsolicited daughters' advice."

"Oh." Candace had told Jameson a bit about all of her children. Pearl had filled in some of the blanks. "Issues with the remodel?"

"If Marianne could, she would remodel my entire life," Candace answered flatly.

"Ouch."

"Then again, so would Shell, just in a different way it seems," Candace laughed.

"Sounds like a spirited weekend."

"I'll tell you something, they never really change and as much as they think they grow up—they never really change," Candace said affectionately. She was still angry with Marianne's line of questioning and her daughter's unfair assessment of Jameson, but that was Marianne. At the end of the day, Candace loved all three of her children more than anything in her life, even with their quirks, habits, and unwanted advice.

Jameson listened to the sudden lilt in Candace's voice. "So, wine to celebrate the remodel or wine to forget about it?"

"Depends on which remodel you are talking about, my house or my life?"

"Do you want to remodel your life?" Jameson asked.

"No," Candace replied. Jameson nodded on the other end of the phone. "Shell was quite interested in your plans," Candace said.

"Oh really? Which would she like to see more of? The Roman statuary or the bird watching motif?"

Candace laughed. "I think you could leave out the well-endowed Romans," she said. "So, I'll assume she will agree with me on the other as well. Seems my daughter and I have similar tastes."

"Apple didn't fall far from the tree, as they say?"

"Not that apple it appears."

Jameson laughed. "Did you know?"

"That Shell was a lesbian?"

"Yeah."

"I knew. I was beginning to wonder if she did though," Candace chuckled.

"You sound like my mother when I finally told her. How is it mothers seem to know these things before we do? Is it a hormone or something?"

Candace laughed at the genuine curiosity in Jameson's voice. "If it is, I am unaware of it. I think it's just that we have years to observe—everything. That's what mothers do the most, you know? Observe. I'm sure my children would disagree, but it's true. You only advise based on what you've come to understand. In my experience, it's easier most times for an outsider to see things objectively."

"Sounds like motherhood was good preparation for the congress," Jameson interjected.

"I think it was," Candace replied honestly. The conversation seemed to come abruptly to a halt; neither woman certain of what to say next. "So? When are you heading back?" Candace asked.

"Not sure yet," Jameson replied. "You?"

"Shell is leaving late afternoon tomorrow. I fly back to D.C. Monday. Tomorrow will be a quiet day for us."

"Chinese food?" Jameson suggested.

"Perhaps….Listen, sorry if I interrupted your…."

"You can interrupt me any time," Jameson said.

Candace took a shaky breath. "Travel safely."

"Don't worry. I promised to obey all the signs on the way here. I'll behave on the way home. I am, after all, working for a lawmaker. Wouldn't be prudent to start breaking them."

"I suppose not," Candace agreed. "I'll see you soon."

"I hope so." Jameson took a deep breath. "Candace?"

"Yes?"

"I'm glad you called. I was getting bored with no one to torture."

Candace smiled. "Glad I could be your willing victim," she said. "I'll look forward to seeing what you devise for future torment." Jameson laughed. "Good night, Jameson."

"Night, Senator."

Jameson felt her heart begin to thunder in her chest as she pulled her car into the long, narrow driveway that led to Candace Fletcher's home. She glanced across to the passenger seat at the large paper bag that sat beside her. "Well, look at it this way," she said aloud. "If no one is home, you won't have to grocery shop for a week."

"Mom?" Candace made her way to the sound of Michelle's voice. "There's a car headed up the driveway." Candace peered out the window with her daughter. The moment she saw Jameson's car, she began to smile. Michelle looked at her mother and fought to conceal her knowing smirk. "Let me guess. Jameson?"

Candace nodded and headed for the front door just as Jameson was exiting her car. She stood on the front step, smiling at the approaching architect. "What are you doing here?" she asked.

"Didn't you request Chinese food?" Jameson held up the bag.

Candace bit her lip gently as Jameson stepped up to her. "You're a lunatic. You do know that?" she asked. Jameson just winked. "You drove all the way back here from Ithaca to deliver Chinese food?"

"Maybe I just missed you," Jameson said without thinking. Candace stared at the woman before her as her heart rate instantly increased. "Besides, Pearl would never forgive me if you drank wine on an empty stomach," Jameson pointed out. "Are you going to let me in?" she asked playfully.

"Depends," Candace said.

"On?"

"How many fortune cookies are in that bag?"

"I don't need a cookie to predict your future," Jameson said.

"Really?"

Jameson closed her eyes and pretended to concentrate. "I see it now…chicken wings, spare ribs, lo mein, and wine." She opened her eyes. "How'd I do?"

"Get in here, you lunatic." Candace pulled Jameson through the door. "Shell!" Michelle sauntered into the hallway from the living room. "Jameson, this is my daughter, Michelle. Shell, this is Jameson Reid, snarky architect and part-time Chinese delivery driver."

Michelle smiled. "Nice to meet you, Jameson."

"J.D.," Jameson said. "For some reason, your mother and Pearl insist on calling me Jameson. Everybody else calls me J.D."

"It's your name, isn't it?" Candace asked.

"That it is, Senator Fletcher."

Candace rolled her eyes, and Michelle reached for the bag in Jameson's hands. "I'll call you anything you'd like," Michelle said, "as long as you feed me." She took the bag and headed off for the kitchen.

"That's the apple nearest the tree, huh?" Jameson asked. Candace nodded. "This should be an interesting lunch."

"You hoping to torture in tandem?" Candace asked. Jameson shrugged. "That's what I thought."

🐴 🐴 🐴

"I never knew you had a pet bird," Michelle looked at her mother. "That's the real reason why you never let us have a cat, isn't it?"

Candace mock glared at Jameson, who in turn snickered. "Don't you have things to pack?" Candace asked her daughter.

Michelle winked at Jameson. "I suppose I do. I am surprised though."

"About what?" Candace asked.

"Mom, you've run against some of the meanest S.O.B.'s in the country and you're afraid of a cat?"

"I am not afraid of a cat," Candace said indignantly. "I just prefer not to have to deal with them."

"What did he look like?" Michelle asked.

"Who?" Candace replied.

"Jinx. What did he look like?"

"Black. He was a black cat. No one should name a black cat Jinx," she groaned. "This is what happens." Jameson hid her face in her hands to quell her laughter. Senator Candace Fletcher had, in an instant, taken on the persona of a wounded eight-year-old girl.

"You know, you always told us we needed face our fears to overcome them," Michelle reminded her mother.

"I am not afraid of cats!" Candace defended herself. "Are you trying to tell me that you think I should allow Jameson to wallpaper this house with cats?"

Michelle shrugged. "No, I think you should get one. Pearl loves them. It would keep her company when you are away. And, Mom…a cat is not going to eat wallpaper. Let J.D. put up the birds. It's pretty."

Candace looked over at Jameson, who kept her face hidden in her hands. "Did you see this in my future?" Candace directed her question to Jameson.

"Well, your cookie did say *Soon you will meet a friend from your past*," Jameson pointed out.

Candace smacked Jameson lightly. "I smell a conspiracy."

Michelle laughed. "I'm out of here before she bombards me with pillows again," she said. "It was nice meeting you J.D."

"You too, Shell," Jameson said. Candace sat shaking her head as she watched Michelle leave the room. "That apple is definitely from the same tree," Jameson said definitively.

Candace shook her head again. "Lunatics," she grumbled.

"Why don't you?" Jameson asked.

"Why don't I what?"

"Get a cat?" Jameson replied.

"Have you completely lost your mind?" Candace wondered.

"No."

"You're serious."

"Well? She doesn't think you will," Jameson gestured up the stairs. She was confident that Candace would take the bait. She enjoyed all of her conversations with Candace, but Jameson took particular pleasure in their banter.

Candace considered the statement for a moment. Jameson was issuing her a challenge, much like Michelle just had. Candace never backed down from a challenge. The youngest of three children, and the only girl, that was a lesson she had mastered early in life. A devious smile edged its way onto her lips. "I'll tell you what," she began. "You find a black, male cat that needs a home and I will agree to allow him the pleasure of Pearl's company."

Jameson pretended to consider the offer. "Done....If you name him Jinx."

"Done," Candace agreed.

"One question," Jameson said.

"What is that?" Candace folded her arms across her chest.

"Whom should I bill for this service I am rendering, you or Jinx?" Jameson asked thoughtfully.

Candace lost all hope of maintaining her stoicism and laughed. "You are certifiable."

"What on Earth is in there?" Pearl asked Jameson.

"In here?" Jameson pointed to the cardboard carrier.

"Yes, Jameson, in there."

"Oh, that. That's Jinx." The look on Pearl's face was comical, and Jameson started laughing.

"Explain yourself, young lady."

"Well, Candace agreed that if I could find a black, male cat that needed a home, she would allow him the pleasure of your company," Jameson explained. Pearl's eyes grew as wide as saucers. "I agreed to find a needy feline as long as she agreed to name him Jinx. It's actually Shell's fault."

Pearl shook her head as if to clear her confusion. "What does Michelle have to do with this nonsense?"

Jameson sighed dramatically and set down the carrier. "We were having lunch and I was showing Shell some of the wallpaper designs. That led to the whole story of the cat that ate the canary...."

"Go on."

"And, later Shell told Candace that she needed to face her fears."

"Oh, no."

"I pointed out that her fortune cookie predicted she would meet a friend from her past...."

"I don't believe this."

"And, so here we are," Jameson said. She opened the carrier and retrieved a small black kitten with bright green eyes. "Jinx, meet Pearl. Pearl, this is Jinx."

Pearl flopped into a chair in disbelief. "Candy let you get her a cat?"

"No, she let me get you a cat," Jameson said with a grin.

Pearl shook her head. "Jameson, I never thought I'd say this, but I think Candy has finally met her match." She took the kitten from Jameson's hands and looked at it in amusement. Candy was full of surprises. Jameson made those all the more interesting.

"Jinx will give her a run for her money," Jameson agreed.

Pearl stood up with the kitten in her hands and laughed. "I wasn't referring to the cat."

Candace played with the glasses that sat on the bridge of her nose. She was making every attempt to concentrate on the papers in front of her. It had been a long and tedious day that lingered in the middle of what had already become an arduous week. She pulled off her glasses and rubbed her tired eyes. Only one more week before the holiday break. She was looking forward to a slight reprieve. She was not at all sure that four days at Marianne's home would provide any tangible refreshment.

"Senator?" Susan's voice broke through Candace's private musings.

"What is it, Susan?"

"Dana is here."

"Send her in."

Dana walked into the senator's office and regarded the dark circles under Candy's eyes. "Long day?" she asked.

Candace looked up and offered her friend a half-hearted smile. "Long life," she quipped. Dana nodded her understanding just as Candy's cell phone buzzed. Candy held up a finger to her friend to give her a moment. "Yes?" she answered the phone a bit playfully.

"Good afternoon, Senator Fletcher," Jameson's voice greeted.

Candace smiled at the sound. Dana watched the transformation and wondered what its cause might be. "What can I do for you?" Candace asked just as her office door opened, and Susan peered in.

Susan held up a paper bag. "Did you order Chinese?" she asked in confusion.

"I don't know," Candace said. "Are there chicken wings in that bag?" she asked.

"There are," Jameson answered on the line.

Candace looked at Susan who was rummaging through the bag. "How many fortune cookies in that bag?" she asked.

"Looks like four or five," Susan answered.

"Let's hope they don't all predict friends from my past," Candace chuckled.

"I'm sorry?" Susan asked.

"It's fine, Susan. Just set it down," Candace instructed as she returned her attention to the phone. "Any predictions?" she asked Jameson.

"Only that you will be eating Chinese food."

"Um. Is this your peace offering for that mangy feline that Pearl is already attached to?" Candace asked.

"He's not mangy, and you were an equal party to that agreement," Jameson reminded the senator.

"So, I was," she admitted.

"Your email seemed….well, you just seemed tired," Jameson said.

Candace noted the concern in the architect's voice. "Long week."

"It's only Wednesday," Jameson said.

"Exactly. Thanks," Candace replied gratefully.

"It's not much."

"The only thing missing was the usual delivery driver," Candace said honestly.

Jameson smiled at the endearment. "She is working with a very demanding client right now. Doesn't give her much time to moonlight."

Candace laughed. "Sounds like a bitch."

"No, but I certainly don't want to disappoint her."

Candace closed her eyes and inhaled the compliment. "I don't foresee that in your future."

"No?"

"No, but I do see you on a plane this weekend," Candace said.

"Is that so? You already opening dessert?" Jameson asked.

"Maybe I am….let's see – it says, *a lunatic will crash your Christmas party*."

"Shell is headed to D.C.?" Jameson asked.

"I was thinking of a certain snarky architect."

"She might be moonlighting that night," Jameson replied. "She relies on tips, you know?"

Candace laughed. "Well, let her know that there will be a tip as to the itinerary in her email later this afternoon."

"I'll check her schedule with the secretary right now, please hold," Jameson said. Candace chuckled while she waited for Jameson to return. Dana pretended to peruse some files as she listened. "Master Jinx says he can clear her schedule for the weekend if necessary. He wants to know if there will be wine."

"Thank Master Jinx for me and assure him every amenity will be provided," Candace said.

"I'll let him know," Jameson said. "Guess, I will see you."

"Jameson?" Candace said. Dana looked up abruptly. "Thanks. I needed that today."

"It's what I do," Jameson said. "Remodeling a day is part of the package."

"I must have missed that in the fine print," Candace returned. "Let me know when you get the email."

"I will. I have to go. Master Jinx has taken up residence on my plans."

Candace laughed. "I told you they were trouble."

"Jinx!" Jameson exclaimed. "Aww, dude! Come on! Gotta go…"

Candace disconnected the call. "Why doesn't anyone ever believe me?" she mused quietly.

Dana looked over at her boss and lifted an eyebrow. "I'm not sure I want to know what that conversation was about."

Candace winked. "Chinese?"

Chapter Six

Jameson looked at her reflection in the mirror. She tugged at her tailored jacket. "Why am I so nervous?" she asked her reflection.

"Why are you so nervous?" Dana asked. Jameson spun on her heels. Dana narrowed her gaze at the architect's startled expression. "Okay, J.D., truth time. What is going on with you and Candy?"

"What are you talking about?" Jameson asked. Dana sat on the edge of the bed in the guest room and waited for an honest response. "Dana, she's a client. That's all."

"Uh-huh. So, you send all of your clients Chinese food randomly when they are having a bad day? Chinese food you have to arrange to be delivered to the Senate offices? Just who did you bribe to pull that one off?"

Jameson shrugged. "I know more people than you think."

"J.D."

Jameson sighed. "She's a friend." Dana raised her brow again. "Okay, I like her."

"You like Senator Fletcher?"

"No, I like Candace," Jameson replied dryly.

"As a friend?" Jameson turned back to the mirror and sighed. "That's what I thought. So, why don't you do something about it?"

Jameson shrugged. "I don't know."

"J.D., I've known Candy as long as I've known you…well, almost. Trust me, she feels the same way." Jameson turned back to face her friend. Dana was surprised to see fear and hopefulness in Jameson's eyes. She smiled knowingly. "You're in love with her." Jameson did not respond. "Are you?" Jameson plopped down beside Dana and nodded. Dana put a comforting arm around her friend. "Can't say I saw that one coming."

"Neither did I."

Dana patted Jameson's knee. "Want my advice?"

"Not really," Jameson said.

"Good," Dana replied. "Wait! What?" she asked. Jameson snickered.

Dana pinched the architect's knee. "Ow!"

"Just take her in your arms and kiss her senseless," Dana said.

Jameson laughed. "Just walk up to Candace, pull her to me and kiss her. That's your solution?"

"Pretty much," Dana said.

"And, she thinks I am crazy?" Jameson asked.

"Hey, if she kisses you back, you'll know."

"Somehow, Dana…I think that plan might be flawed."

"Worked for Steve."

"Happy for you both," Jameson replied.

"Seriously, J.D., no matter what she says or does, you will know."

Jameson gave her friend an uncomfortable smile. "I guess, we'll see."

Candace stretched out on the bed. A quick afternoon nap before all the festivities would begin seemed deserved. She'd been hosting this Christmas party for twelve years. This event had become a sought-after invitation in the halls of the Washington D.C. power structure. Some years, even the president had attended. Candace Fletcher was the perfect host. She had learned that skill from her mother. Her parties were always elegant and ornate. That was not what drew the elite. It was Candace's style and candor that courted her harshest critics and prompted even her political adversaries to seek an invitation. Candace was a rare breed in Washington. Her demeanor, her wit, and her ability to put politics aside for even an evening, harkened back to a different time in the U.S. Senate. The most senior government officials in Washington had nicknamed her The Charming

Maverick. She was not afraid to go against the grain, and with just a few words she could charm her most cantankerous opponents.

Candace looked forward to this event every year. It reminded her of holidays past in her granddad's home. The New York social circuit would be abuzz every year about Governor Stratton's Christmas party. Businessmen, politicians, the aristocratic element of the great Empire State all clamored for invitations. Governor and Mrs. Stratton always invited entire families. The children were entertained by an appearance from Santa Claus, games, and inevitably an old fashioned sleigh ride through the large fields that abutted the governor's home. There were no sleigh rides to offer here in Arlington, Virginia. Candace's townhome was a fraction the size of the house in New York. Still, she strived to capture the feeling she remembered as a child. Invitations were sent to families. Santa would attend, and Candace would delight as much in the sound of children's laughter, and the nervousness of watchful parents, as she did in observing the political jockeying that always entertained her. This year, there seemed to be only one guest that she was truly anxious to see. She reached for her phone.

"Senator," the voice greeted her.

"You made it in safely."

"I did. You do realize that Steven is driving to this shindig of yours?"

"That certainly does have risk factors," Candace laughed.

"You sound tired," Jameson noted.

"It was a long week."

"Are you feeling all right?" Jameson asked.

"Worried about me, Jameson?"

"Maybe," Jameson admitted. Candace had sounded drained all week when the two had spoken. Jameson was positive that the senator had drifted off during one of their conversations earlier in the week.

"I'm fine. It's just that time of year."

Jameson was skeptical, but she let it lie. "Well, can you rest for a bit before this…"

"Shindig?" Candace finished the thought. "Yes, I think I will. Just wanted to be sure you were all set."

"I feel a little funny coming empty handed," Jameson said.

"What do you mean?"

"Should I stop for some chicken wings?" Jameson joked.

"Don't tempt me!" Candace laughed. "I'll see you in a few hours."

"That you will," Jameson promised.

Candace laid back and closed her eyes. Only one picture painted her thoughts as she drifted off to sleep—a snarky architect.

Candace stood at the railing of her upstairs balcony. She was unsure if the chill that suddenly traveled up her arms was due to the brisk December air or the presence that she sensed behind her. She closed her eyes as Jameson's hands caressed her arms. "What are you doing out here?" Jameson whispered.

Candace closed her eyes and struggled to catch her breath. "Why? Did you miss me?"

"Always," Jameson answered, placing a kiss behind Candace's ear. Candace sighed.

"Everyone is gone?"

Jameson's arms pulled Candace closer and traveled slowly from her waist to her abdomen. "Just you and me," she whispered while continuing to place light kisses on Candace's neck.

Candace sighed as Jameson's hands continued their gentle journey upward. "Jameson," she moaned. Jameson smiled as Candace leaned into her. She cupped Candace's breasts through her dress. Candace's breath was becoming shallower as Jameson's fingers played over her cleavage.

Jameson heard her name through another ragged sigh and turned Candace in her arms. Candace looked at the architect and cupped Jameson's face in her hands. Jameson smiled. "I love you," Jameson promised before kissing Candace passionately.

"Oh, God, Jameson," Candace said as Jameson broke their kiss. "I love you."

"Senator," a voice startled Candace. "You feeling okay?" Susan asked.

"Huh? Yeah, I guess I drifted off."

"You look a little flushed," Susan observed.

"I'm fine. When did you get here?"

"Just now. George let me in." Candace nodded. "Are you sure you are feeling okay?"

"I'm fine," Candace reassured her assistant. "But, I'd better get myself together before the caterers get here and the masses arrive."

Susan smiled. "I'll see you downstairs. Anything you need me to handle?"

"Just the usual," Candace said. Susan nodded and left the room. Candace took a deep breath and made her way into the bathroom. She looked in the mirror and shook her head. "Oh, Jameson," she mumbled. "What have I gotten myself into?"

Candace made her way through the house taking a moment to greet each guest and engage in the required pleasantries. Her mind was a million miles away from every conversation she found herself drawn into. If anyone had bothered to ask her what she had been discussing just a moment before, she would have been stumped to give a recounting. The house was full, her glass had run dry, and she had yet to catch a glimpse of Jameson. She offered the congressman that she had been chatting with her best smile when a face in the distance captured her attention.

Jameson stopped a few yards away from where Candace was standing. She stopped so abruptly that Dana failed to realize she was walking alone. She turned to her left to say something to the architect. Realizing she was alone, she glanced behind her to see Jameson smiling stupidly at something in the distance. She followed Jameson's line of sight and shook her head when she saw the subject of her friend's attention sporting the same expression.

Candace was fairly sure that if anyone had been paying attention, they would have noticed the ridiculous smile on her face. "If you'll excuse me," she made her apology to Congressman Stanley.

"Of course," he said.

Candace smiled and slowly turned her attention toward Jameson. Jameson wasn't sure that her feet were moving. She couldn't take her eyes off of Candace. Candace was wearing a dark green dress that hung slightly off of her shoulders. It sported a plunging neckline that Jameson forced herself to lift her eyes from. When she did, she was met with a pair of blue eyes that sparkled in amusement. The next few moments felt like hours to Jameson as one person after another attempted to command Candace's attention. When she finally came face to face with the senator, her words were simple, honest, and unapologetic. "You look beautiful," she said.

Candace smiled. Jameson made a stunning impression. Her black pantsuit was tapered in all the appropriate places. The heels she wore set her about an inch higher than Candace. Her make-up was subtle as it always was, but her hair was curled and framed her face perfectly, bringing out the bright golden-brown eyes that Candace loved. "Loved," Candace thought silently. "My

God," she realized. That was exactly what she felt looking at Jameson standing before her. "You clean up quite nicely yourself," Candace winked.

"I lost you," Dana said, coming even with the pair. "But, I see that you are in capable hands," she commented to Jameson.

"I do know where the bar is located," Candace said without removing her gaze from Jameson.

"You sure you remember?" Dana chuckled.

"What?" Candace finally looked at her friend.

"Oh, nothing," Dana feigned innocence. "I am going to go find that man I call my husband. I'm sure the senator can lead you to whatever you require," Dana smirked.

Candace raised her brow at Dana and then looked at Jameson, who was blushing furiously. "Ignore her," Candace instructed the architect. "Wine?" Jameson nodded appreciatively. Candace stopped and whispered in Dana's ear. "Stop scaring her," she said.

Dana rolled her eyes as the pair walked away. "Is J.D. okay?" Steven sidled up to his wife.

"No."

"No? What's wrong?" he asked.

"Love."

"Huh?"

Dana turned to her husband and patted his chest. "Your best friend," she began. He looked at her in bewilderment as she continued. "Is in love with my boss."

"What? J.D.....Wait, J.D. is in love with Candy?" Dana gave her husband a silly grin. "Are you sure?" Dana nodded. "Oh, shit."

"It gets worse," Dana told her husband.

"Candy knows?" he guessed.

Dana tipped her head. "Pretty sure—yeah."

"Oh, no." He looked at Dana's sheepish grin. "What aren't you telling me?"

"Pretty sure my boss is in love with your best friend."

Steven looked off in the distance to where Candace was handing Jameson a glass of wine. "Oh, boy. Maybe you are just imagining it."

Dana looked at the scene across the room and shook her head. "You think I'm imagining that?" she pointed.

Steve took a large sip from the drink in his hand. "Can't say I saw that coming. What do you think she'll do?"

"Which one?" Dana giggled. Steve looked at her and smiled. "I hope she just kisses her," Dana said, taking the glass from her husband's hand and downing a large swig.

"Which one?"

Dana laughed. "Want to place bets?" she asked.

"I bet on Candy."

Dana handed the glass back to her husband. "You bet on my boss and I bet on your best friend? That's just wrong. What are we betting?"

"Okay…if J.D. kisses Candy first, I will take you for drinks at Red Derby."

"You in a dive bar?" Dana laughed.

"Yeah, so what do I get if I am right and Candy makes the first move?"

"She won't," Dana said flatly. Steve pouted. "Fine, I will take you to dinner at whatever Politico hot spot you choose."

"You hate those places," he reminded her.

"You seem confident, so am I."

"Wait? How are we going to know?" he asked.

"I have my sources," Dana assured him.

"I hope J.D. doesn't get crushed," he said quietly.

Dana sighed. "Me too."

Jameson recognized many of the faces in the room. Candace had tried to keep her company and introduce her to the crowd, but the senator's attention was in constant demand and Jameson inevitably lost track of Candace in the crowd. "Kind of boring, isn't it?" Dana said.

Jameson shrugged. "It's fine."

"She's in her study," Dana said softly. Jameson looked at her friend in confusion. "Sometimes she needs a minute to regroup. She finds her way there every year about this time." Jameson nodded. "Come on," Dana grabbed Jameson's hand.

"Where are you taking me?"

Dana nodded toward a door. "Go on."

"Dana, you just said she needed to step away."

"Yes, I did," Dana admitted. "I'm not sure you are in that equation." Jameson looked skeptical. "Trust me, J.D. Go on," Dana encouraged. Jameson sucked in a nervous breath and walked a few steps to the door. She turned back to Dana for encouragement and received a nod.

Steven found his wife watching as Jameson entered Candace's study and closed the door. "Stacking the odds in your favor, huh?"

Dana shook her head. "I honestly don't care who wins. I just hope someone does," she said.

Steve sighed. "It's up to them. Come on."

🫏 🫏 🫏

"Candace?" Jameson called across the room. Candace turned and smiled. "You all right?"

"I'm fine. Just needed to catch my breath," Candace said. "Sorry, I left you to fend for yourself with the wolves."

Jameson laughed. "I'm was out in college. I've experienced the pack mentality a few times," she joked. "You certainly are popular."

"That's a relative term," Candace said. "Anyone who offers free booze, the ability to network, and decent food can be the star of an evening in this town."

Jameson had made her way to Candace and was standing in front of her. "I think you sell yourself short on that one," she said sincerely.

"Maybe you give me too much credit," Candace replied. "Believe me when I tell you, I would just as soon eat chicken wings with you and Pearl."

"Mmm," Jameson pursed her lips.

"What?"

"You love this too," Jameson commented.

"You think so?"

"I do. I watched you work that room," Jameson said affectionately.

"You watched me?" Candace lifted an eyebrow. Jameson nodded. "Really?" Candace tried to joke.

"People are drawn to you," Jameson commented.

"Because they think I can do something for them." Jameson shook her head 'no'. "Yes, Jameson. They are good people, but they are always working. Looking for an opening…."

"They look to you," Jameson said.

"I've been doing this a while," Candace replied.

"Maybe. That's not the only reason," Jameson said. Candace struggled to catch her breath as Jameson moved closer. "It's not just what you do," she said. "It's who you are," Jameson complimented. She looked in Candace's eyes and instantly lost her heart. "Maybe you just can't see what they see," Jameson suggested. "What I see." Jameson closed the short remaining distance and took Candace's face in her hands. She could see a hint of apprehension mingling closely with anticipation in the senator's eyes. She closed the rest of the distance and placed her lips on Candace's.

Candace felt Jameson's lips on hers and closed her eyes in

surrender. She wrapped her arms around Jameson's waist and allowed Jameson to pull her closer. Jameson coaxed Candace's lips to part and Candace answered the request. Jameson's kiss was so tender that Candace thought for a moment her heart might break from the connection between them. The kiss continued, softly exploring, unhurried and searching. It was as if Jameson were attempting to speak some truth without any words. When Jameson began to pull back slowly, Candace kept her eyes closed. She felt Jameson's hands caress her cheeks.

Candace opened her eyes slowly and looked at Jameson. "Jameson," she said softly.

Jameson smiled. "I just wanted you to know," she said.

Candace was about to respond when the door opened. "Hey," Dana called to the pair. She took note of Jameson's hands as they dropped from Candace's face. "I'm sorry."

Candace moved in front of Jameson. "It's all right, Dana."

"Vice President Miller just arrived," Dana explained.

Candace nodded. She looked back at Jameson apologetically. Jameson offered her an understanding smile. "Go."

"I…"

"I'll see you later," Jameson promised.

Candace nodded again and walked past Dana in the doorway. Jameson closed her eyes, already missing the older woman's presence. "I'm sorry," Dana said sincerely.

Jameson opened her eyes and smiled. "It's okay. I just needed her to know."

🐎🐎🐎

"Hey," Candace caught up to Jameson. Jameson smiled. "You are leaving with the lovebirds?" she asked kiddingly.

"Looks like it," Jameson said.

Candace tried unsuccessfully to smile. She desperately wanted to say something meaningful to Jameson. Emotions and questions were running through her at such an overwhelming pace she thought that she might drown in them. She looked up at Jameson helplessly. "When are you headed home?" she finally asked.

"Monday," Jameson answered. "When are you leaving for Marianne's?"

"Monday morning."

Jameson forced a small smile. She looked ahead to Steven as he opened the car door for Dana. "Looks like my chariot is waiting." Candace smiled weakly. "Merry Christmas, Candace," Jameson said placing a quick kiss on the senator's cheek.

"Jameson?" Candace reached out for the younger woman's arm. Jameson stopped. Candace lost her courage. "Merry Christmas." Jameson winked and headed for the car. Candace watched her climb into the backseat and waved to the threesome as Steven hopped into the driver's seat and shut the door. She watched from the doorway for a moment, wishing she could follow rather than return to the guests that waited for her inside. Why didn't she say something? Anything? Candace wrapped her arms around herself to stave off the December chill. She walked back to the door with one final glance down the street. With a deep sigh, she returned to the world she knew best.

Candace mingled for a few minutes. She found herself wandering back toward her study. She walked into the room and covered her face with her hands. She should call Jameson and say something. "What are you going to say, Candy?" she chuckled to herself. "You know this is a bad idea."

"Now, what on earth is the host hiding from?" a low voice beckoned.

Candace turned around and painted on a contrived smile. "Rachel," she greeted the woman.

Rachel Hutton had been a partner in Candace's ex-husband's law firm. She was six years younger than Candace, tall, slender, blonde, and nothing short of aggressive both in and out of the courtroom. "Bored?" Rachel asked.

"I wouldn't say that," Candace answered.

Rachel took a step closer. "It's never easy to endure these things alone," she said seductively.

Candace sighed. This situation had the potential to devolve into an uncomfortable mess quickly. "I manage," she said lightly.

"Why only manage?" Rachel asked suggestively.

"Oh, shit!" Dana sighed in frustration.

"What's wrong?" Steven asked.

"I forgot my damn handbag."

Steven sighed through a chuckle. "I'll turn around."

"On with the shoes," Dana groaned.

"I'll run in and get it," Jameson offered.

Dana turned in her seat. "J.D., you don't have to....unless, of course, there is some reason you want to."

Jameson just shook her head. "Don't worry about it," she said. She sat silently in the backseat listening to her friends bantering in the front. They had been together since college, and Jameson envied their relationship. They had just seemed to fit instantly. Many of their friends predicted that the real world would signal the end of Dana and Steve's honeymoon. Fourteen years and two children later, the pair seemed as happy with each other as they had been at twenty-one.

Jameson looked at the townhouse as it came into view and readied herself. Perhaps, Dana's handbag was the excuse she needed to say what she had meant to say to Candace. She opened the door and peered back inside. "Do you know where you left it?"

"Yeah, I set it on the table right outside Candy's study when I said goodbye to the vice president unless someone moved it."

"I'll be right back," Jameson promised.

"Take your time," Dana said. "We'll find something to do," she laughed. Jameson rolled her eyes and shut her door. Dana watched her go.

"You left it there on purpose, didn't you?" Steven asked.

"Me?" Dana gasped in offense. "I can't believe you would think that."

Steven laughed. "You watched too much *Spin City*," he said. "And, read too many romance novels. You should have put that on your resume to warn Candy," he told his wife.

"Watch it Russo or you'll be sleeping on the senator's couch."

🫏 🫏 🫏

Jameson made her way through the thinning crowd until she reached the short hallway that led to Candace's office. She spotted Dana's handbag and made her way to retrieve it when she heard voices.

"Candy," Rachel implored the senator.

Jameson could not resist the urge to peek inside the study. She felt her heart drop rapidly in her chest when the tall blonde woman pulled Candace to her. The woman's hands wrapped around Candace's waist tightly. Jameson looked to the ceiling and then closed her eyes in an attempt to banish the image. She turned quickly on her heels and left.

"Rachel," Candace started to pull away.

"We could be so good together," Rachel whispered.

Candace closed her eyes for a moment. She had made this mistake once, lost her senses after one too many glasses of wine and led Rachel to her bedroom. It had been nothing more than a one night stand for Candace. Rachel continued to see it as a potential opening for more. Candace finally pulled away more forcefully. "Stop," she said.

"I don't understand you," Rachel said. "You can't tell me that you didn't enjoy…"

"I never said I didn't find you attractive," Candace admitted. "I'm not in love with you."

"Don't you think we are getting a little old for that kind of fanciful thinking?" Rachel asked.

Candace shook her head. Did she? She thought for a moment. The singular image that played in her mind was Jameson. "Maybe," Candace finally answered. "Maybe it is fanciful. That doesn't make it impossible."

Rachel's sweet expression did little to conceal her displeasure at Candace's assertion. "Candy, are you looking to martyr yourself as the Queen of Broken Hearts?" she asked. Candace's gaze grew petulant. "Love is for the young and fool hearted."

"And, what would you suggest in its place?" Candace wondered.

"The three A's: attraction, acceptance, and alliance."

Candace nodded. "You certainly picked the right town to pursue that equation. I think you might find that theory is flawed," Candace suggested. She went on to explain. "You left out a few A's: arrogance, apathy, and animosity, to name a few."

Rachel threw her hands in the air. "You are impossible."

"And, you are relentless," Candace said with a wink.

"Who is she?" Rachel asked. Candace just smiled. "Oh, so there is someone," Rachel teased. Candace lifted both brows and shrugged. "Well, now that you've broken my heart.…"

"Didn't you sell that old thing years ago?" Candace poked.

"Some of us do have sense, you know?" Rachel returned.

"Come on, I'll buy you a free drink," Candace offered.

"Chivalrous to the end," Rachel said.

"Always," Candace winked.

"J.D. just stay," Dana said.

"No, I have a lot to do. I'm just going to rent a car and drive home."

"What happened last night?" Dana asked.

"Nothing happened, Dana. There are a lot of new projects I need to look over at the firm—that's all."

The change in Jameson's mood from reflective to sullen was evident. Dana wondered if Candy had said something to upset Jameson. That seemed unlikely. She couldn't imagine what had caused Jameson's apparent need to get away. "J.D., Christmas is Thursday. Why don't…"

Jameson set her bag on the bed and faced Dana. "I just need to go."

"Call her," Dana implored her friend. "Whatever happened, and J.D., I know something happened. Just call her."

Jameson's downcast glance nearly broke Dana's heart. "I'm not sure that's such a good idea right now," she said softly. "Thanks for everything," Jameson said, reaching to hug her friend. "The drive will be good for me," she promised.

Dana watched as Jameson retrieved her bag and started to leave the room. She sighed dramatically, wondering if she should intervene somehow. Steven caught her in the hallway and knew immediately what she was thinking. "Dana, whatever it is, you have to let them work this one out."

"I've never seen J.D. like that."

Steven agreed. "She loves your boss," he tried to relieve the tension.

"Yeah."

"Maybe Candy just doesn't feel…"

Dana shook her head. "Steve, I've never seen Candy the way she is with J.D."

"Jessica?" he asked.

"No."

"So, maybe she just…"

"Is terrified?" Dana suggested.

"Candy? Terrified?" he scoffed at his wife's idea.

Dana turned and looked at him. "Yes, terrified. You know what that whole thing did to her."

"Of J.D.?" he asked in disbelief.

"No, of what she feels for J.D. and what that means. Maybe I should call…"

"No. This is between the two of them, Dana. It's not a story you need to spin. It's their story to write. Have a little faith in them. They'll figure it out."

"What makes you so sure?" she asked doubtfully.

"I've never known either of them to back down from a challenge," he said.

Dana snickered at the observation. "Well, that's true," she said.

"Come on, we've got some alone time now before the kids come home."

"Looking to take advantage of your best friend's misfortune?" she asked.

"No, just looking to take advantage of my wife."

Dana laughed and gave into her husband's kiss. "Remind me to thank, J.D."

Chapter Seven

Candace set her phone on the table and put her face in her hands. "Mom?" Michelle called to her quietly. Candace did not move. Michelle sat down beside her mother and put a hand on her back. "What's wrong?" she asked. When Candace looked up, Michelle was startled by the tears in her mother's eyes. "Mom?" Candace just closed her eyes and shook her head. Michelle sighed. "What happened?"

"I really don't know," Candace finally answered.

"J.D.?" Michelle guessed. Candace nodded. "Did you have an argument over something?"

Candace laughed nervously. "Not exactly."

"Okay?"

"She kissed me."

Michelle was puzzled. "And, that is a bad thing?"

"I don't know," Candace answered truthfully.

"Did you kiss her back?" Michelle asked curiously. Candace looked at her daughter indignantly. "Okay....Well, what then? She's a bad kisser?" Michelle was stumped.

"No," Candace laughed nervously.

"Okay, so she's a good kisser?"

"Shell!"

"I guess I don't understand what the problem is," Michelle admitted. "What happened next?"

"I got called away," Candace said. Michelle nodded and waited for her mother to continue. Candace sighed heavily and got up from her chair. "And, I didn't say anything," she admitted in frustration.

Michelle watched her mother carefully. Candace covered her eyes and massaged them wearily. "What did you want to say?" Michelle asked cautiously. Candace closed her eyes, took a deep breath, released it slowly and looked to her daughter helplessly. Michelle smiled. "So, why didn't you tell her?" she asked her mother. Candace shook her head. She felt an enormous sense of self-loathing. "Mom," Michelle made her way to her mother. "You can still tell her, you know?"

"I'm not so sure about that," Candace said.

"Just call her."

"I tried. She hasn't returned any of my calls."

Michelle offered her mother a compassionate smile. "So? Why are you here?" Candace was stunned by the question. "Marianne will forgive you....eventually," Michelle giggled. "You can sulk and worry here or go see J.D. and find a way to be happy."

"Shell, it's not that simple."

"It is that simple," Michelle said flatly. "What's complicated?"

"Jesus, Shell! For one thing, Jameson is only six years older than your sister! Think about that in twenty years," Candace argued. Michelle pursed her lips in defiance. "Michelle," Candace groaned. "My life is not ready made for…"

"For what? For a relationship or for a relationship with J.D.?" Michelle interrupted her mother. "J.D. is old enough to make her own decisions. And, you deserve to be happy, Mom," she said lovingly. Candace's doubtful expression pained Michelle. She grabbed both her mother's arms and looked into her eyes. "Stop making objections like this is a case to argue in the courtroom or on the Senate floor."

"Shell, I don't even know if she wants to see me. I froze. I just…."

Michelle smiled. "Do you love her?" she asked knowingly. Candace closed her eyes in resignation. "Oh, Mom."

"It's Spencer's first Christmas," Candace said tacitly.

"Yes, and you know that he will be here next year. Can you say the same thing about J.D.?" she asked. Candace could not answer. "Go. I'll handle Marianne."

"When did you become so determined?"

"I learned from the best," Michelle said. Candace chuckled as Michelle embraced her. "I love you, Mom."

"I know you do. I love you too, Shell."

"So, go and do something for you, for once," Michelle said. She could see her mother teetering on the edge. "If you can't do it for you, do it for J.D."

"Shell…"

"That must have been some kiss," Michelle guessed. Candace nodded. Michelle picked up her mother's phone and handed it to her. "So, are you calling the airlines, or should I?"

Pearl stood at the sink keeping a close eye on Jameson. Jameson had met with the construction team earlier in the morning. She had been markedly quiet afterward. For the last hour, Pearl watched as the architect stared aimlessly at the same screen on her computer. Occasionally, she would lift her cell phone and look at it, sigh, and then put it back down. Pearl moved beside Jameson with the coffee pot, refilled the half empty mug that sat beside Jameson's computer, and then collapsed into the chair that sat beside the younger woman. "Care to tell me what is going on with you?" she asked.

Jameson shrugged. "Just tired."

Pearl directed Jameson to look at her. "Jameson, I raised two children, not to mention the horde that grew up in this house. I know that look."

"What look?"

"That one. Candy sported the exact same expression for the entire week after Jinx ate that bird. Now, what is going on? Someone eat your canary?"

Jameson laughed in spite of herself. "No."

"Look, your folks are away, my kids are away. If you are going to spend your time moping around here all through

Christmas, I will have to take some drastic measures." Pearl pointed to a small paddle that hung on the wall. It was adorned with basically everyone's name who had ever resided in the house. "So, what is it going to be? You gonna fess up or am I gonna give you your right of passage?"

"I'm an idiot," Jameson said. Pearl was perplexed. "I didn't know Candace was involved with anyone."

Pearl's eyes flew open. "What on earth are you talking about?"

Jameson shrugged sadly. "I just made a total ass of myself, that's all." Pearl looked at Jameson to explain. "I kissed her."

"Candy?" Pearl asked for clarification. Jameson nodded. "And, she told you she was involved with someone?"

"No...." Pearl put up her hands in questioning. "No. She didn't say anything at all."

"And, that made you think she was seeing someone?"

"No."

"Jameson! What on earth are you talking about? Did she push you away?" Jameson shook her head. "What would give you the idea that Candy was involved with someone?"

Jameson groaned. "I had to go back to get Dana's bag. She was with that, well there was this gorgeous blonde that..."

"Rachel," Pearl rolled her eyes.

"I don't know. I just...they were close. I felt stupid. Of course, she would be...she just never said anything."

Pearl's howl of laughter startled and confused Jameson. "I'm sorry, Jameson. Candy would no more be involved with Rachel Hutton than she would become a Republican," she continued to laugh.

"I don't know..."

"Oh, I do know. Look, it's not my place....Rachel's been after Candy for years," Pearl said. Jameson looked at the older woman expectantly. Pearl sighed deeply. "One night, right after everything had blown up with Jessica in the press, Candy had a few too many glasses of wine....Well, let's just say as hard as Candy has tried to forget it, Rachel has never let her."

Jameson felt mixed emotions in the knowledge that Candace had been with the other woman. "How do you know…"

"I know my Candy," Pearl said assuredly. "Jameson, Look....I'm going to tell you something, and I want you to listen to me. Okay?" Jameson nodded. "Candy is…well, there are always people pursuing her, some for the right reasons, most of them with little regard for who Candy really is. It's always been that way, even before she was in office," Pearl explained. Jameson smiled. Candace was a strikingly attractive woman. She was charming and intelligent, and she came from a well-connected family. It was easy for Jameson to comprehend anyone's desire to be with the senator. Pearl continued. "She's beautiful, she's smart, she's wealthy, she's compassionate," Pearl said.

"Yes, she is," Jameson agreed with the assessment.

Pearl smiled. "Mm-hm. You see the real Candace, Jameson. Some people only see the senator now. They don't see the parts of her that she has let you get to know. The mom, the daughter, the woman at the center."

"I'm not sure I follow," Jameson admitted.

"I know you love Candy," Pearl said. Jameson made no comment. "I can't speak for her and I won't, but I'd bet this house that she held on tight when you laid that kiss on her." Pearl saw Jameson's lips turn into a small smile. "I told you, I know my Candy. If you hope to have any kind of relationship with her, you are going to have to accept the fact that there will always be people trying to win her away. And, you are going to have to trust her."

"Pearl, I don't even know how she feels."

Pearl laughed. "Yes, you do. You wouldn't have kissed her otherwise." Jameson sighed again. "She's not as complicated as she likes to think," Pearl said. "Her life can be. To be truthful, that's what happened with Jessica."

"What do you mean?"

"Jessica is not the witch Michelle and Marianne, and the press think she is. She cheated. That devastated Candy. I think Candy also knows Jessica loved her, even then."

"I can't imagine cheating on a woman like Candace."

"No, I know you can't. Jessica was always jealous of the attention Candy received. Candy can make you feel like a million bucks, like you are the only person in the world that exists when she is talking to you. That's her job. And, she is sincere when she is with you, but it's never meant as a slight to the people closest to her. Those few people in her personal life, they are Candy's world. Jessica never understood that. She tried to compete when she never needed to. I think she wanted Candy to feel that—that fear."

"Now, I feel like a bigger idiot."

Pearl winked. "Love will do that," she said. "Now, stop staring at that little box and call her."

"I could have gotten a cab," Candace said to her son-in-law.

Rick smiled. "I really can stand to miss this episode of The Sibling Wars," he joked.

"Sorry about that," Candace said with a smirk.

"Don't be."

"I do feel horrible about leaving," Candace admitted.

"Don't," Rick said as he pulled up to the curb. "I know Marianne comes on a little strong. She does love you."

"I know."

"We all do," he said. Candace smiled. "She just worries. And, I think part of her worries about losing you."

"Losing me?" Candace asked in disbelief.

"Yeah," he said with a sideways grin. "I don't think you realize how much your opinion means to her."

Candace was surprised. "She's my daughter, Rick. I would do anything for her."

"Yeah, I know that. So does she, but she's always trying to prove herself to you, you know?"

"She doesn't have to prove anything."

"You are a lot to live up to," he said earnestly.

Candace shook her head. "Not really."

Rick nodded. "You just don't see it."

"You are the second person to say that to me recently."

"I'm betting the other is the reason you are getting on that plane," he said. Candace smiled. "Sounds like a winner," Rick said. "Shell is right, Mom," he said. Candace was curious. "You deserve to be happy."

"I guess we'll see," Candace said.

Candace took her seat on the plane. She took out her cell phone with the intention of calling Pearl to inform her of her impending arrival. She was surprised to see the missed call and voicemail notification. She wasn't certain she was prepared to hear the message, but she thought at the very least it would prepare her for what she might be confronting soon.

"Hey. It's me. Guess you know that, though, huh?" Candace smiled at the sound of Jameson's voice. *"I don't want to interrupt your visit with your family, so you don't need to call back or anything. I just wanted to say Merry Christmas. I just..."* Candace listened intently as Jameson's voice trailed off. *"Just, have a good holiday. I'll try to get these birds on the wall before the New Year."* Candace laughed. *"Oh, Jinx says hi and... Well, I guess I should*

say....I miss you. Anyway, say hi to Shell. Merry Christmas, Candace."

Candace closed her eyes in relief. Maybe she would get the chance to tell Jameson the truth after all. She put her phone in airplane mode and stowed it in her bag. "A few hours," she muttered.

Pearl was in the kitchen fixing some lunch for her and Jameson. Jameson had headed into the study to do some work after their morning conversation. She had been secretive about the room, instructing the construction crew to leave that room for her personal attention. Pearl had peeked in unknowingly and immediately understood the reasons why. This was Candace's favorite room. Jameson intended to honor that with care. Jameson had been on a ladder hanging familiar wallpaper when Pearl left to start on lunch. Pearl smiled as she put the bread away and went to set the sandwiches she had made on the table. She wondered if Candace had any idea how lucky she was to find someone like Jameson Reid.

"Jinx!" Jameson yelled. A huge crash followed and Pearl dropped the sandwiches in her hand in a mad dash toward the sound.

"Jameson," Pearl called. "Jameson. Hang on, kiddo," she said. She scurried to the front door. "In there," she pointed to the study. She watched as the paramedics tended to the architect. "Oh, Jameson," she sighed. She grabbed the phone in the hallway and dialed Candace. "Voicemail. Figures. Candy, listen, I am on my way to Mercy with Jameson. You need to call me on my cell phone as soon as you get this. I have to go."

84

Pearl paced in the emergency waiting room. She continually checked her phone. There was no answer from Candace. Finally giving in to her frustration, she called Marianne.

"Hello?" Michelle answered the phone.

"Shell? Is that you?" Pearl asked.

"Yeah. Hey, Grandma Pearl!"

"Shell, is your mother there?"

"No. Didn't she call you?" Michelle asked.

"Call me? Why would she call me?"

"She's on her way home," Michelle explained. "She should be home in an hour or so, I would think. Maybe sooner now." Hearing the heavy sigh on the line Michelle became unnerved. "Why? What's wrong?"

"It's Jameson," Pearl said.

"That's why she's coming home," Michelle said. "To talk to J.D."

"No, Shell. I'm at the hospital with Jameson right now."

Marianne came down the stairs and caught the terrified expression on her sister's face. "What's wrong?" Marianne asked her sister.

Michelle shook her head. "Is Jameson okay?" Michelle asked Pearl.

"I don't know. I've been trying to call your mother for an hour. I can't get any answers here."

"What happened?"

"Mrs. Johnson?" a woman's voice called to Pearl.

"Yes?"

"Can you come with me, please?" the nurse asked.

Pearl nodded. "I have to go Shell."

"Wait! What about Jameson?"

"I don't know. If your mother calls, tell her we are at Mercy. I have to go. I'll call when I know anything," she said and disconnected the call.

Michelle hung up the phone and covered her mouth. Tears were beginning to fill her eyes. Marianne took the phone from her sister's hand. "Shell?"

Michelle shook her head. "I don't know," she said. "Something happened to J.D. Pearl is…She's scared, Marianne. I could hear it."

"Grandma Pearl doesn't get scared," Marianne said.

"I know," Michelle said quietly.

Marianne hugged her sister. "It'll be okay, Shell."

"I hope so," Michelle said. "I don't think Mom could handle that."

"She really loves this woman," Marianne said more to herself than to her sister.

"Yeah. She really does."

Candace thanked the agent and slid into her rental car. She put her hands on the steering wheel and took a deep breath. She smiled, wondering if Jameson might be at the house. "I guess I really should call Pearl," she said. She grabbed her phone and was stunned to see the number of missed calls. "What on earth?" Just as she was about to listen to the messages the phone rang.

"Shell?"

"Mom? Where are you?"

"I just got into the rental car. Why? What is going on?" Candace asked.

"Mom," Shell said as steadily as she could.

"Michelle—what?"

Michelle sighed nervously. "You need to go to Mercy."

"Mercy? Mercy Hospital? Why?"

"Grandma Pearl is at…"

"What happened to Pearl?" Candace asked fearfully.

Michelle took a deep breath. "She's fine, Mom. It's…"

"Why is she at Mercy?"

"Mom!" Michelle called for her mother's attention. "It's not Grandma Pearl. She's there with J.D." Candace's heart stopped. "Mom?" Michelle called. "Mom?"

Marianne took the phone from her sister. "Mom," Marianne's voice came over the line.

"Jameson…."

"Mom, calm down, okay? We don't know anything, just that Grandma Pearl is at Mercy and wants you to meet her there," Marianne said. Candace nodded dumbly on the other end of the phone. She felt suddenly paralyzed by fear. "Mom?" Marianne called. "Are you going to be all right to drive? I'll call and have someone…"

"No," Candace snapped to attention. "No. I'm on my way. If Pearl calls, tell her I will be there in about half an hour."

"Mom…."

"Marianne, I'll be fine."

"It will be all right," Marianne said with genuine compassion.

"I hope so."

"It will be. I still have to harass this woman," she said. Candace smiled as best she could. "Call us when…."

"I will."

Candace blew through the emergency room doors like a small tornado. She made her way to the desk, flushed and fearful. "I'm looking for Jameson Reid."

The desk attendant looked up. "Senator Fletcher," he immediately recognized the woman.

"Yes. Jameson Reid," she said pointedly.

He looked at the screen in front of him. "Room four," he said. Candace was already moving forward when he stopped her. "You need this," he said, handing her a visitor sticker with the room number on it. He pressed a button to open the automatic doors and the world slowed down for Candace. People were bustling through the hallway. She saw the room number ahead and willed her feet to keep moving.

"Senator?" a woman's voice called for her attention. Candace turned. "Your friend asked that I make sure you find the room."

Candace nodded. "Is she?"

"Right in here," the nurse said, pushing the door open.

Pearl was standing in front of the bed and Candace could not immediately see Jameson. She stopped just inside the doorway as a wave of fear eclipsed her. Pearl turned and smiled. "Took you long enough," she said. She moved aside and Candace finally saw Jameson.

Jameson smiled as best she could. The relief that traveled through Candace instantly produced a steady stream of tears. She made her way to Jameson's side and gently touched the architect's cheek. Jameson had a bandage over her right eye and a sizable welt on her forehead. Her eye was several shades of green and blue. Candace tenderly traced the injuries, without any words.

"I'm okay," Jameson tried to reassure her. Candace's tears fell more swiftly as she finally looked in Jameson's bloodshot eyes. "Hey, people are going to think you like me or something," Jameson tried to coax Candace to relax.

Candace laughed through a sob. "I more than like you, you lunatic."

Jameson smiled and took hold of the hand that was continually stroking her cheek. "Spoken like a true politician," she said. Candace continued to cry. "And, I love you too," Jameson said.

"Don't you ever scare me like this again," Candace warned the woman in the bed. Jameson kissed Candace's forehead. "I love you," Candace admitted hoarsely.

"I know," Jameson said, allowing Candace's head to fall onto her shoulder. "But, it's nice to hear you say it. So, now, use your clout and get me out of here."

Candace laughed. "I don't know about that. Let's see what the doctors say."

"They say I can go home as long as someone stays with me. Know anyone who might be willing?" she asked.

Candace looked at Jameson. "I might have some connections," she said before leaning in to kiss Jameson's lips softly.

"Is that one of my prescriptions? Because I might look to fall off a ladder every day if it earns me one of those."

Candace pulled back and scolded Jameson with her eyes. "What do you mean you fell off a ladder?" Jameson shrugged. Candace looked to Pearl, who in turn shrugged. "How did you fall off a ladder? Where were you on a ladder? Wait…Why were you on a…."

Jameson stopped Candace's rant with a quick kiss. "Jinx."

"Jinx?"

"Yeah, I guess he wanted to help me with the wallpaper."

"Explain."

"I was hanging wallpaper. I was on the ladder and he jumped off of a shelf onto my shoulder. I fell, the ladder fell on top of me and knocked me out cold," Jameson explained in one long breath.

"I told you! No black cat should be named Jinx! Why doesn't anyone ever listen to me?" Candace said in exasperation.

"I'll change his name, just take me home," Jameson implored the senator.

Candace shook her head. "Is this what I have to look forward to?" she asked.

Jameson smiled. "I'll try not to get a concussion too often. Does that mean you'll keep me?" she joked.

"You, yes. The cat…."

"Aw, it was just an accident," Jameson said. "I survived."

"We'll talk," Candace said, knowing that Jameson could likely convince her of anything. "Keep an eye on her," she instructed Pearl. "I'll see about taking you home," she promised. She leaned in and kissed Jameson's forehead before leaving.

"That went well," Jameson said to Pearl.

"Don't be surprised if she sells that cat to the Chinese restaurant," Pearl laughed. "And, next time you want her to kiss you, do me a favor and just ask. Okay? I almost ended up in the bed next to you with a heart attack."

"Sorry," Jameson apologized.

"Kids," Pearl groaned.

Chapter Eight

Candace felt Jameson's arms around her waist. She snuggled back into the architect's embrace. They had spent a quiet couple of days together. Jameson had slept on and off, and Candace was content to lie beside the woman she loved. She had crept into bed a few hours earlier when Jameson was sleeping. She felt Jameson's lips on the back of her neck. "You're awake," Candace observed softly. Jameson's answer came in the form of more insistent kisses down Candace's neck. Her hands began mapping out Candace's hips and abdomen. Candace closed her eyes and reveled in the feel of Jameson against her. "Sweetheart, what are you doing?" she began to protest. She turned in Jameson's arms.

Jameson's hands continued their methodical exploration, tracing patterns on Candace's back. "I love you," Jameson said.

Candace took Jameson's face in her hands. "We have plenty of time, Jameson. I'm not that old," she tried to joked. Jameson answered with a tender kiss that began to deepen steadily. Her hands began moving up and down Candace's back with more urgency and intention. "Jameson," Candace sighed. "You need to rest."

Jameson kissed Candace and moved her onto her back. She hovered over the senator and shook her head. "I need to make love to you," she said. Candace fought to breathe. Jameson's directness was accompanied by a passionate gaze. She lifted her hands to Jameson's face and held it tenderly. Jameson felt the trembling in Candace's touch. "What are you afraid of?" she asked the older woman.

"Losing you," Candace confessed her heart.

Jameson smiled. "Candace," she said. "I have waited my entire life for you." Candace closed her eyes at Jameson's admission. "I am in love with you. Completely in love with you." Candace opened her eyes and traced over Jameson's eyebrows and cheeks with her fingers. Jameson kissed Candace's forehead tenderly. "The only way you will ever lose me is if you send me away."

"Jameson, when I am seventy-five you will be my age now."

"And, I will make love to you just as slowly and passionately as I am about to now." Candace sighed as Jameson's hands traveled gently over her body. "Do you love me?" Jameson asked directly.

Candace smiled at the woman above her. "You might not believe this, but I love you more than I ever thought possible."

Jameson kissed Candace and felt Candace's hands drop to her back, searching and exploring. She pulled back slightly and smiled. "Let me show you," Jameson requested.

Candace was helpless to do anything but surrender. She could feel the truth in Jameson's declarations and in every delicate touch of the architect's lips and hands. Jameson's kiss remained loving, but grew more insistent and demanding before she moved her lips to Candace's neck. Candace threw her head back to give Jameson better access. She felt the muscles in Jameson's back through the light T-shirt she wore and suddenly had an overwhelming need to feel Jameson's skin. Jameson sat up and allowed Candace to help her pull the T-shirt over her head.

Candace lost her breath at the sight of Jameson's half naked form sitting above her. Her hands reached out and drifted over Jameson's breasts. Jameson smiled at the growing desire evident in Candace's eyes. Candace was wearing a night shirt and Jameson gave a suggestive lift of her brow as she reached down to remove it. Candace sat up at the unspoken direction and Jameson swiftly removed the offending article. Facing each other, Jameson moved in and captured Candace's lips in an ardent kiss that caused Candace to moan.

Jameson's lips traveled over Candace's throat slowly, her tongue softly tracing a line toward the senator's cleavage. Her arms wrapped tightly around Candace's waist. Her hands firmly taking a loving hold of Candace's lower back and pulling her closer as her kiss traveled over Candace's breasts. She heard Candace whisper her name and looked up to see Candace close her eyes in submission. Jameson watched as need etched the expression of the face she loved and dropped her kiss deliberately over Candace's right nipple. She kissed it reverently, slowly, so softly that Candace could barely detect the sensation. A small moan encouraged Jameson and she sucked the small bud into her mouth firmly.

"Jesus!" Candace gasped. Jameson sucked harder and then pulled away, leaving faint kisses across Candace's breasts before capturing the other nipple in the same way. Candace felt an electrical current travel straight through every nerve in her body and settle directly south. Jameson began to pull away again and Candace grabbed hold of her to urge her continued exploration. "Please," Candace begged.

"Please what?" Jameson asked playfully.

"Please, don't stop," Candace said.

"Don't stop this?" Jameson asked, taking a nipple into her mouth and sucking on it gently. "Or this?" she asked, sucking harder.

"God!" Candace gasped.

Jameson obeyed the unspoken request. She moved her right hand to Candace's other nipple and pulled at it gently, careful to give equal attention to both. Candace's breath was beginning to grow quick and shallow. Jameson could feel the arousal growing in them both. She sucked in a ragged breath when Candace's hand cupped her breast and the senator's palm grazed her nipple.

Candace felt the response from her lover and squeezed Jameson's nipple gently. Jameson's automatic reaction was to bathe both of Candace's breasts in a flurry of small nips and kisses. Jameson understood Candace better than Candace realized. She pushed Candace back onto the bed and lifted the senator's hands over her head, holding them there. She kissed Candace deeply, allowing their tongues to dance and battle for dominance. She gently tugged at Candace's bottom lip with her teeth and then pulled back to look into Candace's eyes. "Let me make love to you, Candace," Jameson said. Jameson watched desire and confusion play across Candace's face. "Just let me love you," she said softly before lowering her kiss back to Candace's breasts.

"Jameson," Candace moaned.

Jameson's hands roamed over Candace's stomach and thighs while her lips and tongue continued to make love to each of Candace's nipples. Jameson felt Candace's hips rise to meet her touch when her hand reached Candace's thigh. Jameson looked up briefly and smiled. Candace's need and anticipation were evident in her breathing, her deep sighs, and the mixture of frustration and ecstasy that caused her eyes to close tightly.

Jameson allowed her fingers to faintly cover the soft curls between the senator's legs. "Oh my God," Jameson sighed as she felt the softness beneath her touch.

"Jameson, please," Candace encouraged her lover. She moaned loudly when Jameson slipped a finger inside of her. "Jameson!"

Jameson had become lost in the sensations that touching Candace produced in her body. She was beginning to crave release for herself, but she was determined to spend every ounce of her energy and effort on Candace's pleasure. Her kisses began to wander lower, her tongue tasting the skin of Candace's stomach and legs. Her fingers kept a steady rhythm with the grinding of Candace's hips against them. She would pull them back as far as possible without breaking all contact and feel Candace's hips rise in desperation. Jameson thrust deeper and harder and Candace cried out.

Candace's heart was thrumming so fast and hard that she could barely remember to breathe. Jameson's exploration of her body was driving her closer and closer to the edge of sanity. She wanted to let go. She wanted Jameson to take her completely, and yet she did not want the delicious torture she was experiencing to end. She felt Jameson's fingers move inside of her and held her breath when a soft, warm, wetness traveled the length of her need.

Jameson dipped her tongue inside Candace for a split second, before allowing it to find Candace's greatest need. She flicked it lightly over the small, sensitive area that seemed to grow with each kiss, then sucked gently while her fingers continued their assault. "You feel so good," Jameson said through a small moan before tasting her lover again.

Candace could feel her muscles gripping Jameson's fingers. The more her body responded, the faster the pace of Jameson's efforts became. "Oh, God!" Candace screamed as she drew closer to her release. She had never made a declaration in the throes of passion before, but as she felt Jameson bring her over the final precipice she called out for the woman she loved. "Jameson…I love you….I love you," she cried.

Jameson was amazed at the rush of emotion that surged through her with Candace's release. She heard Candace's words and it compelled her to gentle her touch without stopping it. She slowed her pace and drew out Candace's orgasm until it rolled into another wave, and then another. Jameson finally lifted herself and noted the tears that bathed Candace's cheeks.

"Why are you crying?" she asked in concern.

Candace reached for Jameson and kissed her tenderly. "I love you so much," she said.

Jameson smiled. "I know you do," Jameson said. She narrowed her gaze at an unfamiliar expression in her lover's eyes. In an instant, Candace had reversed their positions and was straddling Jameson's hips. She didn't say another word. She claimed Jameson's lips in a kiss that would have brought Rome to its knees. Jameson swallowed hard as that same fervent kiss found its way to her breasts. She sighed.

Candace could tell that Jameson was aching for release. There would be time for her to make love to Jameson slowly, and she had every intention of delivering the same methodical torment she had just happily endured soon. Right now, she could sense the urgency in Jameson. Her tongue teased every inch of Jameson's flesh and she delighted in the way the younger woman began to writhe beneath her.

"Candace…I need you," Jameson confessed.

"What do you need, Jameson?"

"You," Jameson repeated.

Candace found Jameson's sudden shyness endearing. It seemed the architect's boldness withered under the senator's touch. Candace understood. Making love with Jameson, Jameson making love to her had been the most vulnerable she had ever felt. "I'm right here," Candace promised as she took a nipple into her mouth. Jameson moaned. Candace pulled back and looked at her lover. "What do you need?" she asked. Jameson's body moved against her will and Candace pressed her weight against her lover to steady her. Candace lifted her kiss to Jameson's mouth. When Jameson's searching became desperate, Candace pulled back and replaced the fiery battle for dominance with the most delicate kiss Jameson had ever experienced. Candace brushed the hair from Jameson's eyes. "What do you need, Jameson?" she asked gently.

Jameson met her lover's reassuring gaze and closed her eyes. "I need you inside me," she confessed.

Candace smiled and moved her hand to comply with the request. She held Jameson's eyes as she entered the younger woman tentatively. Jameson was so wet Candace had to fight the desire to taste her. She understood what Jameson needed. "Look at me," she instructed the woman beneath her. Jameson complied. Candace moved gently in and out of Jameson, stroking her with her thumb at the same time. Jameson was struggling against the urge to close her eyes, but Candace's gaze held her firmly in place. It was the most erotic thing she had ever experienced. Candace's eyes conveyed all the love and desire that she felt for Jameson. Jameson desperately wanted to let go. That had always been difficult for her. Somehow, it seemed that Candace was aware of that.

"Let go," Candace told Jameson. Jameson held onto Candace tightly. Candace allowed her fingers to search deeper and she increased the pressure with her thumb, softly stroking in a circular pattern. She placed her forehead against Jameson's and whispered. "Let go, Jameson. I'm right here."

Jameson's world exploded into an array of color and light unlike she had ever seen. She could swear that Candace had become part of her somehow as her body lifted from the bed. Part of her wanted to pull away. She had no control. She screamed Candace's name in desperation. Candace held her close and whispered continually in her ear while Jameson's body continued to succumb to shudder after glorious shudder. "I'm right here," Candace promised. "Right here," she kept repeating until she felt Jameson's body finally begin to relax.

Candace laid down beside Jameson and pulled her into an embrace. "Candace?" Jameson whispered.

"Hum?"

"Is it always like this for you?" she asked.

Candace smiled and turned to look at the woman she loved. They had never discussed their previous relationships or lovers in any detail. She did know that Jameson had never had a committed relationship. She kissed Jameson's forehead. "No," she said. "It's never been that way for me until you."

Jameson nodded. "Me either. Do you think that's strange?"

Candace laughed. "No, I don't."

"Really?" Jameson asked in surprise.

Candace kissed over the small bandage on Jameson's forehead. "Really," she assured her lover before pulling Jameson back into her arms.

"Still want to keep me?" Jameson asked kiddingly.

"As long as you don't bring home any more cats."

"Deal."

Candace closed her eyes in contentment. Jameson nestled against her lover and followed suit. "Oh shit," Jameson said.

"What's wrong?" Candace opened one eye.

"I didn't get you anything for Christmas. I didn't think I'd see you and…" Candace laughed and kissed Jameson soundly. "What was that for?"

"Jameson, sleeping next to you is the best and most unexpected Christmas present I've ever gotten."

"The best, huh?"

"Yes."

"I'm in trouble next year. How am I going to top that? I'll have to find something new to design….maybe…"

"Go to sleep, you lunatic."

"Merry Christmas, Candace. I love you."

"I love you too, even if you are a lunatic. Now go to sleep or Santa will never come," Candace warned.

"You really are connected," Jameson said as she closed her eyes.

Candace chuckled. "Good night, Jameson." She waited for a response. A soft purring was emanating from Jameson. "Snoring already," she laughed. Candace looked down and saw a small kitten cuddled beside her sleeping lover. "I'm watching you," she said sternly. "Merry Christmas, Jameson. It's going to be an interesting New Year," she laughed before closing her eyes. "Very interesting."

Candace stepped into the doorway of the kitchen and smiled. Jameson was humming, engaged in some task at the counter. She stepped behind Jameson quietly and wrapped her arms around Jameson's waist. "Merry Christmas. What are you up to?" she asked.

Jameson leaned into Candace's embrace happily. "Me?"

"Yes, you."

"I'm making you Christmas breakfast. What does it look like I am doing?" Jameson chuckled. Jameson poured some coffee into a cup and turned to face her lover.

"How are you feeling?" Candace asked.

Jameson smiled and kissed Candace gently. "You worry too much," she said honestly. "I'm all right. It would take a lot more than a bump on the head to get rid of me."

Candace sighed and traced the edges of the cut that adorned Jameson's head. She had spoken at length with the doctor in the emergency room. Jameson had been lucky. The concussion she had suffered was not a joking matter. Had it not been for Jameson's persistent demands to get out of the hospital, and Pearl and Candace's assurances that she would not be left alone, Jameson would have been admitted. It still had Candace slightly rattled.

"Jameson, that head injury was no joke and you and I both know it."

Jameson nodded. "I really am okay. I promise. I feel a thousand times better. Besides, the doctors said after forty-eight hours I should be fine to resume normal activity unless I got dizzy," she reminded Candace.

Candace frowned slightly. "No dizziness?"

Jameson smirked. "Maybe a little last night."

Candace rolled her eyes at the comment. She had become swept away by Jameson's advances. Jameson's playful banter assured her that Jameson was feeling like herself. Jameson had been quiet for the last two days. "Mm. I guess we should table any physical activity until you can handle it," Candace quipped.

Jameson jumped slightly. "What?"

Candace laughed and set down her coffee. She put her arms around Jameson's neck. "You really are easy sometimes," she winked.

"That was evil. You are an evil woman, aren't you?"

"I do have a black cat," Candace replied.

Jameson kissed Candace's forehead. "Come on, let me make you breakfast."

"Sweetheart, you don't have to do that," Candace said.

"You have been taking care of me for the last couple of days. You flew home to be with me," Jameson said a bit regretfully. "You're away from your family. I just…"

"Stop," Candace said firmly. "There is no one I would rather spend the holidays with. No one." Jameson nodded and grabbed Candace's hand. "Where are we going?" Candace asked as Jameson led her from the room. Jameson remained silent. She directed Candace to sit on the sofa in the living room and moved to the small tree in the corner. Candace watched as Jameson retrieved an envelope and brought it over to Candace. "What is this?" Candace asked.

Jameson shrugged. "I told you last night. I wanted to do something for you. Just open it."

Candace was perplexed. She opened the envelope. It was a simple Christmas card with a winter scene. She opened it and found a folded piece of paper inside. Candace looked at Jameson curiously. Jameson smiled. Candace read the inscription on the card:

Candace,

I already know what you are going to say when you see this. I hope that we spend many holidays together. You already think I am a lunatic so I might as well be honest. If I had my way, I would never spend another one apart from you.

Candace looked up at Jameson and smiled. She returned to the note.

I didn't think I would see you this Christmas. I didn't know what to get you. I know a few things about you. You love Chinese food. You are always curious what your fortune cookie will say. That's why you always want extras. You love this old house. More than anything, you love your kids. I know that. You talk about them all the time. You should be with them for the holiday. I got to wake up with you this morning. They should get to see you tonight.

I love you. I never thought I would say that to someone. I do. Merry Christmas.

Jameson

Candace unfolded the paper in the card and smiled. She looked over at Jameson with tears in her eyes. "When did you…"

Jameson made her way to Candace and sat beside her. "I wanted to give you something special for our first Christmas. Since I couldn't go shopping at five in the morning, I booked you a flight. I talked to Shell just before you came downstairs. She'll pick you up at the airport."

Candace shook her head and kissed Jameson tenderly. "I'll go on one condition."

"You have conditions?" Jameson laughed. "You never stop negotiating; do you, Senator?"

"Comes with the territory."

"What's your condition?" Jameson asked. "Want to make me dizzy before you leave?"

Candace chuckled. "No. It might affect your ability to fly."

"Huh?"

"I want you to come with me," Candace said.

"To Austin?"

"Unless I have children someplace else that I am unaware of, yes." Jameson shifted nervously. "Jameson?"

"You want me to meet your kids?"

"As I recall, you have already met one and called her this morning."

"Yeah, but that's Shell," Jameson observed. "What if they hate me?"

"Impossible."

"Candace, I don't want to intrude on your…"

"You are not an intrusion in my life, Jameson," Candace said. She looked at the card in her hand. "Did you mean what you wrote?"

"Of course."

"Well, if you plan to be with me, you will have to endure The Three Stooges and their shenanigans."

"You call your kids The Three Stooges?" Jamison asked.

"Not to their faces," Candace feigned innocence. Jameson laughed. "I'm not going to pressure you. If you aren't ready…"

"It's not that," Jameson said. "I'd love to go. I just…"

"What is it?" Candace asked gently.

"I don't ever want to disappoint you."

Candace smiled and kissed Jameson's cheek. "The only way that you could ever disappoint me, Jameson is to lie to me. That's it. Trust me on that. If that were not the case…If I didn't already trust you, we would not be having this conversation," she said. Jameson looked at Candace hopefully. "I didn't plan on falling in love. To tell you the truth, I never imagined wanting to be with someone again."

"And now?" Jameson asked.

"And now, I want to take things as slowly as we both need when we need to. I do know one thing."

"What's that?"

"I don't want to imagine my life without you. That frankly scares the hell out of me," Candace admitted.

"Are you sure you want me to come with you? I don't expect…"

"I'm positive."

"Okay," Jameson agreed.

Candace smiled and rose to her feet. "Wait here."

Jameson sat contemplating the conversation while she awaited Candace's return. Slow? She wondered how they would manage to take things slowly. Just a couple of nights sleeping beside Candace, just once making love and Jameson already hated the idea of being apart. She would have expected that to unnerve her. Oddly, she seemed to find the feeling comforting. Being with Candace could be exhilarating. There was always a sense of contentment in Jameson's time with Candace. Jameson closed her eyes for a moment, thinking how lucky she felt.

"Napping already?" Candace asked lightly when she reentered the room.

Jameson opened her eyes. "Must be all the exercise," she said. Candace laughed. She approached Jameson with a wrapped box and handed it to her. "What is this?" Jameson wondered.

"It is Christmas," Candace observed. Jameson looked at the box in her hands. "Well, open it already. I know it's killing you."

Jameson tried not to laugh at the impatient tone of Candace's voice. She was curious. She also found Candace's obvious eagerness amusing. Jameson wondered if people would believe how excited the powerful senator could become over the simplest of things, things like extra fortune cookies. Candace's expression always took on a childlike quality when she was about to unwrap a surprise. Jameson's eyes began to twinkle with mirth remembering the gleam in Candace's eyes the night before when she had removed Jameson's T-shirt.

"What are you grinning about?" Candace asked.

"Just thinking how much you love unwrapping things," Jameson replied as she set about unwrapping her gift. Candace pursed her lips and sat beside Jameson.

"Oh my God," Jameson said in disbelief when the

contents of the box were revealed. "Candace....This had to cost you a fortune. Where did you even find it?" Jameson wondered.

"Do you like it?"

Jameson opened the lid of the box that read J.B. Perry. Her fingers lightly brushed over the set of antique drawing tools. "It's incredible," she said as she explored the contents. "This is too much. I've seen these, but never…"

Candace watched Jameson as she lifted each instrument delicately. "It's not too much," she said. Candace would have paid a million dollars gladly to see the expression on Jameson's face, although it had not cost her anywhere near that amount of money to purchase the antique set. "The gentleman in the shop told me that these would have been similar to the type used when this house was designed and constructed."

Jameson nodded. "Yes. These are definitely from the early nineteenth century. They're in amazing condition." Jameson finally pulled her attention away from the box and looked at Candace. "When did you…"

"When did I buy it?" Candace guessed. Jameson nodded. Candace took a deep breath. "I made the inquiry when I got back to Washington after Thanksgiving," she said. Jameson was stunned. "They arrived the morning of the Christmas party."

"You had someone search for them?" Jameson asked in disbelief.

"I wanted you to have something special."

Jameson kissed Candace tenderly. "I love you, Candace."

Candace smiled. "Does that mean I am booking you a seat to Austin?"

"No."

"No?" Candace asked.

"No. This trip was my present to you. I will take care of it."

"So, you'll come?"

Jameson nodded. "I just hope I don't…."

"They will love you."

"How can you be so sure?" Jameson wondered.

"Because I do."

"Pretty sure of yourself," Jameson chided with a wink.

"No," Candace said. Jameson looked at her inquisitively. "I'm sure of you."

UNDER CONSTRUCTION
Chapter Nine

Jameson Reid sat at a long table in a conference room studying plans for her firm's latest project. Her eyes were tired. All of her was tired. The last two weeks had seemed endless to Jameson, and she had another full week to endure before she would get any reprieve from the stress of work. Worse still, it would be another full week before she got a reprieve from the loneliness of home. She closed her eyes and rubbed her forehead in a feeble attempt to banish her lingering headache. Her patience was running low. Her energy was running even lower.

Two weeks ago, the senior architect in her firm, Bryan Mills was forced to take an unexpected leave of absence. His wife was experiencing complications during her first pregnancy. There had been no question in Jameson's mind that he needed to be home. Bryan had argued that he could work part-time. Jameson would not hear of it. Family first was not just a motto that Jameson Reid had adopted, it was the philosophy she lived by. People came first. Business came second. End of discussion for Jameson. Bryan's absence happened to coincide with beginning one of the largest projects the firm had acquired to date.

Jameson loved a challenge and she had confidence that her team could create something amazing for this new client. The project entailed designing a state of the art medical building and rehab center. The new structure would replace the outdated buildings currently being utilized at a large urban hospital in Maryland. Designing complex structures to house medical facilities was time-consuming and often daunting. Technology had to be considered in every nook and cranny. Safety, while always at the core of Jameson's designs, took on a different significance in health care facilities. Patients were often immobile.

That meant that there had to be alternative ways to access and exit the structure in case of an emergency. Jameson prided herself, and her team's work on innovation, functionality, safety, and lastly, style. Style, in Jameson's mind, was useless if the other three points were not executed efficiently.

Jameson took her work seriously. She sought to please her clients, but she also understood that the work her firm was contracted to perform had both significant applications and implications. The problem she was having lately was with her ability to concentrate. Jameson's need to be in Albany took her away from the project that commanded her greatest interest. It also inhibited her ability to see the person who commanded her heart. That was beginning to take as much of a toll on the architect as the heavy workload in front of her.

"J.D.?" Melanie called for her boss's attention. Jameson looked up. "Maybe we should take a break, huh?" the young woman suggested.

"Worried about me?" Jameson asked lightly. Melanie pursed her lips. Jameson chuckled. "I want to finish up with this before I head home."

"To your home or to Candace's?" Melanie winked.

Jameson grimaced. "Mine," she said.

"Really? I thought for sure you would be headed there for the weekend. You can't work 24/7, J.D.," Melanie said.

"Thanks, Mom," Jameson winked. "I'm not working….Well, actually, I probably will be working," she groaned. Melanie shook her head and sighed. "Candace is stuck in D.C. until next Friday," Jameson explained.

"That sucks," the younger woman turned up her nose. Jameson offered her an awkward smile in agreement. "How long since you've seen her now?"

"Two weeks," Jameson said softly. "It'll be three by the time next Friday rolls around."

"I thought politicians didn't work?" Melanie quipped. Jameson squinted at her assertion. "Well, I do read the news!"

"What news is that? E! Online?" Jameson laughed. "Mel, your friends' Facebook rants do not qualify as news."

"Funny," Melanie wrinkled her nose at Jameson. "I'm serious. I thought politicians had more vacation days than work days. Isn't that what everyone complains about?"

"Not this politician," Jameson said affectionately. Candace's workload sometimes frustrated her, but she adored her lover. She missed Candace when they were forced to be apart. "She is the definition of a workaholic," Jameson said.

"I thought you were the cure?" Melanie poked. "You know…to get her to stop and slow down."

"No, Chinese food is the cure."

"She likes Chinese food more than you?" Melanie asked doubtfully.

"She might," Jameson answered with a twinkle in her eye. The conversation was making her think about Candace. She took a deep breath and let it out slowly before rolling up the plans in front of her.

"Thought you wanted to finish this?" Melanie asked in confusion.

"I will. Just need a break," Jameson said. "I'm going to head into my office for a bit. You should head out early. It's Friday. I can finish this without you."

"J.D., I'll stay. I don't mind. I can go get us some food."

"No. You go. Who knows how long I will be here," Jameson told her.

"Okay? J.D.?" Jameson turned back to the younger woman. "Why don't you just fly down and see her?"

Jameson smiled. "I would. She's supposed to attend some fundraiser tomorrow. She'll be tied up all day, and I know she is working late tonight."

"Two of a kind," Melanie smirked. "You have a lot in common."

"Mm. I guess so," Jameson said. "We're both alone," she whispered to herself.

Candace was sitting around an enormous table listening to the people around her argue. She had tuned out the majority of the conversation. It reminded her of the days when both Marianne and Michelle insisted on playing the same song over and over....and over again. She consistently wondered what made people get so stuck on one thing that they became unable to hear anything else. She looked down at her phone to check the time just as a message popped onto her screen.

New Message: JAMESON
Candace smiled and opened the new screen.

JAMESON: "Busy?"
CANDACE: "Bored."
JAMESON: "Meeting?"
CANDACE: "Maddening."
JAMESON: "Are we playing word games?"
CANDACE: "That would be refreshing."
JAMESON: "That bad?"
CANDACE: "McGuire and Steele must have mixed up their vitamins with their little blue pills."
JAMESON: "????"
CANDACE: "The most excitement in this meeting happens whenever Dana pops in. That's the only time they pop up."
Jameson read the message and started laughing.
CANDACE: "How about you? How's the new project?"

JAMESON: "Good. Working on the rehab center. State of the art stripper poles right in the middle. What do you think?"
CANDACE: "Never fly."
JAMESON: "Why not? It's innovative."
CANDACE: "They wouldn't need to prescribe all those blue bills. They love those things."
JAMESON: "You're sick."
CANDACE: "Good thing you're designing a new hospital then."
JAMESON: "I miss you."
Candace sighed softly and traced the screen with her finger.
CANDACE: "I miss you too."
Candace tried not to laugh out loud at her next thought. *I even miss that mangy cat.*
JAMESON: "Late night?"
CANDACE: "Unfortunately, looks that way."
JAMESON: "Me too. Talk to you in the a.m.?"
CANDACE: "Yes. I will call you."
JAMESON: "I'd rather give you a wake-up call." Jameson included several emoticons.
CANDACE: "Lunatic."
JAMESON "You like lunatics."
CANDACE: "Good thing."
JAMESON: "Love you."
CANDACE: "I love you too. Lunatic."
Candace settled back in her chair and covered her tired eyes. "Will this day never end?" she thought silently. "Who am I kidding? Will this week never end?"

"Hello?" Pearl answered the phone.
"Hey, Pearl."
"Jameson? Everything okay?" Pearl asked cautiously.
"Yeah, why?" Jameson asked.

"Jameson, you never call me on the house phone."

"I wanted to see if you were still there."

"Why? Someone coming to look at something?" Pearl wondered.

Jameson had been away, but she still had contractors at Candace's house working. Once the project to restore Candace's home got underway in earnest, Jameson had discovered a few hidden issues. Thankfully, nothing in the house had been structurally unsound, but the roof had not been replaced correctly. Jameson was amazed it was not leaking too badly. There were places in many of the walls that needed addressing. She had uncovered plumbing issues, and the electrician that Candace's brother had hired had basically cut every corner he could and still be able to manage to pass an inspection. Candace's reaction was to tell Jameson to do whatever she thought needed to be done and send her the bills. Jameson did as much of the work herself as she could to cut costs. Being called away had changed that situation. That meant even more contractors.

"No. No contractors. I just wondered how much Chinese food I should pick up," Jameson said.

"Why? Are you coming home?" Pearl asked.

Jameson smiled. She had never considered her condo in Albany a home. Home had always been her parent's house in Ithaca. Being back in Albany the last two weeks had made Jameson homesick. This time it wasn't for her parents or the house she was raised in. Jameson missed Candace. She missed Pearl. She missed Jinx. She missed home. "At the Chinese place now," Jameson said.

Pearl chuckled. "Missed Jinx, huh? He misses you too."

"He misses Candace," Jameson laughed. As ironic as that was, it was also true. Jinx, the cat, had a strange obsession with Candace, the senator. The one person who never wanted to see a cat again in her life after the age of nine was Jinx's favorite human. It delighted both Jameson and Pearl. They both knew that secretly it pleased Candace as well. Jameson had caught her lover talking to Jinx in the kitchen more than once. She never commented. There were certain things that Jameson just liked to enjoy at a distance. Watching Candace pretend that she loathed the creature and sneaking in the doorway to watch her coo at the cat was one of Jameson's favorite pastimes at home.

"Well, if you are bringing dinner, should I break out some of Candy's wine?" Pearl asked.

"Coffee would be better."

"Coffee? She's corrupted you completely," Pearl admonished Jameson. "It's already after six."

"I know. I still have a lot of work to do," Jameson said.

"On the house? Oh, no…You are not climbing any ladders at night. No way," Pearl said.

"I fell once!" Jameson exclaimed into the phone.

"And nearly put us all in the hospital with you!" Pearl reminded her. "I'll make you your coffee. You stay away from anything tall, sharp, or with an electrical current."

Jameson laughed at Pearl's stern warning. She had gotten injured once and that was six months ago. Neither Pearl nor Candace let her forget it. They teased her endlessly, but underneath their teasing there was an honest undercurrent of fear. The truth was, Jameson had been both very unlucky and very fortunate that day. If she had been standing higher on the ladder when Jinx jumped on her, or if the ladder had hit her just a fraction of an inch to the right, she might not have fared so well. As it was, she had ended up with a concussion that almost kept her in the hospital. Jameson could recall Candace's face that day in the hospital vividly. Relief and fear painted Candace's expression. It wasn't until that night when they got home that Jameson realized how terrified Candace and Pearl had both been.

Pearl had found Jameson unconscious on the floor. Jameson's head was bleeding heavily although, Jameson was sure that it looked far worse than it really was. Pearl had not been able to get to Candace directly. The vague message Candace did receive that Jameson was at the hospital had rocked her to the core. She had no idea what had happened or how badly hurt Jameson might be. Neither Jameson nor Candace had confessed her feelings for the other until that night. That night, Candace broke down with Jameson in her arms, refusing to let go. If Jameson had any lingering doubts that Candace Fletcher was in love with her, that night silenced them all.

"I promise," Jameson said. "Actually, I have to work on a different project. So, you make the coffee. I'll get the Chinese food and you can catch me up on all the gossip," Jameson said.

"About who? Jinx? Not much gossip with just me here," Pearl laughed.

Jameson smiled at the older woman's comment. Pearl knew all the gossip. Everyone went to Pearl. Michelle, Marianne, and Jonah all called Grandma Pearl when they were afraid to tell their mother something. Jameson had figured that out in the first two months of her relationship with Candace. All of Candace's children used Pearl as a sounding board and a resource. Everyone in Candace's small town told Pearl everything, in the hopes that she might tell them anything at all about the popular senator. Pearl never shared anything confidential. She was the perfect mother and grandmother figure to them all, even to Jameson. But, she did have her share of anecdotes and amusing tales about all the colorful characters in Candace's world. Jameson loved to listen to them.

"Well, just be hungry," Jameson said.

"Bring extra fortune cookies," Pearl ordered.

Jameson snickered. She often wondered if it was somehow possible that Pearl actually was Candace's mother. They were two peas in a pod. "Check. I will see you shortly."

Pearl hung up the phone and shook her head in amusement. Jameson was homesick. She could hear it. She grabbed her cell phone off the counter and called the woman she had always considered her daughter.

"Candy? Yes, It's me….Hold on…Candy….No, no one is in the hospital, but I might put someone there if you don't be quiet and listen to me!"

🐴 🐴 🐴

Candace walked in the front door and made her way into the kitchen. She stopped and chuckled when she flipped on the light. Jameson had left her plans spread across the table. Candace threw her keys on the counter and looked at the plans. Jameson had notes stuck everywhere. Underneath the long white sheet of drawings, one blue sticky note caught her attention. Jameson had a tendency to doodle when she was contemplating something. Candace picked up the note and smiled. There were no comments about changes, measurements, or questions. This note had just three words on it. "I miss you." That was all it said.

"Meow!" a tiny voice greeted her from below.

"Well, well…Did you miss me?" Candace asked the small black feline that was rubbing up against her legs. She knelt down and scratched behind his ears. "I missed you too, you mangy little brat," she said.

"Meow!"

"Where's your Mommy?" she asked. Jinx circled Candace's legs a few more times and then started rolling around on the floor. "Oh, you are hers all right," Candace laughed.

She looked back down the hallway toward the stairs. It was late and Candace was certain that Jameson would be sleeping. She was anxious to slip into bed beside her lover. Two weeks had been too long. Pearl didn't need to do much convincing to get Candace to cancel her plans for the next day. She had paid more than her share of dues over the years. The Democratic Party did not need her as much as she needed

Jameson. That was just a fact. Frankly, she felt she'd earned the right to say no once in a while.

Candace climbed the stairs slowly. Her entire body seemed to be crying out for rest. She turned the corner into her bedroom and smiled at the sight before her. The curtains were open and the moon offered just enough light to see Jameson's figure sprawled across the bed. Jameson was hugging Candace's pillow tightly. Her hair was tussled and hanging in her face. Candace sucked in a deep breath and closed her eyes for a brief moment. She opened her eyes, let out her breath slowly and made her way to the edge of the bed. She stood there for a few minutes just watching Jameson sleep until the temptation became too great. Candace reached out and brushed the hair from Jameson's eyes.

Jameson slapped lightly at the sensation. "Jinx," she groaned without opening her eyes. "Knock it off," she said.

Candace bit her bottom lip to keep from laughing. She leaned over and kissed Jameson's forehead and let her lips linger.

"Jinx!" Jameson complained again but did not open her eyes. "No offense, but I wish your Mommy were here."

Candace stroked Jameson's cheek and Jameson finally started to pry her eyes open. "Hey, sleepyhead," Candace whispered.

"You're home," Jameson commented in wonderment.

"Apparently," Candace said.

"What time is it?" Jameson asked.

"A little after two in the morning."

Jameson sighed and pulled Candace down to her. She kissed her tenderly but deeply. "I can't believe you are here."

Candace leaned over and kissed Jameson again in reply. Jameson took the opportunity to pull Candace down on top of her. "What are you doing, you lunatic?" Candace giggled, still looking in Jameson's eyes. Jameson studied Candace's face silently. "Jameson?"

"I missed you," Jameson said with a gentle kiss.

"Mmm. I missed you too," Candace said. "Let me go get changed."

"Why? I can take care of that for you right now," Jameson said suggestively.

"If you take care of that for me, neither of us will get any sleep and both of us need it," Candace said. She kissed Jameson on the nose and pulled herself off the bed. "Stop pouting," Candace called as she walked into the bathroom.

"Who says I am pouting?" Jameson called out. She rolled over and sighed. She was exhausted and she could see the weariness in Candace's eyes. She longed to be close to Candace again, to hold her, to make love to her softly. The thoughts were making her dizzy and she groaned in frustration. Jinx jumped up on the bed and rubbed against her. Jameson shook her head. "Not what I had in mind. What does she mean pout? I don't pout."

"Yes, you do," Candace disagreed as she slipped into the bed behind Jameson and wrapped an arm around her. Jameson immediately turned and faced her lover. Candace raised her brow. "Mad at me?" she asked a bit playfully.

"No," Jameson said quietly.

Candace pulled Jameson into her embrace. "I love you, Jameson. We have all weekend. I don't leave until Monday morning."

"How did you get out of that fundraiser?" Jameson asked.

"I just told them I had a more urgent matter to attend to."

"What's that?" Jameson asked.

"You," Candace said with a kiss. "Now, go to sleep."

"You didn't actually tell them that?" Jameson marveled.

"Sure did," Candace said. "Now, go back to sleep."

Jameson cuddled closer. She was already losing the battle to stay awake. "Can you pass some legislation to ban Mondays?"

Candace kissed Jameson's head. "Don't tempt me," she said before giving in to her exhaustion.

Jameson was still groggy when she awoke and unsure if she had dreamed Candace's homecoming. The light scent of a familiar perfume, the warm body pressed behind her, and the hand that held hers convinced her that Candace was very real. Jameson took the first deep breath she had in days. She ran her fingers gently over Candace's hand and realized just how much she had missed the woman holding her. Jameson turned in Candace's arms. She watched her lover sleeping peacefully, feeling an enormous sense of gratefulness. Jameson had never considered herself someone clever with words. She tried to show Candace, tried to tell Candace what she felt. Often, she felt inadequate in that capacity. Jameson's teasing was often her way of saying "I love you" to Candace. It's not that she didn't say the words. She did. She feared that if she said them too often they would somehow become meaningless, and yet she felt she could never express her love enough to the woman beside her.

Jameson kissed Candace's eyelids and her nose softly before placing a tender kiss on Candace's lips. "What are you up to?" Candace whispered sleepily.

Jameson stroked Candace's hip lovingly with her left hand and raised her right to caress Candace's cheek. She brought her lips to Candace's again and felt Candace immediately respond. The kiss continued slowly. It was an achingly emotional rediscovery for them both. Jameson heard a faint moan escape from the back of Candace's throat, and she pulled away to explore Candace's neck.

"Jameson…"

"Shh," Jameson whispered in Candace's ear. She nibbled on Candace's earlobe and delighted in the sigh that escaped her lover. Jameson's hands worked to lift the long T-Shirt Candace had worn to bed and remove it. She looked at Candace as if she were seeing her for the first time. Candace watched as love and desire flickered in Jameson's eyes. Jameson had become entranced by the smattering of freckles that adorned the swell of Candace's breasts. She was tracing patterns with her fingers around them. "So beautiful," she breathed. Candace closed her eyes when Jameson's touch was replaced by faint kisses.

Jameson positioned herself above Candace and looked down on her longingly. Slowly, she kissed her way over Candace's throat. Jameson continued bathing her lover in light kisses. She moved from Candace's right shoulder across her chest, deliberately tasting every inch of skin along the way. Candace watched as Jameson continued her delicious assault. Jameson kissed both of Candace's breasts, just over the tops before circling each of Candace's nipples with her tongue. Candace arched her back instinctively. Jameson gently took a nipple between her lips and sucked lightly. "Oh…" Candace moaned.

"Mm…" Jameson agreed. She lifted a hand to play with Candace's other nipple and Candace threw her head back. Jameson played with Candace's nipples, teasing and taunting her until Candace's body began to move involuntarily.

"Jameson…God, you have no idea what you are doing to me," Candace said through a ragged breath.

Jameson knew exactly what she was doing to her lover. She had learned how Candace liked to be touched, and what sensations made Candace beg for release. Jameson had memorized every inch of the woman she loved, down to the freckles spread across her chest that reminded Jameson a bit of constellations in a night sky to the faint scar that ran across the bottom of her belly from the C-section she had needed to deliver Jonah. Jameson loved every piece of Candace, every freckle, every tiny scar, the laugh lines at the corner of her eyes, even the little stretch marks that could barely be seen on her hips. They were the unique physical parts of Candace that made her Candace Fletcher, and Jameson was completely in love with her.

Jameson's hand ran over Candace's abdomen as it worked its way intentionally lower. She pulled back and looked at Candace whose face was flushed with desire. She stopped for a moment and kissed her lips sweetly, taking a moment to whisper in her ear. "I am going to make love to you until you beg me to stop," she promised. She felt Candace's breath hitch and her body shiver.

Candace ran her hands over the muscles of Jameson's back and moaned. Jameson drove her wild, not only the way that Jameson touched her, but Jameson's mere presence. Candace marveled at the way softness and strength mingled in her lover. The combination was evident in everything from Jameson's intelligence and humor to the way her body moved, and the way it felt beneath Candace's hands. Jameson could be strong and commanding in one moment, and soft and vulnerable in the next. That made their lovemaking exquisite. It was like nothing Candace had ever experienced, every time. Candace lifted Jameson's shirt and pulled it over her head. She let her hands glide over the curves of Jameson's hips and up to her breasts. When her fingers brushed over Jameson's nipples, Jameson moaned loudly. Candace leaned forward and kissed an already erect nipple lightly before making small circles around it with her tongue. She watched as Jameson's eyes lost their ability to stay open against the wave of pleasure.

Jameson should not have been surprised when Candace pulled her in for a heated kiss. The kiss set Jameson on fire. Nothing in the world could arouse her more than Candace's kiss. She prayed that would never change. She pulled away and licked a steady trail down Candace's middle. She stopped when she reached the top of a quivering thigh. Jameson pulled off

Candace's panties deliberately. She kissed her way up Candace's legs, allowing her hands to continually caress Candace's thighs and hips. She looked up to see the anticipation in Candace's eyes. Jameson pulled Candace closer to her and breathed in the scent of her arousal. Just the sensation of Jameson's breath on her made Candace writhe. Jameson held her firmly. She kissed Candace's thighs and gradually moved her kisses inward.

"Jameson…please," Candace barely whispered. Jameson licked Candace gently, softly, slowly. "Oh, God…Oh my, God….Jameson."

"Mm," Jameson moaned. Her hands massaged both of Candace's thighs as she continued exploring Candace leisurely with her tongue. Candace was shifting desperately beneath her in an attempt to focus Jameson where she wanted her. Jameson intended to take her time. She had missed Candace. Phone calls, emails, internet chats, text messages, they were all a sorry substitute for holding, touching, and feeling Candace. Jameson loved making love to Candace. She felt Candace's hands entwine themselves in her hair and she reached out to take hold of them.

Candace thought she might lose consciousness soon if Jameson didn't relieve the ache that had taken up residence in her body. Jameson was tracing over every inch of her center. Jameson would tease her with just enough pressure to start a slight flickering pulse through Candace, and then she would change direction as though she were searching for some treasure. Now, Jameson held her hands tightly. Candace screamed Jameson's name when Jameson finally circled Candace's clit deliberately with her tongue. "Please," Candace begged. "Please, Jameson. I need you…I need to feel you…Please."

Jameson responded immediately. She could sense Candace's climax building from deep within. She circled the small point beneath her tongue again before capturing it between her lips and flicking her tongue over it in quick, repeated bursts. Jameson felt her own arousal building swiftly. The closer

Candace came to release, the more Jameson's center began to throb with need. She swirled her tongue in one direction and then the other, repeating the action over and over, increasing the pressure ever so slightly until she heard Candace cry out.

"Yes…Oh….Oh my God," Candace managed between explosions of blissful shudders.

Candace's entire body lifted from the bed. It took more strength than Jameson had expected to hold Candace in place. Candace was still trying to catch her breath when she felt Jameson begin again.

"Jameson…What…Oh, God!"

Jameson couldn't stop herself. She savored every moment of Candace's release and she wanted more. She let go of Candace's hands and swiftly entered her lover with two fingers. Candace closed her eyes in a futile attempt to banish the flashing lights that accompanied the orgasm that followed. It came in an instant, without warning. Her entire body shook as Jameson's finger's twirled inside her in time with the constant flicking of her tongue.

Jameson finally stopped. Candace was still quivering and Jameson moved to take her lover into an embrace. "Shh," she whispered, kissing Candace's head as Candace folded herself into Jameson. "I just missed you so much," Jameson said. Candace didn't answer. "Are you okay?" Jameson asked. Candace was trying to calm the rapid beat of her heart and catch her breath. She didn't know how to tell Jameson that she was still reeling from the ripples of pleasure that had not fully subsided. "Candace?" Jameson asked again. Candace was shaking in her arms.

"Just hold me," Candace said. Jameson pulled Candace closer. "I don't want to do that again." Jameson was alarmed. "Be apart for that long," Candace clarified. Jameson let out a nervous sigh. Candace finally moved to look at her. "Oh, no…you thought I meant," Candace stopped and kissed Jameson.

"Sweetheart, you can wake me up that way whenever you want," she said. "Unless I have to go to work." Jameson was confused. Candace chuckled. "I just woke up and I need a nap," she laughed.

Jameson smiled. She would be happy to hold Candace, but she was feeling more aroused than spent. "Oh," Candace said as realization dawned. She raised an eyebrow. "Not sleepy?" she asked.

"I'm fine," Jameson said unconvincingly. She startled at the feel of Candace's hand removing her shorts.

Candace bit her lip to quell another wave of tremors when she was finally able to feel Jameson's arousal. "I see," she said. Jameson's breathing had become rapid and shallow. Candace stroked Jameson tenderly. The warm wetness beneath her hand was intoxicating. She kissed Jameson and then looked in her eyes. Candace moved to her back and pulled Jameson over her. "Come here."

Jameson's heart began to pound furiously as Candace gently guided her. She felt Candace hold her hips and sighed when she settled above her lover. Candace groaned in excitement at the first taste of Jameson. "Perfect," she said as she explored every inch of the softness that was Jameson. She heard Jameson's frantic sighs. Even after all their months together, Jameson's boldness faded when Candace made love to her. It only made Candace love her more, the raw vulnerability in Jameson that made itself known in these moments. Candace drew lazy circles around Jameson with her tongue.

"Candace," Jameson urged softly.

Candace could feel the frustration in Jameson's movements. She reached up and fondled Jameson's breasts until she heard Jameson begin to faintly moan above her. She sucked gently and then moved her tongue up and down Jameson with hard, deliberate strokes. It was only a few seconds before she felt Jameson's legs begin to shake. Wave after wave pounded over and through Jameson. She felt as if she were caught in an undertow. She would surface for a brief second, only to be held under again as the waves crashed over her. She pulled away, fearing that if it continued she would no longer be able to support her own weight.

"I'm sorry," she apologized as she crawled up beside Candace.

"What are you sorry for?" Candace asked, stroking Jameson's hair.

"I just...You are amazing, you know that?"

"I love you," Candace gave as her explanation. Jameson held onto Candace and breathed her in. "Tired?" Candace asked. Jameson was already asleep. "See what I mean?" Candace chuckled. "Good thing we don't work until Monday."

Chapter Ten

Jameson walked into the kitchen. Candace was at the counter making coffee and Jameson snuck up behind her to cuddle close. Candace closed her eyes and leaned back into Jameson's arms. "Good morning," Jameson whispered in Candace's ear.

"Yes, it is," Candace said. Jameson was nuzzling her neck and Candace sighed. "Jameson," she giggled.

"What?"

"Are you trying to send me to an early grave?" she asked.

"Why? Is your heart beating faster or something?" Jameson teased. "You haven't even had coffee yet." Candace laughed and finished the task before her with Jameson's arms still holding her. "What are your plans today?" Jameson asked.

Candace turned in Jameson's embrace. "That depends."

"On what?"

"On what your plans are," Candace said.

Jameson smiled and kissed Candace gently. "I thought maybe…antiquing?"

Candace pursed her lips and squinted at Jameson curiously. "Antiquing?"

Jameson knew that Candace loved to wander in and out of eclectic shops. Although, she was loathed to admit it, she enjoyed it too. Every item had a story and Jameson enjoyed imagining what those stories might have been. Who had owned that lamp or that ring? How did it come to be where it was now? And, she loved spending time with Candace. She felt a sense of pride watching how people responded to her lover, and how Candace engaged people so effortlessly.

"Don't you have to work?" Candace pointed to the plans still spread across the kitchen table.

Jameson shrugged. "I have more important things to attend to," she winked. "So? What do you say? Antiquing? Lunch? You and me?"

Candace kissed Jameson's cheek. "It's a date."

"A date? Oh my God! I have a date with Senator Fletcher!" Jameson exclaimed playfully.

Candace smacked Jameson and rolled her eyes. "Lunatic."

Jameson and Candace walked through the front door laughing. It had been a perfect day for them both. They had wandered through small shops, purchased a few items for the house, stopped for lunch at a small, hole in the wall café. They spent time talking about the renovation and even about their future. They traded playful banter on and off and sat on a bench under a large tree, eating ice cream cones and talking about their families. Candace had decided in May that they should start a new annual tradition and had been planning a large Fourth of July picnic. She had even convinced Marianne to come for a long weekend with Rick and Spencer.

Jameson was a tad nervous. It was the first time their families would be together. Candace seemed completely unfazed by the impending event. Jameson was continually impressed by Candace's ability to take a great many things in stride. She asked Candace when they began planning the barbecue how she managed not to worry about what people said and thought about her. Was it from spending so many years in political life, Jameson wondered? Candace laughed.

"No. Well, I guess that is part of it," Candace said. "You have to have a thick skin in my job, Jameson. It's true."

"I don't know how you do it."

Candace laughed. "Mostly, it's just a product of living," Candace told her. Jameson looked bewildered. "You grow up, you get married, you work, you give birth to your children and you mourn your parents....I don't know, you just learn along the way that you have to be true to yourself. I've lived long enough to know that some people will love me and some will loathe me. That's life. I try to concentrate on the ones in my life and not worry so much about the rest."

"Yeah, but what about when they don't approve?" Jameson asked nervously.

Candace nodded. She knew that Jameson's greatest anxieties surrounded Candace's children's acceptance of her, and Jameson's siblings' acceptance of Candace. "In my experience, if they love you, they'll find their way to where you are. It just takes some people a little more time than others. If they don't? Well, sometimes you just have to accept that and move on." Candace watched tension etch Jameson's features. "Relax," she said. "You worry too much about things you can't control, sweetheart."

They had been discussing the impending arrival of their families on the way home. That led to Jameson playfully calling Candace, Nana as they entered the house. "One title I will never earn!" Jameson stuck out her tongue behind Candace's back.

"Watch it," Candace warned. "You'll be sleeping with Jinx."

"Throwing me to the pussy ca…." Jameson almost ran into Candace, who had stopped abruptly.

"Shell?" Candace looked at her daughter who was fast asleep on the living room sofa.

"Shell?" Jameson repeated in surprise. She put her hands on Candace's shoulders and felt the tension there. "I'm sure everything is okay," she whispered in Candace's ear.

Candace sighed and made her way to her daughter. "Shell," she called gently.

Michelle opened her eyes and immediately started crying. "Mom," she sniffled and grabbed onto her mother.

Candace looked back at Jameson helplessly. Jameson sighed. "I'll go start some coffee," she said softly. Candace nodded.

Jameson made her way into the kitchen and started the coffee. She flopped into a chair and sighed. Jinx hopped into her lap and Jameson chuckled. "This is about the extent of my parenting skills," she said. One of the things she admired most about Candace was how she interacted with her children. It left her breathless on many occasions, just listening to Candace talk on the phone with one of her children. It wasn't something she had ever shared with Candace. It was one of those things that Jameson kept to herself and admired from a distance. It was also one of the parts of Candace that Jameson was positive made her fall even more deeply in love with the woman. It was interesting to Jameson, watching how Marianne, Michelle, and Johan morphed from grown adults into small children in their mother's presence at times, each searching for her affection and approval. She wondered how they could not realize that the sun rose and set in each of them for their mother. Candace bragged about all of her children incessantly, just like Pearl waffled on about Candace without even knowing it. Jameson wondered if it was the same with her mother.

Jameson was watching the slow drip of the coffee maker contemplating what she should busy herself with when she heard Candace's footsteps approaching. "She okay?" Jameson asked.

Candace let out a heavy sigh and Jameson got up and headed toward her. "It doesn't get any easier," Candace said as she collapsed her head onto Jameson's shoulder.

Jameson held her close. "What happened?"

"I don't know."

"She didn't tell you?"

Candace sighed again. "She was too busy crying and apologizing for screwing up our weekend. She didn't think we would be here."

"I don't get it," Jameson admitted.

"I don't either," Candace said with a shake of her head. "I think she just needed to get away. Our conversation, or rather her crying was interrupted when I got a message," Candace said quietly.

"Don't tell me."

Candace pulled back and looked at Jameson apologetically. She cupped Jameson's face in her hands and smiled. "I'm not leaving. I do have to take a call in fifteen minutes. I have no idea how long it will last."

"Don't you get weekends off? I thought that was a perk," Jameson tried to make light of the sudden chaos in their romantic weekend.

"Not when the president requests you, no." Jameson's eyes grew wide. Candace couldn't help but giggle. "We're old friends. I'm not even sure what it is regarding," Candace said, pulling away from Jameson and taking a seat in one of the kitchen chairs.

"But, you have some idea."

Candace groaned. "I do."

"What is it? Secret squirrel stuff?" Jameson laughed. Candace grimaced. Jameson sometimes did forget that Candace had knowledge of and dealt with issues that Jameson could not fathom. "That bad?"

"Nothing you need to worry about," Candace assured her lover. "And, I promise to make it as short as I can."

Jameson nodded. She grabbed a large mug, poured in a dash of cream, and filled it with coffee. She turned and handed it to Candace. "You might need this," she said.

Candace stood and accepted the offering with a quick kiss on Jameson's lips. "I'll make it up to you, I promise."

"I'll hold you to that. Unless, of course, you are too tired from all the excitement, Nana."

Candace laughed. "Jameson, a twenty-five-year-old would need Geritol to keep up with you."

"I'll take that as a compliment."

Candace kissed Jameson on the cheek. "You should." She started out of the kitchen and stopped. "Will you…"

"I'll check on her in a few," Jameson read her lover's thoughts. Candace nodded with a smile and took her leave.

"Hey, Shell," Jameson wandered out to the backyard where Michelle was lying in a lounge chair by the pool. Jameson handed her a beer. "Thought you might like one."

Michelle offered Jameson a halfhearted smile. "Thanks," she said as Jameson flopped into the chair beside her, taking a sip from her beer. "I'm really sorry J.D."

"For?" Jameson asked.

"Crashing in on you guys. I thought Mom was still in D.C."

Jameson smiled. "Shell, this is your home. You don't have to apologize for coming home. Not ever." Michelle took a sip from her beer and nodded silently. "Want to talk about it?" Jameson asked without looking directly at the younger woman.

Michelle took another long swig from her bottle. "Women suck."

Jameson laughed. "Sometimes, they really do," she agreed. "Let me guess? Girl trouble."

Michelle sighed. "More like Shell is an idiot. Seriously, J.D., how can someone raised by my mom be such a total pushover?"

"I'm not sure I know how to answer that," Jameson conceded. "But, I'm pretty sure your mother would say when it comes to women, we are all a pushover at times."

Shell chuckled slightly. "I thought she loved me," she said softly.

Jameson turned her attention to Michelle. She was

positive that Candace had no idea Michelle was even seeing anyone. "Love, huh?"

"Yeah…I know. Sounds crazy? Four months and I thought it was love."

Jameson laughed. "You do realize who you are talking to?"

"Okay, point taken," Michelle giggled.

"If you don't mind putting the backup lights on…"

"Lisa. Her name is Lisa," Michelle said.

"That's a start," Jameson said. "And, how do you know Lisa?"

"We've worked together for the last two years. She's an art teacher," Michelle explained. "We were friends. It turned….well, it turned." Jameson nodded her understanding. "I thought this was it. I'm such a fucking moron."

"I doubt that," Jameson assured Michelle. "So? You two were dating?"

"Yeah. Dating, sleeping together. I guess that's where we took separate tracks."

"You lost me."

"I thought we were making love. She thought we were fucking." Jameson spit out the sip of beer she had just taken. Michelle couldn't help but laugh. "I am of age, J.D."

"Yes, I know," Jameson returned. "Okay, so different tracks. What happened?"

"Yeah….more like different railroads. She was apparently making love to one of the science teachers while she was fucking me."

Jameson was not accustomed to hearing Michelle swear like a sailor. She wondered what Candace would say if she could hear Michelle now. Then again, she had heard Candace drop a string of 'F' bombs a few times after a conference call. "Not good."

"No. Not at all."

130

"Umm...and the science teacher? Did she know about the two of you?" Jameson asked.

Michelle let out a burst of caustic laughter. "Oh, he knew all right. I think he encouraged it. Asshole." For the second time in less than five minutes, Jameson lost the beer in her mouth violently. Michelle giggled. "You are wasting that beer, J.D.," she teased.

"No shit, Shell," Jameson rolled her eyes. "Are you telling me she was with this douchebag the whole time?"

It was Michelle's turn to spray beer through her nose. "Do you kiss my mother with that mouth?" Jameson wiggled her eyebrows. "Don't answer that," Michelle held up her hand. "I don't want to know....at all."

Jameson winked at the younger woman. "So, I take it, it's over."

"From her point of view it never started," Michelle said sadly.

"I'm sorry, Shell."

"Yeah, well. Fools do foolish things," Michelle said.

"Why didn't you tell your mom?" Jameson wondered.

Michelle shrugged. She adored her mother. She admired her mother. She felt utterly stupid. "Tell my mother, who is the best judge of character I know, that I am a total moron?"

Jameson sighed and shook her head. "Your mom would never think that," she said honestly.

"My mom is the smartest person I know, J.D."

Jameson smiled. "Me too," she agreed. "But, she hasn't had perfect success in the relationship department, Shell. And, she would never judge you. She might find a way to ban this Lisa person from life itself though," Jameson chuckled thinking of how protective Candace was of her kids.

Michelle laughed. "I know, it's not just that."

"Okay?"

Michelle let out a heavy sigh. "I quit," she said. Jameson's confusion was evident. "My job, J.D. I quit my job." Jameson waited for her to continue, unsure of what to say. "I cannot go in there and face them every day next year. I can't do it. He's told half the staff that I tried to steal his fiancée."

"They're engaged?"

"No. Well, I guess they are now. They certainly were not when Lisa and I started seeing each other."

"Jesus."

"Yeah, no shit," Michelle said.

"What are you going to do?" Jameson asked.

Michelle shook her head. "There's a position in Albany. It's mine if I want it."

"Okay?"

"I don't know…my lease isn't up until January. It pays a little less than my district now. I can't afford two apartments. I might be able to sublet in the fall, but there's no guarantee," Michelle explained. Jameson started to open her mouth and Michelle silenced her. "I can't ask my mom, J.D. I've never asked my mom for money. Not once. We all have a trust fund that we get when we turn twenty-eight. I'm not asking her for anything now. It's my problem."

Jameson took a sip of her beer to conceal her smile. She loved Michelle. She realized it might not be right for her to have a favorite when it came to Candace's children, but she did. Shell was her ally. Shell, when she thought about it, was a lot like a little sister. They were only nine years apart in age. Jameson recognized Michelle's affection and admiration for her mother immediately. What impressed her was Michelle's respect for Candace. That went a long way with Jameson. She sipped her beer for a minute, replaying the conversation she and Candace had over lunch.

"Jameson, keeping three residences is crazy."

Jameson nodded. *"Are you asking me to move in?"*

"I suppose that is exactly what I am suggesting."

"You know I want to," Jameson said.

"But?"

"It's not about us," Jameson said. She saw Candace tense. "It isn't. I would much rather be here with you. You know that," she said assuredly.

"Okay?" Candace questioned.

"The firm is in Albany. I can't ask my whole staff to relocate because I fell in love," Jameson explained. Candace smiled. "I might hate it, but even when Bryan comes back, there will be times I just can't work remotely. I have to be there."

"I know," Candace said in a defeated tone.

"I could sell the condo," Jameson said. "Or, I could rent it, but with as much time as I am there, well….I'd rather not be relegated to crappie hotel rooms. I'd rather be…"

"Home?" Candace guessed.

"Comfortable," Jameson corrected her. "If that were home, I wouldn't have come here this weekend." Candace nodded. "Honestly, I'd rather be wherever you are….even when that's in Washington."

Candace was surprised at Jameson's honesty. "You would want to stay in D.C.?"

"I have a lot of clients in the area. I've been thinking of opening a small office there," Jameson said. "Before you say anything, I've been considering it for over a year. I guess I just have added incentive now."

"And, a place to stay," Candace teased.

"There's that," Jameson admitted with a wink.

"I know that it's inevitable," Candace admitted. "That we will have to be apart at times." She took a deep breath. "I'd like to limit that," she said quietly.

Jameson smiled. She knew this was difficult for her lover. Candace had resigned herself to being alone. In many ways, so had Jameson. Their relationship was still new. Six months was hardly a lifetime, but Jameson felt sure it was only the beginning of their life together. Candace's decision to broach this subject assured her that *they were on the same page. Both had fears. Both had insecurities. Both were certain they wanted to be together, and that trumped everything else.*

"We'll figure it out," Jameson said. "That is if you could stand me being around more often."

"I think I could survive your presence," Candace said. "Besides, Pearl misses you."

Jameson smirked. "Oh, I see. Looking out for Pearl."

"Of course," Candace winked. "And, you wanted that cat."

"Mm-hm. Worried about Jinx getting lonely?"

"Don't be ridiculous. I just want to make sure someone is there to keep an eye on him. The last thing we need is fleas in the house."

Jameson couldn't help but laugh. "That would be a travesty."

"And ticks."

"Mm."

"Jameson, it's true!"

"Yes, since he is indoor all the time he might get fleas from the mice he catches," Jameson said.

"What mice?" Candace jumped slightly. "Mice? I haven't seen a mouse in that house in forever."

Jameson finally laughed. "More like six months," Jameson mumbled.

"What?"

"Nothing. You are right. Pearl can't be expected to supervise Jinx all the time."

"Glad we agree," Candace said.

"I know better than to argue with a politician." Candace threw her napkin at Jameson. "We'll work it out," Jameson said earnestly. Candace just smiled.

"What are you grinning about?" Michelle asked Jameson.

"Huh? Oh, just thinking about your mom and Jinx."

"The cat?" Michelle asked.

"Yeah. Listen, I think I might have a solution to your problem. Not the asshole problem, the Albany problem," Jameson clarified.

"J.D., I'm not moving home."

"I wasn't going to suggest that you should," Jameson responded.

"I'm not asking Mom…"

"Shell! God! You really are your mother's daughter. Stubborn," Jameson laughed. Michelle pursed her lips. "Would you just listen?" Michelle groaned but acquiesced. "Thank you," Jameson sighed. "I have my condo in Albany…"

"J.D. I am not…."

"Shell! Shut up already!" Jameson ordered in exasperation.

"Wow. That was authoritative, J.D. I am impressed."

Jameson laughed. "Can you just….Please, let me finish?" Michelle waved her hand for Jameson to continue. "The thing is, your mom and I, well….I get stuck in Albany a lot and I don't really want to have to impose on friends or stay in hotels."

"Ha! You and mom are moving in together!"

Jameson sighed. "I probably should not be telling you this."

"Why not?"

"Look, you could stay at my condo. Keep an eye on things for me. I'd have a place to crash when I need to be there…."

"I'm not freeloading off my mom's girlfriend," Michelle protested.

"You wouldn't be. You'd be helping me out. And, for the record…I would hope you consider me as much your friend as your mom's girlfriend."

"J.D. it's a generous offer. I don't want to take advantage of you."

Jameson nodded. Michelle was sincere. "Shell…you wouldn't be. Six months when your lease is up we can talk. If you want to stay there, we can talk about you renting the place. It actually would solve both of our problems. And, you couldn't freeload off me. You're family. That's not how it works," Jameson said honestly.

Michelle's lips had turned up into a genuine smile. "I'm happy for you," she said.

"Huh?"

"For you and Mom," Michelle said. "Can I think about it?"

"Of course," Jameson said.

"J.D.?"

"Yeah?"

"Thanks." Jameson just nodded with a smile.

"Here you two are!" Candace called. She walked up and picked up on the genuine emotion between Jameson and her daughter. She raised a brow at the pair. "I miss all the good stuff, don't I?"

Jameson pulled Candace into her lap. "Is that really how you feel?" she flirted.

"Gross!" Michelle exclaimed in amusement. Candace kissed Jameson in response. "Get a room," Michelle laughed.

"You're just jealous," Jameson teased.

"Yeah…and that is wrong on so many levels," Michelle said with a shake of her head.

Candace looked at Jameson inquisitively. "Assholes and railroad tracks," Jameson explained. Candace shook her head in confusion and then laid it on Jameson's shoulder. Jameson relaxed and held her lover close.

"I need another beer," Michelle stated. "Anyone else?"

"Sure," Jameson agreed, giving Candace a quick kiss.

"Mom?"

"Sure."

Michelle rolled her eyes in amusement at her mother and Jameson. She looked back over her shoulder and smiled at the pair. She'd never seen her mother so relaxed. She hadn't told Jameson the entire truth. Michelle wanted to be closer to home. She wanted to be closer to her mother. She'd never been close to her father. She'd always felt awkward around Candace's former partner, Jessica. It was different now. Michelle felt more at home than she could ever recall when she was with her mother, Jameson, and Pearl. She was reeling from Lisa's betrayal. It had blown up just when Michelle was preparing to invite Lisa home to meet her family. Now, it was her family that Michelle needed. She worried about intruding on their life, but selfishly she felt she needed them both. Jameson was…What was Jameson? A friend? She was that, but it was somehow different. Michelle cared what Jameson thought almost as much as she worried about her mother's opinion. She shook off her musings. Jameson was too young to be a parental figure. "Maybe another big sister," Michelle thought. She looked back when she heard her mother's laugh and felt it fill her heart. *I hope I find that someday.*

Chapter Eleven

Jameson could hardly believe that it was already Thursday. She was anxious to finish out the next two days in Albany and get home. The Fourth of July was only a week away. Monday, Jonah was due to arrive. Tuesday, her brother Toby and his wife Liz were expected to make their appearance with Jameson's two nephews. By Wednesday, all three of Candace's children would be home, and then on Thursday, Jameson's parents planned on making the trip with her younger brother and Jameson's niece. Candace's brother David and his brood, along with Dana, Steve, and their two children were also expected to join them. Friday was the official barbecue, but the event itself was more like three days of unofficial festivities. Candace thrived on being around people. Jameson was a bit more reserved in that manner. She was praying that there would be no drama.

Marianne had been civil, even cordial bordering on kind to Jameson when they had met. Jameson was certain that Candace's oldest child had reservations about her relationship with Candace. Jameson's younger brother had expressed concerns to her as well. While his reasoning to Jameson was the constant distance between the pair, Jameson suspected it had more to do with Candace's political beliefs and public persona. Doug was two years younger than Jameson and the family conservative. They always joked about her father's Republican affiliation, but Jameson's father, Duncan had long ago shifted alliances. Jameson imagined that was a product of so many years loving her mother and having a lesbian daughter. Doug somehow got what Jameson called the recessive gene. She loved her younger brother, but she often wondered how they could have been raised in the same house by the same parents.

"J.D.?" a familiar voice came from the doorway to Jameson's office. She swiveled her chair around.

"Shell?"

"Yeah, sorry. I seem to be showing up unannounced a lot lately, huh?" Michelle said sheepishly.

"Everything okay?" Jameson asked.

"No," Michelle chuckled. "But it will be. I was hoping maybe you might possibly have a minute to talk," Michelle asked hopefully.

"Wow, that was a mouthful," Jameson laughed. "I need a break anyway. How about lunch?"

"I don't want to take you away from…."

"From all this?" Jameson shook her head. "Come on, let's go. I need some fuel. Food and a gigantic coffee."

"Dana, please," Candace tried to keep her rising temper under control.

"I understand, Candy. Aren't you at least going to consider it?" Dana asked her boss. Candace frowned. "What does J.D. think?" Dana asked.

"I don't know."

"What do you mean? She didn't have any thoughts at all?" Dana was amazed.

"I don't know because I haven't told her," Candace said flatly.

"Don't you think you should?"

"There is nothing to tell. I'm not doing it," Candace said.

"Candy, you would make a fabulous governor. And, think about where that would position you in six years?" Dana said enthusiastically. Candace groaned. "Candy! Come on! They are lining you up as a heavy hitter and you know it. If you wanted to make a run for…."

"I don't," Candace stopped her friend's diatribe.

"No offense, but I think you are full of shit," Dana challenged the senator.

"No offense, but I didn't ask for your opinion," Candace replied in kind.

"Why are you so set against this?" Dana asked. Candace put her face in her hands. "It's J.D., isn't it?" Dana softened her tone. Candace sighed. "Candy, I know you love the Senate. I do. This is a huge chance."

"If I won, you mean."

"You'll win if you run," Dana said confidently. "You know it as well as I do." Candace's lips upturned into a small smirk. "So, let's have it. Is it really because this is where you want to stay? You have some aversion to governing the State of New York? Or…is it something else?"

Candace huffed and removed her glasses to rub her tired eyes. "Would I win? Probably," Candace agreed. Dana perked up. "I said probably," Candace tempered Dana's enthusiasm. "State politics are different, Dana. I've been in Congress now for fifteen years. Election battles are not so difficult now for me. People know me in the role. They trust me in this role. No one wants to fund a lame horse. The odds of a payoff in betting against me in a Senate bid are just not that great, not yet anyway. It's simply not their best investment."

"That's my point!" Dana said.

"Yes, but this is a different ball game. Different players. Different positions. Different strategies," Candace reminded her friend.

"You love campaigning. And, you are incredibly popular at home. Look at your approval ratings."

"I know all of that. New York is a different state in a state election. There are different issues and concerns. I don't know that I want to invest all of that. The research into campaign strategies, the money….the time," Candace said.

"Are you worried about J.D.?"

Candace smiled. "No….not in the way that you are thinking," Candace said.

"What way am I thinking?" Dana asked.

"Dana, Jameson will tell me to do what I want to do. That is what she will say," Candace said.

"So? What's the problem?"

"I don't know that it *is* what I want to do," Candace replied honestly.

"Part of you wants to and…"

"I love Jameson."

Dana smiled. "I know you do. What does that have to do with this? You just said that J.D. will support whatever you decide."

Candace sighed heavily, flipped her glasses onto her desk and took a deep breath. "Yes, she will. I see that gleam in your eyes, Dana."

"Would you jump to do it if you weren't involved with J.D.?"

"I don't know," Candace answered honestly. "I love what I am doing. You know that is the truth," Candace said. She could see the skepticism in Dana's eyes. "I had the chance last go round for a cabinet appointment. You know that too."

"Yes, but you were worried about Jonah then."

"And, I resolved myself that this is where I wanted to be."

"And?" Dana urged.

"And, my life is different again. I like my life right now," Candace said. She saw Dana studying her. "There's still a lot to learn how to balance. I'm not sure I want to shake the apple cart so soon."

"Candy, the election is two years off. You have time."

"Not really, and we both know it. If I want to do this, I need to make that clear and I need to start looking at my team now," Candace said bluntly.

"You have to talk to J.D.," Dana said. "She's going to hear the chatter and you know it."

Candace smiled. She was not afraid to discuss the

possibilities of her career with Jameson. She had hoped to get through the holiday before doing that. Jameson had tried to conceal her apprehension about the big family barbecue. Candace could see the clues to the trepidation that lingered in Jameson's mind. If Candace were to be honest, she felt a few jitters when she allowed herself the time to stop and consider the upcoming event.

Candace had immediately clicked with Jameson's parents. She adored Jameson's mother, Maureen. She wasn't worried about anyone's approval, but she hoped that the two families would find some common ground. Family meant a great deal to both her and Jameson. Family gatherings were stressful in the best of circumstances over many years. This would be the first go-round for the new couple. She wanted to limit the stress in both their lives until they were on the other side of next weekend.

Still, the political chatter was bound to start soon. Candace knew that as well. The fact was that the party was exerting a comfortable pressure on her to consider a bid for the governorship. She fully expected that they would be turning up the heat in the coming months. She was a viable candidate with national name recognition. The governorship of New York would place her as an excellent Vice Presidential nominee, or if she chose, a candidate for The White House herself. That had never been her ambition. She was skeptical about a middle-aged lesbian's viability in such a high powered candidacy. She could not deny that fact that attitudes were changing. Six years from now, it might be a different ball game. The Democratic Party wanted a strong, well-placed candidate when that tide finally sifted. She would have been lying if she suggested that the idea did not, at the very least, intrigue her.

"I was going to wait until after the festivities on the Fourth," Candace said.

"But?" Dana asked, sensing a slight shift in Candace's mood.

"There's no point in waiting," Candace admitted.

"Candy? Can I ask you something? I mean, as your friend, not as an adviser in any capacity?"

"Of course."

"Are you afraid that this....possibly taking a different course will scare J.D. off?"

"No," Candace answered immediately. She wasn't. "That's not it at all, Dana," Candace noted the inquisitive expression on the younger woman's face. She laughed quietly. "I know you may not understand this, I like the downtime. It's nice to just come home and be with someone. No kids under foot. They visit. It's a nice change of pace. I raised three kids while juggling two careers my whole adult life. I barely saw Jessica and Jonathan when you think about it. Jameson is....well, it's entirely different. Jessica always wanted to be going. We were on the go constantly. Jonathan was the same way. That has never been me and you know it."

"I know. I know that you like your down time, Candy, but you love the social piece as well. You thrive on it," Dana smirked.

"Yes, but not incessantly. I like balance," Candace said. Dana nodded. "I won't make this decision by myself, Dana."

"I am happy for you, you know?"

Candace smiled. "Me too."

"But, selfishly....I hope you do it," Dana admitted.

Candace laughed. "I would never have guessed."

🐎 🐎 🐎

"J.D., are you sure you would be okay with this? I mean, it's your place and…"

"Shell, I already told you, you would be helping me out," Jameson said.

"What did Mom say?" Michelle asked.

"I didn't say anything to her yet," Jameson said.

"Really?"

"Shell, I love your mom, but I would not betray your confidence unless I thought I needed to for some reason. She knows that."

"Thanks," Michelle said. "I did tell her a bit about things with Lisa."

"I know," Jameson replied.

"Do you think she will be mad?"

Jameson smiled at Michelle. "Mad? About what?"

"Me quitting my job," Michelle said.

Jameson nodded and took a sip from her iced coffee. "No. I don't. She won't want to admit it, least of all to you," Jameson chuckled, "but she will be happy that you will be closer to home."

"You really think so?" Michelle asked hesitantly.

"Yes, but you already know that," Jameson said with a wink.

"Are you excited about Mom's big party?" Michelle changed the subject. Jameson tried to smile, but it failed in its sincerity. "That's what I thought," Michelle laughed. "Don't let Marianne scare you," she said. "She's got a loud bark, but no real bite. Trust me." Jameson sighed. "J.D., seriously…."

"It's not just Marianne," Jameson said honestly.

"Jonah?"

"It's all of it," Jameson said. "My brothers, Marianne, Jonah, my parents…It's just…"

"Mom's a master. She can make anyone feel like they belong. Besides, Grandma Pearl will be there. No one messes with Grandma Pearl," Michelle said. Jameson had to smile at the truth in that assessment. "Don't worry," Michelle took Jameson's hand. "If all else fails, I'll protect you," Michelle winked conspiratorially.

Jameson laughed out loud. "My bodyguard?"

"Sure. I can be scrappy if necessary. You live with my mom for twenty-six years, you learn."

"I believe it," Jameson said. "I'll whistle if I need you."

"Deal," Michelle said. "J.D.?"

"What?"

"I just….Thanks again….for everything."

"You don't owe me any thanks, but you are welcome."

Jameson was stretched out on a lawn chair, relaxing as the sun began to set when she sensed a presence above her. She felt Candace's lips on her forehead and smiled. "Napping?" Candace asked.

"Relaxing. You're home early," Jameson said happily.

"Yes, I am," Candace replied. "Seems I have a date tomorrow with my daughter." Jameson bit her lip gently. "Something about moving closer to home?" Candace posed her statement as a question. "You wouldn't happen to know anything about that, would you?"

Jameson was unsure if Candace was upset or simply being playful. "Well, I didn't want to say anything…I mean it's…well, you know…it was…."

Before Jameson could continue her rambling explanation, Candace silenced her with a kiss. "I love you," Candace said.

"Huh?"

Candace laughed. "Have I not told you that lately or something?"

"No, I just…I didn't think it was my place to tell you. It was…"

"Jameson," Candace took the opportunity to sit on Jameson's lap. "I know why you didn't tell me. I appreciate it. Michelle is a grown woman, but to me…"

"She's your baby. I know."

"Mm. You don't know how much it means to me that she felt she could confide in you or what it means to her that she could."

"I love Shell," Jameson said as a point of fact. "She's like mini-Candace."

"Mini-Candace?" Candace raised a brow.

"Yeah," Jameson said wistfully. She adored Candace and Michelle was the most like her mother of all three children. She resembled Candace more in mannerisms than in her physical appearance, but she also had a similar personality and sense of humor. Jameson had been immediately comfortable with Candace's middle child. Jameson's friendship with Michelle in some odd way made her feel even closer to Candace. Seeing the earnest affection in Jameson's eyes, Candace ceased the opportunity to tease her.

"You don't have a crush on my daughter, do you?" Candace asked.

Jameson jumped. "What?" Jameson asked nervously. Candace fought to remain stoic. It was sometimes far too easy to playfully rattle her lover. "Oh, God, that would be like crushing on my sister…if I had one," Jameson said.

"Oh?" Candace was finding great humor in the unintentional ditch that Jameson was digging for herself. "I see. So, that would make me a mother figure."

"You're a great mom," Jameson praised and then realized how it might have sounded. Candace raised her brow a little higher. "I mean….that's not what I meant."

"Oh? I'm not a great mom?"

"Of course, you're a great mom…just not my great mom…I mean not my mom…You know what I mean!" Jameson sighed.

"Mm. Maybe I should send you to bed without dinner, let you think about this a little," Candace said thoughtfully.

Jameson narrowed her gaze at her lover, finally realizing her game. "Oh? No, I think you might need some rest, though." She grabbed hold of Candace and stood up carrying her.

"Jameson! What the hell are you doing? You're going to hurt yourself!"

"Nah, I'm young. I need to take care of my old lady and put her to bed," Jameson chided.

Candace smacked Jameson. "Put me down, you lunatic!" she laughed. Jameson ignored her and headed for the house. "Jameson!"

Pearl was walking through the kitchen when Jameson kicked open the back door with Candace in her arms. "I've heard of sweeping them off their feet, or is this a threshold thing? Something I should know?" she called out to the pair.

"No!" Candace yelled.

"Just putting Nana here to bed," Jameson laughed.

Pearl shook her head. "Well, don't drop her down the stairs whatever you do. I've seen enough emergency rooms this year, thank you very much!"

"One time! I fell one time!" Jameson called back.

"They never grow up," Pearl chuckled. "Heaven help me with a house full next week."

🐴 🐴 🐴

Wednesday was upon them faster than either Candace or Jameson could have imagined. Candace rolled over and snuggled closer to Jameson. "I'd better get up and help Pearl with breakfast," she yawned.

Jameson kissed Candace's head. "You stay," she said. "I'll go help Pearl. Sleep a little while longer."

"Mm. Aren't you tired?" Candace asked. "You were up late with Toby last night. Everything okay?"

"Yeah. Just talking," Jameson said. She had enjoyed her one on one time with her older brother and was relieved to see that Candace hit it off immediately with her sister-in-law.

Candace propped herself up to look at Jameson. "I know you are nervous."

"You are better at these things than I am," Jameson reminded her lover.

"What things?" Family things?"

"People things," Jameson said.

"Not true. I am just more accustomed to dealing with different personalities all at once. You are every bit as personable as I am. I've just learned to hide my apprehension."

Jameson chuckled. "If you say so."

"I do," Candace yawned again.

"Seriously, go back to sleep for a bit," Jameson said. "I'll go help Pearl. It'll give me some more time to catch up with Toby before everyone else arrives anyway."

Candace sighed. She was not used to being given this kind of opportunity. "I don't want you to feel like you need to…"

Jameson kissed Candace gently. "I'll set the alarm for 7:00. Okay? I'll see you in a bit," she said as she made her way from the bed. Candace grabbed Jameson's pillow and almost immediately fell back to sleep. Jameson shook her head. She was tired, but she could tell that Candace was exhausted, and the planned chaos was only beginning. She stretched and headed for the shower hoping it would somehow bring her to life. "I'm ready for vacation already," Jameson laughed.

By noon, Candace's house was full. Dana and Steve had decided to make their way to the area a day early. Jameson was grateful. She spent the majority of the afternoon playing with her nephews and Dana and Steve's two children. She found herself enjoying the day far more than she had expected and looking forward to her parents' arrival the next day. Everyone seemed to be enjoying themselves. Rick and Toby had seemed to cultivate a fast friendship. Jameson liked Marianne's husband a great deal. He was mild mannered and it was clear that he not only loved Marianne, Rick's affection for Candace was also evident. Jameson did not know Rick's whole story. She did know that he had lost his mother when he was quite young and she suspected that Candace filled that role for him in many ways. As the sun began to set, and the kids began to tire, the party moved indoors. Jameson found herself sitting with Marianne and Dana.

"So, what do you think?" Dana asked Jameson.

"Think? Think about what?" Jameson laughed.

"Oh come on, J.D.! What do you think about Candy running for governor?"

"Mom's running for governor?" Marianne piped up.

Jameson shook her head. "She doesn't know yet," she said to Marianne. "As far as what I think, I think she should do whatever she wants to do."

"Uh-huh. You know, J.D. if she does, she will be in a prime position to run for higher office," Dana said. Jameson just smiled.

"You mean you think my mother might run for president, don't you?" Marianne asked. Dana just smiled. Jameson's gaze had drifted across the room to where Candace was cuddling Spencer happily. "That's crazy," Marianne said.

Dana shrugged. "Why? She could do it if she wanted to."

"She could do anything," Jameson said proudly. She was enjoying watching Candace's expression as she held her grandson.

"She could. She won't," Marianne said emphatically. "She never wanted any of that."

"Things change sometimes," Jameson said softly. "Sometimes, you think you are heading one way and all of a sudden you are forced to take a detour. You find out you like the scenery on the new road better."

Marianne frowned slightly. She followed Jameson's eyes to where they were focused on her mother. She looked back at Jameson, who seemed oblivious to anything at the moment except Candace. Marianne looked at Dana. "My mother is about as likely to run for The White House as she is to have more children," she said. "I wouldn't bet on her coming home to New York. She's been pretty clear that she likes her life the way it is," she said bluntly.

Dana forced a smile. Marianne often challenged her patience. She wasn't certain what it was that Marianne struggled with about Candace's life. Part of it, she suspected, was the difficulty that Marianne had with her parents' divorce. She was seventeen when her parents split. Dana would have thought that would have made it easier. Marianne was off to college before Candace had even become involved with Jessica. Michelle was only fourteen, and Jonah twelve. Both of Candace's younger children seemed to accept, if not always support their mother's decisions both personally and professionally. It was always Marianne who seemed to need to stir the pot.

"You never know," Jameson said softly as Candace looked up and caught her attention, offering a soft smile.

"You never know what?" Marianne asked pointedly.

Jameson turned to Candace's eldest child. "You never know what the future might have in store," Jameson winked. She smiled at Dana and made her way across the room to Candace.

Dana looked over and saw Jameson place a kiss on Candace's cheek and whisper something in her ear. "Truer words," Dana chuckled.

"Excuse me?" Marianne asked.

Dana motioned across the room. Jameson's nephew Eli was trying to climb up her leg. Candace was laughing while

Spencer slept in her arms. "Looks good on them. You never know, Marianne. Your mother might surprise us all."

Marianne's posture grew rigid. She watched her mother pass Spencer to Rick before she and Jameson led two overtired little boys toward the kitchen. "Oh, I do know," she thought silently.

"I hear there's a little buzz about the senator," Maureen Reid goaded her daughter.

"Buzz?" Jameson played dumb.

"J.D.?" Maureen smacked her daughter lightly. "Lots of talk about the future," she lifted an eyebrow.

Jameson laughed at her mother. Maureen Reid had spent her entire career teaching history. She relished anything political or historical in nature. Jameson was confident that it delighted her mother to no end to have a senator in the family. "Whose future?" Jameson winked.

"She could do it, J.D. I mean it. If not her own candidacy, she could easily end up in a cabinet position, Attorney General, Secretary of State, even Vice President," Maureen said.

"Yes, I know," Jameson agreed.

"Do you not want her to do that?" Maureen asked.

Jameson caught a wayward beach ball from the pool and tossed it back to her brother. "No."

"No! You don't want her to?" Maureen was shocked.

"No," Jameson laughed. "I want her to do what she wants to do."

"What about you? Do you think you could handle that? I mean, even governor. Geez...J.D., you would be really in the spotlight. A lesbian couple in the governor's mansion?" Maureen said with a grin. Jameson wiggled a bit in her chair. "That isn't what you want, is it?" Maureen asked quietly.

Jameson gave an uncomfortable grin. "I just want her to be happy."

"What about you?" Maureen asked.

"You won't believe me."

"Try me?" Maureen replied.

"I'm just happy to be along for the ride. I really don't know what to expect, Mom. I have no idea where she might be headed. I just hope she wants me to be a part of it. It scares me sometimes."

"Why?"

"Because I don't want to let her down. And, because I really don't want to be without her. As weird as it sounds, I don't want to be without Shell or Pearl or God, or any of this."

"It's not weird J.D."

Jameson grinned. "You thought it might be weird having a daughter-in-law a few years younger than you. Imagine having your daughter-in-law in The White House someday!" Jameson laughed.

"J.D.? Are you and Candace getting married?" Maureen asked.

"Huh?"

"You said, daughter-in-law."

"Oh…Hmmm. Don't know," Jameson laughed. "Think she'd want to?" Jameson asked.

Maureen rolled her eyes. "You'd have to ask *her*," she winked.

"Guess that makes sense."

"Are you going to?" Maureen grew wide-eyed.

Jameson shook her head. "Not today," she laughed as a splash of her.

"Spencer seems to love the water," Candace commented to Marianne as they watched Rick swing the baby through the water.

"Yeah. I guess he takes after his father," her daughter answered.

"What do you mean? When you were a kid, we couldn't get you out of the water," Candace chuckled at the memory. She watched in the distance as Jameson's nephew Eli splashed his aunt who was sitting near the edge of the pool. "Having the kids here reminds me of those days," she said wistfully. Candace listened to Eli daring Jameson to jump in. Candace laughed when Jameson stopped her conversation with her mother abruptly and obliged her nephew's request by splashing into the pool with her shorts and T-Shirt on. "Lunatic," she mumbled affectionately.

Marianne looked at her mother seriously. "You might want to be careful taking that trip down memory lane," Marianne said.

"What does that mean?" Candace asked.

Marianne sighed. "Mom...What happens when J.D. wants to fill that pool back up with screaming toddlers?"

"What are you talking about?"

"I'm talking about you and J.D. What are you going to say when J.D. wants to have a family?" Marianne asked.

Candace was completely taken off guard. "Marianne, where is this coming from? Jameson hasn't given me any indication that she wants children....at all."

"Have you two talked about it?"

Candace's face was beginning to flush. She was both irritated and embarrassed by her daughter's line of questioning. "Not directly, no. In general, yes."

"What does that mean?" Marianne challenged her mother.

"It means it's none of your business," Candace answered abruptly.

"I'm just raising a point."

"Marianne, Jameson and I are not planning on having a family. In all the things we have discussed, Jameson's desire for children has not once come up...and before you say another word, I am certain that if it were something she wanted, she would have raised the issue numerous times by now."

"Uh-huh. Mom," Marianne said. "J.D. is thirty-five. Look at her! How can you be so sure that she won't change her mind in two years? People change what they want sometimes. You of all people know that. I saw her looking at you last night when you were rocking Spencer," Marianne said.

Candace sighed. The conversation was making her extremely uncomfortable. She and Jameson had never discussed family in this manner. They had considered Candace's children, Jameson's family, and how they would navigate everyone's questions, concerns, and personalities. They had not once delved into the subject of whether or not Jameson wanted children. Candace had just assumed that they were on the same page. "Jameson loves kids," she admitted. "That doesn't mean she wants her own."

Marianne nodded. "Now," she remarked. "What about you? You really want to open up that can of worms, Mom? I mean....seriously? Can you see yourself with babies again?"

Candace swallowed hard. She felt herself becoming unsteady and was grateful when she heard Pearl call out to her from the kitchen. "I have to go help Pearl," she said.

Candace made her way across the yard at a brisk pace, holding back mounting tears. Michelle caught sight of her mother's expression as she moved away from Marianne and headed directly for her sister's location. "What the hell did you say to her?" she asked her older sister.

"What?" Marianne snapped.

"What did you say to Mom to upset her this time?" Michelle asked.

"Why do you assume it's my fault? I just raised a question. If it upset her, that's not my fault."

Candace was cutting up vegetables silently when Pearl removed the knife from her hand and set it down. "What is going on with you?"

"What do you mean?"

"Candy," Pearl warned.

"I'm fine."

"And, I'm an eighteen-year-old swimsuit model. Out with it," Pearl ordered. Candace looked up with watery eyes. "Who do I need to ground?" Pearl joked.

Candace chuckled and wiped away the hint of a tear. "Oh, Pearl. Am I being realistic?"

"Realistic? You lost me."

"About Jameson," Candace said sadly. "What if I am keeping her from the things she deserves? I've raised my family. For Christ's sake, I'm a grandmother!"

"Still lost. You went left somewhere back there and I'm still at the stoplight. What are you talking about?" Pearl asked.

"Jameson wanting children."

"Oh. Does Jameson want children?" Pearl asked.

"I don't know. She's never said that, but…"

"Never said that to me either," Pearl offered. "So, just ask her."

"What?" Candace startled.

"If you're worried about it, ask her. I think she would have said something by now," Pearl shrugged, seeming unfazed by the conversation.

"I agree," Candace said. "That doesn't mean she might not change her mind."

"True," Pearl replied.

"You are not helping!" Candace said. "How can you be so calm?" Pearl shrugged again and leaned against the counter. Candace covered her eyes. "I don't want to lose her."

"So don't," Pearl said.

"Pearl…"

"What? Why are you so worried about what might happen? You know better than that," Pearl said.

"I don't want to do that again," Candace said. "I did that part of my life."

Pearl nodded. "Where did you get this idea anyway?" Candace sighed. "Well?"

"Marianne just mentioned that…"

"Candy," Pearl scolded. "Listen to me," she said. "I've lived a little longer than you. Not much, but just enough," she said with a wink. Candace sighed again. "You love Jameson?"

"Of course, I do."

"Um-hum. That's why you are hesitant to make certain changes. Am I right?" Pearl asked.

"You mean running for governor."

"I do. Am I wrong? You're not sure you want to do that. Part of you does and part of you doesn't. Mostly because you're afraid that where it might lead is not what Jameson will want," Pearl surmised.

"It's not just that," Candace said. "I'm not sure if it's what I want. If I do it everything will change for us."

"And, I will bet that you are right, Jameson would probably rather not rock the boat, but I will also bet that she will stay beside you if that's what you want. She'll make the compromises if I know Jameson. And, I do know Jameson."

"I know that," Candace said. "That's why I want to be sure before I make that decision, before we make that decision. She'd do anything for me. I know that too." Pearl smiled and raised her brow. Candace shook her head as she followed the older woman's train of thought. "Not the same thing," Candace said.

"Yes, it is," Pearl said. "You are worried about something that hasn't even come to pass. And, you don't even know how you would feel if it did." Candace's jaw fell open. "First of all, I'm not sure Jameson would ever even want children," Pearl said.

"Did you see her with those boys?" Candace chimed.

Pearl nodded and noted the smile on Candace's face. "Yes, and so did you. You look me in the eyes and tell me it doesn't make you love her all the more," Pearl challenged. Candace groaned. "That doesn't mean she wants her own," Pearl said. "Things change, Candy. People even change. You can't predict tomorrow. You just have to trust that you and Jameson will be able to get through whatever comes your way."

"I know."

"So, trust her."

"I do," Candace said.

"Than trust that she will tell you what she needs, not Marianne." Candace sighed heavily. "Don't try to predict the future, Candy," Pearl said. "It has a way of surprising you." Candace nodded with a smile as Pearl enveloped her in a hug. "And, for once…consider the source. I love Marianne, but she has a vivid imagination and she doesn't think things through sometimes."

"I know," Candace said.

"Yes, but you sometimes forget."

"What did you say to make Mom cry?" Michelle demanded of her sister.

Jonah heard Michelle's voice raise and made his way over to his siblings. "What do you mean Mom's crying?" he asked.

"It's not my fault," Marianne defended herself.

"Bullshit, Marianne. What did you say?" Michelle barked.

Rick noticed the argument beginning and discretely asked Jameson if she would hold Spencer. "What is going on?" he asked as he toweled off his short hair.

"Ask your wife," Michelle answered without removing her gaze from her sister.

"I didn't do anything," Marianne insisted. "I just asked her a simple question."

"What kind of question?" Jonah asked.

"I just asked if she had considered the fact that Jameson might want kids someday. What would she do then?" Marianne explained as reasonably as she could.

"Why the hell would you even ask that?" Michelle asked.

"Come on, Shell! You can't seriously see Mom with another baby! Jesus! You want brothers and sisters the same age as your own kids? I'm just trying to help her be realistic."

"No, you're just trying to cause trouble for her and J.D.," Michelle said in disgust.

"Jonah?" Marianne implored her brother.

Jonah shook his head. "Why can't you just let them be?"

"Don't tell me you are suddenly all for this relationship?" Michelle asked her brother.

"Why wouldn't I be? J.D.'s been nothing but good to all of us. I don't give a shit about their age difference."

"It's not the age difference, Jonah. It's the reality difference. You didn't see J.D. watching Mom yesterday with Spencer. I mean....come on! You're twenty-four. You seriously want to have little brothers and sisters?"

Jonah shrugged. "Why do I care?" he asked. "I'm not raising them." Rick snickered at his brother-in-law's response.

"You're not helping!" Marianne chastised her husband.

Rick nodded. "I don't actually see your point in any of this," he said honestly. "Your mom and Jameson are adults. They can do whatever they want."

"You want Spencer playing with his uncle?" Marianne asked pointedly. Rick shrugged again, unaffected by the scenario.

"God, you can be such a bitch," Michelle chimed.

"I'm just trying…"

"To what? Be the center of attention?" Michelle's voice was rising fast. "What are you afraid of? That Spencer won't command center stage or something? Why do you care? How about if I have a baby? How about Jonah!"

"Don't look at me," Jonah put up his hands. Rick snickered again.

"I'm looking out for Mom," Marianne defended herself.

"Bullshit. You are looking out for you, just like you always do. What the hell is your problem?" Michelle nearly screamed.

"My problem? What are you talking about? Look at J.D. with Spencer! Look! Don't you think they need to consider this stuff! My God! Are you two completely stupid?" Marianne yelled.

"Why don't you just shut up, Marianne. It's none of my business and it's none of yours," Michelle said angrily. She was coming dangerously close to hauling off and punching her sister.

"The hell it isn't! Shell, Mom is fifty-five…almost fifty-six. The last thing she needs…"

"The last thing she needs," a voice came upon them. "Is you three fighting over something that not one of you knows anything about," Pearl said firmly.

"We were just," Marianne began.

Pearl folded her arms across her chest. "I'd like a moment with your sister," Pearl said to Michelle and Jonah. They both nodded and shook their heads as they walked away. Rick started to follow.

"Where are you going?" Marianne asked her husband.

"Going to go talk to Granny J.D.," he tried not to laugh at his comment. Marianne bristled.

"Are you through?" Pearl asked the younger woman.

"What do you mean?" Marianne answered. "All I did was ask a question."

"No, all you did was suggest an issue to your mother that doesn't even exist."

"Yet," Marianne interjected.

Pearl took a deep breath. "Marianne, I love you like you were my own flesh and blood," Pearl said. Marianne braced herself. "Candy is as much my daughter as my own two children. You are a mother," Pearl said.

"Yes," Marianne agreed.

"What would you do to protect Spencer?"

"Anything," Marianne answered honestly.

"Mm. Glad we agree on that. I feel the same way. And, how would you feel if Spencer tried to tell you how you and Rick should live your lives?" Pearl asked.

"That's ridiculous," Marianne said.

"Really? You seem to think you know how your mother should live hers."

"Grandma, she's not…You can't tell me…."

"I can tell you that whatever happens with your mother and Jameson is between them."

"You don't honestly think this is a good idea?" Marianne asked in disbelief.

"I'm not certain what *this* is. I am certain that your mother is happy, happier than I have seen her in many years. If you really care about her, you will stop trying to undermine that."

"I don't want to see her get hurt," Marianne said softly.

Pearl guided the younger woman to a chair off in the distance and sat down beside her. "I know," she said softly.

There were things that Pearl understood about this family that no one else did. She had the advantage of being able to watch them all as they grew. Michelle and Jonah had not seen a great deal of what Marianne had. What they had witnessed in their mother's relationships, they often did not understand. It had been Marianne who found her mother crumpled on the floor after discovering Jessica's affair. It had been Marianne who had caught her father with another woman while Candace was away in Washington. Marianne's tactics were often brash. It made her appear self-centered. In fact, Pearl and Candace both understood that Marianne's brazenness was often a cover for her fear and sensitivity.

"I don't want to see her like that again," Marianne whispered.

"And, you don't want to lose her," Pearl surmised. Marianne looked up in shock. "Oh, I know you, sweetheart. I changed your diapers. I watched you with your mother. You fool them all….even her sometimes. You don't fool me, Spitfire," Pearl called the younger woman by her childhood nickname. "Not one bit."

"You didn't see her," Marianne said.

"Oh, but I did," Pearl said. "I saw her scraped knees. I sat at her wedding. I held her hand when she went into labor…three times…"

"I meant…."

"I know what you meant," Pearl interrupted Marianne. "I held her the first time she caught your father cheating on her." Marianne winced. "I rocked her the night Jessica moved out. If you are lucky, you will get to do all those things with your children," Pearl said. "To me, Candy is still the little girl who sat on the kitchen counter. I know she's not, but that is who she is to me. I would do anything to protect her. I also know that she doesn't need protection from Jameson."

"How can you say that?" Marianne asked. "What happens when…"

"What happens when she loses an election? What happens when she gets sick or Jameson does? What happens when, what? There is no what happens when, Marianne."

"I just can't imagine that…"

"You don't need to. You do need to let this go. Whatever this fear you have about Jameson and your mother is. No one will ever replace you, or Spencer," Pearl said. Marianne looked up and swallowed hard. "My kids certainly didn't replace Candy….and their children take nothing away from any of you."

"It's different," Marianne said.

"No, Spitfire. It isn't."

"I just…"

"You just need to apologize to your mother. Stop trying to be her mother and just tell her you love her for once."

"She knows that," Marianne said.

"Yes, she does. But that doesn't mean she couldn't use to hear you say it," Pearl said. "As for the rest, I think you had better start finding a way to accept Jameson. No matter what, I don't think she's going anywhere. Give her a chance. You might find you like her."

"I'm not the enemy," Marianne said.

"No. Neither is Jameson," Pearl said. She stood up, kissed Marianne on the head and smiled. "No family is perfect, Marianne. Not one. Not even this one. They change over time. Jameson is part of yours. I'd get used to it."

Chapter Twelve

Jameson snuck up behind Candace just as she finished putting Spencer in his portable crib. "Worn out? Huh?" Jameson whispered, putting her arms around Candace.

"Yeah, I envy him. Being able to just decide to sleep," Candace said.

"He's a lot of fun," Jameson said. Candace turned in Jameson's arms and looked at her thoughtfully. "What?" Jameson asked.

"Jameson...Do you want kids?" Candace asked hesitantly.

Jameson wrinkled her nose in thought. "Why? Do you?"

"I have kids," Candace said. Jameson grinned. "Jameson, I'm serious."

"I love kids."

"I know. That's not what I asked," Candace pointed out.

"Candace? Are you pregnant?" Jameson joked.

"Jameson!" Candace snapped. "I'm serious!"

Jameson softened her gaze. "Where did this come from?"

"I don't know. You love kids. I know that, but we've never talked about it."

"No. I guess not. We never talked about you having aspirations to be president either," Jameson said.

"Because those aren't my aspirations," Candace said.

"Mm-hm. You love politics, though."

"Yes, but..."

Jameson raised an eyebrow. "I love kids. Doesn't mean I have always aspired to be a parent."

Candace sighed. "You don't want kids?"

Jameson led Candace to the queen sized bed across the room and sat her down. "If the person I was with wanted to have children, I would consider it. I don't know that I'd be any good at it, but I would try," Jameson said honestly. Candace let out a heavy sigh. "And, if the person I was with wanted to say, run for governor or even president one day, I'd do my best to be what she needed. I don't know that I'd be any good at that either, but I'd try."

Candace smiled. "Jameson…"

"I heard the kids earlier," Jameson said. "They were arguing over our imaginary progeny while my mother was making the assumption that I was about to propose to you."

"What?" Candace asked.

"Mm-hm. Seems everyone knows what we are doing," Jameson smirked. "Your children have me pregnant before my mother even got the ring on your finger," she chuckled.

"Your mother thinks you were going to ask me to marry you?" she asked. Jameson nodded. "Why?" Candace asked. Jameson shrugged with a gleam in her eye. "Were you?" the question slipped out.

"Why? Do you want me to? I'm already down on my knee, so I'm half way there," Jameson said.

"I'm sorry," Candace blushed. "I wasn't trying to put you on the spot."

"I would marry you, if that's what you wanted to know," Jameson said. Candace's jaw fell open. Jameson put two fingers under Candace's jaw and gently closed it. "I would also follow you to the Governor's Mansion or The White House if you wanted me to. I'd even consider one of those," she gestured to the crib. "If you asked me to."

Candace smiled. "What about what you want, Jameson?"

"I have what I want. I have my job. I have my family. I have you." Candace kissed Jameson gently. Jameson smiled at her lover. "I have a feeling, deep down you want to do this…make this run for governor and see where it leads," Jameson said. Candace sighed. "I see that sparkle in your eye when it comes up," Jameson observed. "It's part of who you are, Candace."

"What about you?"

"Well, I think it might take me some getting used to. Campaigning. Being front and center. Sharing my lover with the world more than I do already," Jameson admitted. Candace nodded. Jameson was sure that Candace was about to interrupt and continued before she had the chance. "But, I'm pretty sure I can handle that. The thing is, I don't really want to share you with anyone else when you come home," Jameson said. "Don't get me wrong. I love this. I actually am having fun this week, but it's enough to share you with this family and with a whole nation. I don't really feel like competing at three in the morning with a Spencer sized rival for your attention."

Candace smiled. "Are you sure about that?"

"Yeah. Pretty sure," Jameson said with a wink. "We can take them on loan. That works for me."

"You might change your mind," Candace said.

"Maybe," Jameson admitted. "Or you might, and then what?" Jameson said. Candace laughed. "You laugh now," she said. "I don't say it enough."

"Say what?" Candace asked.

"That I love you."

"You say it all the time," Candace said.

"No. You do. The truth is, I do. I love you so much that it hurts some days. That's the truth. Marianne is right," Jameson said.

"What?" Candace asked.

"I love watching you with Spencer," Jameson admitted. Candace smiled. "Because I love you and you love him....and that makes me love you even more."

"I love you too," Candace said. "I want you to be happy."

"I am. Well, except when you steal all the fortune cookies."

"I do not!" Candace argued.

"You so do," Jameson laughed. "Listen, I have my hands full with the addition to this house, work, and keeping up with you. Besides, I can't imagine being pregnant. You won't let me climb ladders now. I wouldn't be allowed near a step stool."

Candace laughed. "I'm not that bad, but I get your point."

"Do me a favor?" Jameson asked.

"Anything."

"Just ask me. Whenever you want to know something, just ask me. I can't promise you'll always like my answer. I can promise it will always be the truth," Jameson said. She held her hand out to Candace. "Now, come on. I heard something about S'mores."

"Jameson?"

"Hum?"

Candace stopped their movement suddenly. "I would do it for you too. I would try."

Jameson smiled. "I know."

"Everything okay?" Shell asked Jameson.

"I'm not pregnant or engaged," Jameson chuckled.

"What?" Shell asked.

"Neither is your mom," Jameson said.

"J.D.?"

Jameson laughed and patted Michelle's knee. "But, I think your mom might end up running a lot more than this crazy family one day," she said.

"I'm sorry you heard us fighting," Michelle apologized.

"Me too," Jonah said, taking a seat next to his sister.

"Eh. You've met my brothers. Trust me, we've had our share of knockdowns. Don't worry about it," Jameson said. She caught sight of Marianne trying to avoid them. "Sit down and have a S'more," Jameson beckoned to Marianne and Rick. Rick smiled at Jameson and nodded, leading his reluctant wife over to the group. "Pull up a piece of grass," Jameson said. "Think I might have to call a lawn care company after this weekend," she laughed.

Marianne kept her eyes on the fire in front of them. Jameson handed her a stick and a marshmallow. "Thanks," Marianne said.

"I was just telling Shell that I am not pregnant," Jameson raised an eyebrow.

"J.D., I didn't mean to upset Mom or you," Marianne said.

Jameson held up a hand. "Since I have you all here, let's just put this to rest. Okay?"

Jonah looked at Jameson. "J.D. you don't owe any of us any explanations."

"No, I don't," she agreed. "But, if it were my mom, I would worry." Marianne looked up in surprise. "That surprises you?"

"No," Michelle answered for them all.

"Well, I would. She might kill me for telling you this, but I'm going to," Jameson said.

"Tell us what?" Michelle asked.

"I love your mom." Jonah, Rick, and Michelle all laughed. Marianne listened intently, instinctively understanding that this was mostly for her benefit. "I don't picture your mom and me changing diapers and filling bottles in the morning. Unless, of course, one of you is visiting."

"Jonah hasn't worn diapers in at least ten years," Michelle cracked, receiving a swift punch from her brother. "Ow!"

"Just remember, you two will be in Depends before me," he reminded her.

Jameson sniggered. Candace's children reminded her of her own brothers. "Well, it's good to know that you are all potty trained," Jameson said. "I was worried there for a while."

Across the yard, Candace was sitting on the patio with Jameson's parents, Pearl, Dana, and Steve. "What do you think is going on over there?" Dana pointed to where Jameson was seated by the fire, flanked by Candace's kids.

"Trouble," Pearl smiled. Candace grinned along with her.

"Yeah, you don't need to worry about us, J.D.," Michelle said. "I can barely get a date, so you'll have to rely on Marianne and Rick for diaper duty."

Jameson nodded. "The thing is....We don't have that planned." Marianne looked directly at Jameson. Jameson continued without missing a beat. "If any of you have a concern or a question, you can ask me. I can't promise you I will answer it, but I will listen and if I can, I will answer."

"J.D.," Michelle said quietly.

Jameson held up her hand. "I would like to be your friend because I know how much that would mean to your mom and because you are all a part of her. That means something to me," Jameson said honestly. "What I won't stand for is seeing her hurt. She doesn't deserve that."

Jonah smiled at Jameson. "No, she doesn't," he agreed.

"I can't promise I will never hurt her," Jameson added. "But, I would die before I would ever do that on purpose. That's the best I can promise you. Now eat your S'mores," Jameson instructed.

"You've been spending way too much time with Pearl," Michelle laughed. Jameson chuckled.

"For what it's worth J.D., I think you'd make a hell of a parent," Rick said. Marianne shot her husband a confused look. "Well, I do," he said. Jameson nodded her appreciation.

"Hey, if you can smack us down, a kid would be no problem," Jonah laughed.

"Yeah, but those diapers," Jameson cringed. "I kinda like it when they come already potty trained. Speaking is optional.

Potty trained…" The entire group laughed, even Marianne was left chuckling.

"You sure she doesn't want to run for office herself?" Pearl asked Candace and Maureen.

Jameson's mother laughed. "My daughter? She's lucky she remembers who the president is."

Candace laughed. "That hasn't stopped many before her," she winked.

"All I know is, if she managed a smile from Spitfire, she could charm a den of Republicans in a heartbeat," Pearl said.

"That's good since she is one," Maureen laughed.

"A spitfire?"

"No, a Republican," Maureen laughed.

"What?" the entire table erupted at once.

"That's like having a fish on land. There are no lesbian Republicans," Dana said.

"She did it when she registered just to ruffle me," Maureen laughed. "I don't know if she ever changed it, though."

Dana looked at Candace. "Ohhh…boy."

Candace just raised an eyebrow. "Well, that certainly is not the elephant in the room I expected," she laughed. Maureen laughed immediately. It took the rest of the table a moment to understand Candace's pun. When they did, the entire group fell into a fit of raucous laughter.

"What's wrong with them?" Jonah pointed to the patio.

"Is Mom drinking wine, J.D.?" Michelle asked, concern coloring her voice.

Jameson smiled watching the group at the table. "Nah, she's just being Candace," Jameson said.

"Mom?"

Candace was just about to head up the stairs when she

heard Marianne's voice. "Hey, thought you went up to bed?" Candace asked. She looked at her daughter's face and sighed. "Come on," she grabbed Marianne's hand and led her into the kitchen. Marianne watched as her mother filled a kettle for tea. Almost everyone had retired for the evening. Jameson and her brothers were still out back with Jonah. She startled slightly when Jonah and Jameson walked through the back door in tandem.

"Hey, you two," Candace greeted the pair. "Where are Toby and Doug?"

"Camping in my old tent with the kids," Jonah said.

"Is that what you were up to out there?" Candace asked.

"Yeah. I thought they might have fun with that. J.D. helped me pitch it while they got the boys ready. Do we have any more flashlights?" he asked his mother.

"I think there might be a couple in that old box in the back of the barn," Candace said. She rummaged through a kitchen drawer and handed Jonah some batteries. "Pearl's not so secret stash. I discovered it when I was ten. She's never moved it," she winked.

"Thanks, Mom," Jonah said. "I'll see you in the morning."

"You sleeping out there?" she asked.

"Yeah, should be fun," he said with a kiss to his mom's cheek. "Love you, Mom."

"I love you too," Candace said as she made her way to the whistling kettle.

"Night J.D, thanks letting me hang out with you guys," he said.

Jameson laughed. "Don't thank me. You'll be begging my forgiveness by morning. You've never shared a tent with Doug after a barbecue and beer."

Jonah laughed. "Noted. Night, Sis." Marianne nodded. She watched as her brother bounced back out the door as if he were twelve again. She tried not to focus on the scene unfolding a few feet away.

"Need anything before I head up?" Jameson asked Candace.

"Nope," Candace replied.

"Okay, don't stay up too long," Jameson whispered, but Marianne heard her clearly.

"Why? Afraid of the dark?" Candace teased Jameson.

"Yes, and you gave away all the flashlights," Jameson replied.

"I'm confident Jinx will protect you," Candace reassured her lover.

"Big help he'll be. What's he going to do, knead the monsters to death and purr?" Jameson whined.

"You really are a bit touched," Candace observed affectionately.

Jameson winked and kissed Candace tenderly. "I'll see you in a bit."

"Yes, you will."

"Good night, Marianne," Jameson said.

"Night, J.D."

Candace took the opportunity to wink at Jameson when Marianne looked down the table. She placed a cup of tea in front of her daughter, sat down, and waited.

"I'm sorry," Marianne said. Candace sighed. "I love you, Mom," Marianne said so honestly that it nearly took Candace's breath away.

"I know that," Candace said, reaching across the table and taking Marianne's hand. "Tell me the truth. What is it that has you so worried about Jameson?" Marianne looked up with unshed tears. "Go on," Candace encouraged her daughter.

"I don't want to see you hurt again."

"Yes, I know. It's more than that," Candace said.

"Sometimes, I don't want to share you," Marianne admitted. Candace smiled and moved across the short distance to embrace her daughter. "I already have to share you with too many people. What about Spencer? He has to share you too," she said. "I know…I'm selfish."

"Maybe, but I appreciate what you said more than you know," Candace replied. "It's funny, you know? That's exactly the reason Jameson gave as to why she doesn't want to have children."

"What do you mean?" Marianne asked.

"Well, our time is so divided now. We both have careers that occupy much of our week. I have you kids and Spencer. Jameson has her family, not to mention all of our friends and the people we both employ. If I decide to pursue anything else, well…that will add another layer. It's a lot to juggle," Candace said.

"You almost sound disappointed," Marianne noted.

"No….Well, maybe I am, just a little," Candace confessed.

"Really?" Marianne asked.

Candace nodded. "Yeah. Maybe a little, just a little. I guess as much as it would scare me, seeing Jameson with those kids…hell, seeing her sitting with you three made me realize how much she has to offer, and not just to me."

"Did you tell her that?" Marianne asked.

Candace smiled. "No. I have a feeling she knows how I feel. That's not something I want now. It isn't something she does either. I don't really want to share her any more than I already do either."

Marianne nodded. "I do like J.D."

"I know you do," Candace said. "That's what worries you. You love your dad. You and Jessica were close. Closer than Jonah and Shell," Candace said. "I already know."

"She really loves you," Marianne said. "I knew that, but…"

Candace was beaming. "Yes, she does."

"And, you really love her, don't you?" Marianne asked.

"Yes, I do," Candace smiled. "Not more than I love you, though." Candace felt Marianne's tears begin to flow. "In some ways, you are my greatest treasure," Candace said. Marianne cried in her mother's arms. "I don't think I understood what it meant to love completely until I held you. You taught me that," Candace said.

"I'm sorry, Mom. I really…"

"Marianne, no one knows you better than me. No one. Sometimes I would like to throttle you," Candace chuckled and Marianne chuckled along with her. "I do know you. I do love you. No one that comes into my life will ever change that."

"I know. I'm still sorry."

"So am I," Candace said.

"For what?" Marianne asked.

"For all the loss you've experienced—all of it. For my disappointments also being yours," Candace said honestly. "I wish more than anything that you never had to go through any of that," Candace said as she battled her own tears.

"Sometimes, I feel like I'm five when I'm with you," Marianne confessed.

Candace laughed. "I hope you always feel a little bit like that."

"You do?"

"Of course, it means you still need me," Candace said.

Marianne looked at her mother. "I do."

Candace nodded. "I know. There are two important people upstairs waiting for you. They need you right now," she said.

"Yeah, and there is someone waiting for you," Marianne smirked.

"I guess there is," Candace smiled.

"Do you think you and J.D. will make it, Mom?"

"No one can predict the future," Candace said. "You just prepare for it as best you can. Relationships are the same. All you can do is build a solid foundation and hope it holds up against the inevitable cracks. It's always under construction."

Marianne laughed. "She's rubbing off on you."

Candace winked at her daughter and held out her hand. "Yeah, I know. Who would have thought I'd have a cat!"

Marianne laughed and followed her mother as Candace shut off the lights. "At least Jinx doesn't need his diapers changed," Marianne joked.

"No, he has a whole box to himself. And, that was in the negotiations. That is Jameson and Pearl's territory. One that I have no desire to encroach upon—ever. Not even if they throw up the white flag!"

"Night, Mom," Marianne laughed.

"Night, sweetheart," Candace said.

Candace slipped into bed and kissed Jameson sensually on the neck. "What are you doing?" Jameson asked.

"What do you mean?" Candace feigned innocence.

Jameson closed her eyes against Candace's sensual assault. Candace's hands had slipped underneath Jameson's T-shirt and were massaging her abdomen. Her lips and tongue were tracing patterns on Jameson's neck. Jameson moaned. "If you don't stop, I cannot be held responsible for myself."

"Surrendering so soon?" Candace teased.

"To you? Yes," Jameson giggled and then sighed.

"I want you," Candace breathed in Jameson's ear.

"Marianne is next door," Jameson whispered.

"So? She knows how babies are made," Candace said as she pulled off Jameson's shirt and quickly sucked a straining nipple into her mouth.

"Jesus!" Jameson moaned.

"Shhh," Candace cautioned. "Your parents are across the hall, you know?"

"You are evil," Jameson breathed.

Candace teased Jameson's nipple with her tongue and teeth. They had not made love in days and Candace had found herself thinking about touching Jameson all day long. She loved to watch Jameson playing in the pool, much like she enjoyed watching Jameson work on the house or in the yard. Jameson had a delicately sculpted body. She was not overly muscular, but when she moved certain ways, Candace could note the lines of muscle definition in her back, abdomen, arms, and legs. Now that summer had fallen upon them, Jameson had developed the hint of a golden tan. She was still fair, but unlike Candace, when the sun kissed Jameson's skin it left a lasting reminder of its presence. There were moments that Candace found Jameson irresistible. That was still a new sensation for the senator, one that she hoped would last the rest of her life.

Jameson stroked Candace's hair while Candace continued to play with her breasts. Candace flicked her tongue over the tip of one nipple while she rolled the other between her fingers gently. This night would be soft. She wanted to make love to Jameson slowly, deliberately searching out every piece of flesh beneath her. She lowered her other hand to Jameson's thigh and brushed over it lightly with her fingertips. Her kiss strayed from one nipple to the other sucking gently, her teeth raking lightly over the tips just enough to produce a visible shudder from Jameson's body.

"Candace," Jameson called as softly as she could. Her voice was low and desperate. Candace lifted her mouth to Jameson's lips and kissed her slowly, taking the time to explore

Jameson's lips and tongue thoroughly with her own. "Tell me, love," Candace whispered.

"I love you so much," Jameson nearly cried.

Candace smiled down at the woman beneath her. She caressed Jameson's face and kissed her again gently. "I love you, Jameson," she said. "Do you know what I love?" she asked. Jameson shook her head and bit her lip gently. "I love this little scar right here," Candace said, taking a moment to kiss the small scar that was left as a reminder from Jameson's mishap on the ladder at Christmas. "And, I love this little freckle right here, right next to your ear," Candace breathed in Jameson's ear. She kissed the freckle and then licked behind Jameson's ear slowly.

"Mm," Jameson moaned.

"I love your eyes," Candace said as she kissed both of Jameson's eyelids. "And your nose," she said nuzzling her nose against Jameson's. "I love your mouth." She traced Jameson's lips with a finger and then dropped her mouth over Jameson's and kissed her soundly. "So sweet," she whispered. Candace let her fingers trace a slow trail over Jameson's throat to the swell of her breasts, which were heaving noticeably. "I love this, kissing this," Candace said as she allowed her kisses to follow the trail her fingers had just blazed down Jameson's throat. She let her tongue dance over both breasts and circle each of Jameson's nipples. "I love this," Candace said. She took Jameson's nipple into her mouth and Jameson gasped. Candace felt a jolt of excitement pass through her body. She was beginning to struggle against the rising tide of her own arousal.

"Candace," Jameson sighed again, dropping her hands to Candace's head and gently encouraging her.

"Mmm," Candace moaned seductively. Jameson was spiraling in a swirling array of sensations. She had become lost in the emotions Candace's declarations and passionate touch evoked in her.

Candace pulled back slightly, needing to calm the brewing storm within her veins. Jameson's words were echoing in her mind. "I love you so much that it hurts some days." The look in Jameson's eyes when she spoke those words had penetrated any remaining doubts Candace had about their relationship. She looked down at Jameson and closed her eyes for a moment to still her emotions.

Jameson reached for Candace's face. "Hey?" she called. "What's wrong?"

Candace opened her eyes and searched Jameson's. She thought for a moment that she might drown in them. "I love you so much it hurts," she whispered. Jameson smiled and pulled Candace to her for a kiss. "I want you to know," Candace said.

"I do know," Jameson promised. She caressed Candace's back as Candace rained kisses all across Jameson's abdomen until she reached her thighs. She lowered the boxer shorts that Jameson was wearing with a questioning raise of her eyebrow.

"What? You don't find Wonder Woman sexy?" Jameson asked.

Candace continued pulling off the bright red boxer shorts. "I find everything about you sexy." She looked up at Jameson affectionately before beginning a lazy ascent up both of Jameson's legs, kissing and caressing every inch of skin on her way. "I love your legs," Candace breathed seductively. "I love watching you swim in that pool. I love watching you in the shower," she said. Jameson was beginning to feel lightheaded. Candace watched as her lover's eyes grew dark with desire. "I love feeling you beneath me," she told Jameson. "Touching you, feeling you, tasting you," she said. She placed a feather-light kiss on Jameson's leg and inhaled deeply. "I love making love to you."

Jameson threw her head back when she felt Candace's tongue begin to delicately trace the outline of her center. "Oh, God!"

Candace's hands reached out and held Jameson's. She

savored her lover's softness over and over with her tongue, gliding back and forth and slipping inside for just a second to tease Jameson into a frenzy. Jameson's hips were beginning to gyrate and arch in desperation. Candace slowed her pace. "Relax," she said. "Just feel me." Jameson felt Candace's thumbs both brush over the tops of her hands. Candace's tender exploration gradually increased in intensity. She finally curled her tongue around the soft bud that always sent Jameson soaring. She circled Jameson's clit again and again, tasting it, flicking it lightly until Jameson's body began to grow tense. "Relax, love," she called to Jameson, tightening her grasp on her lover's hands. She returned to her task with fervor, moaning at the multitude of sensations that besieged her senses. The soft wetness of Jameson's excitement mixed with the heat of her mouth and tongue. Candace felt a steady stream of tremors beginning to flutter in her core. She felt Jameson shift slightly and allowed Jameson's leg to slip between her thighs. Her lips wrapped around Jameson's clit and she sucked firmly as Jameson pressed against her.

"Oh…Candace!" Jameson cried out, no longer concerned about who might hear them.

Candace felt Jameson's body rise and fall. She struggled to keep Jameson in place as they crested and fell together repeatedly. She wanted to cry out, but she resisted, desiring to draw out Jameson's release as long as she could. Jameson's body was quaking with so much power that Candace was finally compelled to pull away and hold her lover. "I'm right here," she promised, cradling Jameson in her arms as a series of aftershocks coursed through them both. Slowly, Candace's breathing returned to normal, a satisfying tingling still traveling up and down her body. She pulled Jameson closer. "And, I love this," Candace whispered.

"What?" Jameson panted.

"Holding you close after we make love," Candace said honestly.

Jameson labored to take a full breath. She laid her head on Candace's breast and sighed. She was happily spent. "I'm glad because I think you might be in this position for a while," Jameson chuckled. Candace kissed Jameson's head. "You think they heard us?" Jameson asked a bit sheepishly.

"I think they might have heard you in Jonah's old tent," Candace giggled. She felt Jameson's head burrow into her chest and laughed. "It's okay. They'll probably just think you were in trouble for something."

"Yeah, I'm sure," Jameson mumbled. "Maybe you should gag me next time you want to make love and your kids are here."

"Your mother is across the hall," Candace reminded her lover with a chuckle. Jameson groaned in embarrassment. "I can do that when we have company if you like," Candace said. "I didn't think you Republicans were into such daring endeavors."

"What are you talking about?" Jameson asked.

"You've been holding out on me," Candace said. "Your mom told me."

"My mom has no idea about my sex life," Jameson said.

"She might now," Candace giggled. Jameson groaned. "I meant your political affiliation. How come you never told me you were a Republican?" Candace asked.

"Would it have mattered?" Jameson wondered.

"No. I seem to have a thing for lesbian lunatics. Party affiliation doesn't matter, just the lunacy and the lesbian are prerequisites."

Jameson chuckled. "Good to know. And, I didn't tell you because I'm not."

"Not a lunatic or not a lesbian?" Candace asked. "Have to make sure we check the right boxes."

"Not a Republican. I never was."

"What?" Candace asked.

"I had my friend make up the card. I never voted at

home, so Mom never knew the difference. I just like to let her think I went to the wild side."

Candace snickered. "Jameson, you may be the only person I have ever heard refer to the Republican Party as the *wild side*. Your poor mother thinks you're an elephant."

"Well, I know I've put on a few pounds," Jameson was interrupted by a pinch to her back side. "Ouch!"

"Behave," Candace said with a yawn.

"I think you should do it. Run for governor."

"Really?"

"Yep."

"Why do you think that?" Candace asked.

"Because, I think you'd be terrific. And, imagine living in that house!" Jameson said.

Candace smiled. "So it's all about the house?"

"No. That's just a bonus," Jameson said through a yawn. "It's up to you."

"No, it's up to both of us. I'm not going into anything unless you are comfortable with it," Candace said. "I promise you that."

"Hey. Just out of curiosity…"

"Hum?" Candace replied. Jameson was rubbing slow circles on her belly and it was putting her to sleep.

"Would you want me to?"

"To what?" Candace asked groggily.

"Propose."

"Of course," Candace yawned.

Jameson smiled. "Good to know," she said, sensing that Candace was almost asleep. "What would you say if I did?"

"What?"

"Propose," Jameson explained. There was no reply. "Candace?" Jameson pulled up slightly and shook her head. "Of all the times to fall asleep."

"I think J.D thinks your mom is God," Rick laughed. "Want to see if we can wake them up now?"

Marianne jabbed her husband. "I need therapy."

"Well, I think you just lost your Republican daughter. That sounded like conversion to me," Maureen laughed.

"Is that your theory?" Jameson's father laughed.

"Why? What's yours?"

"Torture," Duncan Reid answered. Maureen's eyes flew open. "Safer."

"Safer? For whom?" she asked.

"Me," he said. "I need to sleep."

"Shell?" Jonah asked as his sister approached the small fire that he, Toby, and Doug were sitting around.

"Yeah."

"I thought you were bunking down with Liz for the night."

"We came out here to see if you were still awake," she said as Toby's wife took a seat between his legs.

"Why?" Jonah asked.

"I think Mom killed J.D."

"What?" Jonah asked. Toby, Doug, and Liz started laughing. "What am I missing?"

"Umm. Good thing they can't procreate if they don't want to have kids," Michelle said.

Jonah's eyes grew wide. "Oh, God."

"More like *Oh, Candace*," Liz laughed.

"Oh, no," Toby chuckled.

"Oh, yes!" Michelle howled loudly into the night.

"What the hell was that?" Jameson startled at a sound from the yard.

"Ask me in the morning," Candace mumbled.

"What?"

"Whatever you are mumbling about," Candace said. "Ask me in the morning."

"I was trying to ask you to marry me," Jameson mumbled under her breath. "Before you passed out and I was so rudely interrupted by some howling creature." Jinx chose that moment to jump on the bed and nestle against Candace. "Well, I managed to convince her to get you so anything is possible," Jameson surmised, closing her eyes and snuggling closer to her lover.

Candace opened one eye and looked down at her lover. "So easy," she mused silently, trying not to laugh. She closed her eyes again and took a deep breath, feeling a sense of completion and happiness with Jameson in her arms. She heard Jameson's soft snoring. "I love you, you lunatic," she said softly. "Ask me in the morning," she chuckled.

Chapter Thirteen

"Do you think she'll do it?" Michelle asked Jameson.

Jameson was entertaining Spencer on the floor in front of the Christmas tree. She rolled a small ball to him and looked up to Michelle. "I don't know, Shell. Just do me a favor and let it be for the next few days."

"I just don't get it. She sat us all down and asked us how we felt about her running at Thanksgiving and now it's taboo table talk or something."

Spencer jumped into Jameson's lap and she laughed. "It's not taboo. It's just that your mom is more relaxed than I have seen her in weeks. I don't think she wants to think about work. She just wants to enjoy the holidays. That's all."

Michelle looked at Jameson and pursed her lips thoughtfully. Spencer was climbing all over Jameson to Jameson's delight. "Is there some reason she wouldn't want to run?"

"Easy buddy," Jameson chuckled before turning Spencer upside down in her lap. "I don't know, Shell. It's her decision. She has her reasons. Give her time. She'll let us know what she wants to do when she's ready."

"Jay Jay. Up-down!" Spencer giggled.

"Upside down?" Jameson asked him. Spencer nodded. Jameson tickled him lightly.

"Jay Jay!" he yelled through his laughter.

"Enough?" Jameson chuckled.

"Yes!" he laughed. Jameson stopped her teasing. "Again, Jay Jay. Again!"

Michelle shook her head. "Trying to have a conversation with you is pointless," she said flatly.

"What do you mean?" Jameson asked as Spencer attempted to climb onto her back.

"Spence is like your own personal growth," Michelle

laughed.

Jameson shrugged. She adored Spencer and for whatever reason, Candace's grandson had adopted her as his favorite adult. Spencer managed to make his way onto Jameson's back and wrap his arms around her neck.

Michelle started laughing. "Seriously, J.D. if he gets any closer we'll have to call Mulder and Scully to have him removed."

"Spence! Auntie Shell just called you an alien!" Jameson said. "Are you?" she asked. "Where are your tentacles?"

Spencer laughed. "Ride, Jay Jay!"

"Ride, Jay Jay," Michelle teased. "Mom never told me you doubled as a horse." Jameson wrinkled her nose and stuck her tongue out at Michelle. "Real mature, J.D."

Jameson ignored her. "You want a ride, buddy?"

"Ride!"

Jameson made her way to her feet. "Want to go find Nana?" she asked knowingly.

"Jay Jay…Nana!" he yelled. "Nana!"

Jameson jostled Spencer to a secure position on her back. This was one of his favorite games. Candace would hide and Jameson and Spencer would search her out. Candace would pretend to be startled by their discovery. Spencer was just about twenty-one months old. He was already sprinting, albeit with the occasional wobble. He was incredibly articulate for his age, talking a blue streak most days. He loved playing with his Nana and his Jay Jay.

"Nana!" Jameson called through the house to warn Candace of the impending assault. "Where are you, Nana?"

"Nana!" Spencer called. "Nana!"

Michelle chuckled as Jameson took off in search of her mother with her nephew in tow. Marianne passed Jameson in the doorway, rolled her eyes and plopped down beside her sister. "The dynamic duo is off again, huh?" Marianne asked.

Michelle nodded. "I know how you feel, but I swear

sometimes I think Mom and J.D. should have their own kids."

"Bite your tongue," Marianne scolded her younger sister.

"Oh, come on. Admit it. They would be fabulous. Plus, you love J.D. and you know it."

"It's not that," Marianne said. Michelle looked at her sister curiously. Marianne shrugged. "Free babysitting. You wait. You won't want to give up that either."

"Me? Wait? I don't think so. That is all about you and Rick."

"What is all about us?" Rick asked as he entered the room.

"Nana!" Spencer yelled through the house followed by an eruption of laughter from Jameson and Candace.

"That," Michelle said.

"Shell swears she is going to die a spinster," Marianne explained.

"Cute," Michelle replied dryly. "I never said I would be alone. Maybe I will pull a Mom."

"What the hell does that mean?" Marianne wondered.

Michelle smirked. "I'll wait to find my true love until I am Mom's age and make sure I find a big kid like J.D. Kill two birds with one stone."

"Uh-huh," Marianne said doubtfully. Rick laughed.

"What? It's a good plan!"

"Except that you fall in love over the Walgreens counter if the clerk is cute enough," Marianne teased.

"I do not!" Michelle argued.

"She's right, honey. That was Target, I think," Rick said.

"Shut up!" Michelle said. "I didn't fall in love with her."

Rick shook his head. "How many times did you offer to go buy Spencer's diapers that visit?"

"Okay…So…I was scoping out the scene. That's what single people do," Michelle said. "You old married folk get senile fast."

"I'd rather be old, married and senile than young, available and desperate," Marianne returned.

"I'm not desperate!"

"Rick, maybe we should let Shell go to the grocery store. She might get lucky and find some poor woman to accost while perusing the melon bins," Marianne suggested.

"What do you know about melons?" Michelle said to her sister. Marianne smiled. "Ah! Ha!"

"Sorry, Sis. I did not get that gene," Marianne said.

"Yeah, because you are the recessive mutant one. First try is always a bit off."

"How am I the recessive one?" Marianne asked.

Michelle shrugged. "You're the only one with a melon aversion."

Spencer came running at full tilt. "Mewon!" he yelled.

"You want melon?" Candace asked from behind him.

"See! Melon!" Michelle said.

"Mewon, mewon, mewon," Spencer sang happily. Rick put his face in his hands and shook his head.

"Why is everyone talking about melons?" Jameson asked as she and Candace made their way into the room.

Spencer ran into Jameson's legs. "Jay Jay! Like mewon?"

Jameson lifted Spencer onto her hip. "Yeah, I like melon, buddy."

"Nana? Like mewon?" Spencer reached out for Candace.

Candace took him gently from Jameson and smiled. "I like melon, Spencer. Do you like melon?"

"Mewon! Mommy! Mewon?" he asked his mother.

Michelle lifted her brow at her sister and waited. "Yeah, Mommy…Tell us how you feel about melons," Michelle challenged her older sister. Candace gave Jameson a puzzled look.

"Well," Marianne began to answer.

"Me mewon?" Spencer asked innocently. "Pwease?"

"I don't think we have any melon, sweetheart," Marianne

said.

Spencer frowned and looked at his nana. Even as a toddler, he understood that Nana solved problems. "What about something else?" Candace suggested. Spencer pouted and shook his head.

"Ha!" Michelle goaded her sister. "Rick, I think you'd better take your wife to the grocery store so she can peruse the melon bins."

"Mewon!" Spencer said again.

"Shell, shut up," Marianne whispered.

Candace looked at her children suspiciously. Spencer began wiggling in her embrace. She set him down and he took off yelling the word melon repeatedly. "Why am I sure that I don't want to know what this is about?" she asked the trio seated across the room.

"Jay Jay!" Spencer yelled. "Mewon!" Jameson looked at Candace and headed off to follow Spencer.

"Just proving a point, Mom," Michelle said.

"Uh-huh. I don't want to know," Candace said.

"Nana!" Spencer yelled suddenly. "I-cweam! Jay Jay, i-cweam day!"

Candace laughed and shook her head again at her children. "Coming!" she called out. "Guess Jameson solved that problem," she said. She started to leave and then turned back. "Just a suggestion. You might want to pick up some hot fudge with those melons."

"What?" Marianne was puzzled. Candace winked and left the room. Michelle and Rick burst out laughing. "Oh. My. God," Marianne's face flushed in embarrassment. "I need therapy."

"I agree," Michelle laughed. "For your melon aversion."

"Tired?" Jameson asked Candace as she flopped down onto the bed beside her.

"Beat."

"Me too," Jameson agreed. She pulled Candace into her arms and felt Candace's head collapse onto her breast. "Can I ask you something?"

"You can ask me anything," Candace replied. "You know that." Jameson hesitated. Candace caressed Jameson lightly. "What is it?" she asked.

"Shell wanted to talk to me about you running for governor today." Candace nodded against Jameson. "It just got me thinking."

"About?"

"I don't want to upset you."

Candace sat up and looked at Jameson seriously. "I need to know how you feel, Jameson, you most of all."

Jameson propped herself up on her elbow. "I told you already, I am okay with whatever you decide. It doesn't matter to me what you choose to do. It does matter to me that you make the choice that you want to make."

"I know," Candace said. "There are a lot of things to consider."

"Yeah. I've heard you voice your concerns, at least, some of them. You haven't told me why you would want to leave Washington. I have a feeling part of you does."

"Part of me would welcome the change," Candace admitted.

"Tell me."

"Things are not the way they were when I started, Jameson. Life in the Senate is all about money. It's about who gets the money to fund which projects and where. There are moments that we pass meaningful laws. There are. But, mostly we affirm or deny requests for money. Legislation costs money."

"And, you don't like that?" Jameson wondered.

"It's not that. You can hold up anything by withholding funding. You can progress many great things by greasing the wheels. Once upon a time, we found ways to keep the wheels turning forward. Lately, we seem to be spinning backward. People don't listen to each other. Legislators aren't writing legislation. Corporations are. Lobbyists. It's become so polarized that we are effectively rendered paralyzed. There is no debate, just public shouting. There is no accountability, just complaining. There has always been finger pointing. That's part of posturing. But, that used to be part of the propaganda machine. We still did work. Now? I don't know. People will hold up important legislation just to be oppositional. It doesn't actually serve anyone, even them. Our actions directly impact people. That just doesn't seem to matter most days. That isn't what I went there to do," Candace said sadly.

Jameson had noticed Candace's fatigue over the last few months had grown. She was positive that the debate she was waging over whether or not to launch a campaign was part of it. There was more to it than that. Jameson knew that as well. "And, if you were to become governor?"

Candace smiled. Jameson noted the slight twinkle in her eye. "Don't get me wrong. There are good people in the Senate. It's just that things have gotten stagnant. There's not any real accountability. We are largely removed from our constituents. State politics are different. They have different challenges. They also require accountability. There are still all the uphill battles. But, you can't close the roads. You can't close the schools. You can't allow people to go without resources. If you do? You will be taken to task. You see the people you represent. That means that you have to listen. You have to deal. It's not easier. In fact, it's a great deal harder in a lot of ways. But, you can accomplish things."

Jameson reached out and stroked Candace's cheek. She loved to listen to Candace talk about what she did. She loved to hear Candace debating someone, arguing a point or explaining an idea. "I'd vote for you," she said with a wink.

"Bias to the last."

"Not at all. I've always voted for you," Jameson said honestly. "I'm sorry if you didn't want to think about this now."

"Don't be sorry. You have every reason and every right to ask me."

"I just want you to be happy," Jameson said.

"I am happy," Candace said. "Honest. I love what I do, Jameson."

"I know that."

"I don't love it more than I love you or those lunatics downstairs," she laughed.

Jameson smiled. The faint sound of Candace's children laughing downstairs was drifting upward every so often despite the late hour. "I know that too," Jameson said. "But, you are not ready to not do what it is that you love."

"No, I'm not. I just am not sure where I want to do it yet…for a lot of reasons," Candace replied. Jameson guided Candace back into her arms. "Thank you," Candace said.

"For what?" Jameson wondered.

"For caring how I feel. For listening. For supporting me."

"I wish I could do more," Jameson said.

"That's far more than anyone has ever given me."

"I love you. I'd give you anything if I could," Jameson replied.

"That's all I need," Candace promised. "Well, the occasional fortune cookie is a plus."

"Mm. I figured out the answer to your heart a long time ago," Jameson said.

Candace giggled. "Well, there are ways to earn extra credit."

"Oh, really? What might those be?"

"The first," Candace said with a kiss. "Is to put a nice

cantaloupe on Marianne's plate tomorrow instead of the pancakes I make every year."

"What?" Jameson chuckled. "You are worse than Shell," she observed. "What do my extra credit points earn me?"

Candace moved over Jameson and smiled seductively. "Me," she said.

"Melon it is," Jameson declared before flipping Candace underneath her. "Now, about that hot fudge you…"

"Lunatic," Candace laughed.

SOLID FOUNDATION
Chapter Fourteen

"Well, Daryl...I would have to say that Senator Fletcher is the logical choice for the Democratic candidate. New York loves her."

"I agree with you. She is extremely popular in the party. But, the question is, how will that play out for them down the line? She is out in front by twenty points in early polls for the governorship. You have to think that the party will want more from her sometime in the future. But, why would she leave Washington? One would think that she could position herself just as well from her current position in the Senate where she has considerable influence."

"There could be personal reasons," the female pundit offered.

"And those personal reasons could be a hindrance down the line for Senator Fletcher and the party."

Candace grimaced and clicked off the television.

"Candy," Dana called gently. "No one in the party believes that."

"Yes, they do," Candace laughed. "And, they would be right."

"Look, I've heard all of your arguments. I have. I just don't understand this hesitancy of yours. J.D. supports you. The party wants you. Christ, Candy, the people want you to run," Dana said.

Candace flopped into her office chair and sighed. "I know."

"All right? We've been going round and round this for months."

Candace looked at her friend. "I promised the president I would give the party my decision by April 1st."

"That's less than a month away," Dana observed.

"I know."

"Candy? Look, I know you think we are all pushing you."

"You are."

"You've worked your entire career to be in this position. I don't get it. I'm sorry, but I don't. J.D. will be thrilled for you. She's proud of you, you know?"

Candace smiled. "I know."

"You seem to be saying that a lot. For a woman who is so in the *know*, you certainly are indecisive."

"I guess that is true," Candace laughed. "I promised to make a decision and I will."

"Will you.."

"When I know, you'll know," Candace said. She closed the laptop on her desk, packed it in her briefcase, and made her way to the coat rack in her office. "Now, I am heading home for five days. Away from this chaos."

"You know, if you were governor, you would be in New York most of the time. Close to home. Close to Shell. Close to J.."

"I know," Candace laughed. "Someone paying you under the table?"

"No," Dana answered. "I just want you to be happy."

Candace paused in the doorway of her office. "I don't need to be governor to be happy, Dana."

Dana nodded. "I know."

Candace shook her head. "I'll see you on Wednesday morning.

"You will. Any big plans?" Dana wondered.

"No. No plans at all, and that is exactly what I need."

Candace drove down the winding driveway that led to her house, thankful to be home. She needed to escape Washington. She needed to escape politics. She needed to be

Candy, not Senator Fletcher, not potential candidate Candace Fletcher. Candace's time of waffling, debating, protesting, and avoiding making any career decision was coming to an end. She'd attempted to sift through her reservations quietly. She'd discussed the pros and cons with her lover and her family. She'd listened to the pitches and arguments of her colleagues. She'd paid attention to the fervor of the pundits. No amount of time, reasoning, listening, or debating seemed to have brought Candace any closer to a resolution. For a moment, she would think she had come to a decision only to change her mind the next day. Right now, she needed to step away from it all. Perhaps she was grasping at straws, but she hoped a quiet weekend at home would put life in the proper perspective.

Candace looked up toward the house and her heart stopped. She could see Jameson's father, Duncan standing on the roof. He was looking up and Candace followed his line of sight through the branches of a large oak tree that hung over the house. What was he looking at? Jameson? What was Jameson doing in the tree? Candace had learned to deal with Jameson's acrobatics. She'd seen Jameson on ladders, the roof, and crawling into tiny spaces countless times over the course of the last year. It was part of who Jameson was. Candace had learned that while Jameson Reid was a talented architect, there was nothing her lover enjoyed more than construction. Jameson liked working with her hands. That thought would have conjured images that brought a smile to Candace's lips normally. Jameson above the roof in a tree produced a dramatically different reaction.

"What in God's name are you doing?" Candace called out as she exited her car hurriedly. Jameson and Duncan both looked down at the senator as she approached.

"Hey!" Jameson called out excitedly. "You're home early!"

"And, you are in a tree!"

"Can't fool you," Jameson tried to joke.

"What are you doing in a tree? Get down from there!" Candace said a bit harshly.

Jameson was puzzled. She looked at her father who conveyed his silent advice to comply with the demand. Jameson moved down through a couple of branches and hopped back onto the roof. She turned for her father to unclip her safety harness and swiftly made her way down a ladder to the ground. Candace was walking toward her quickly.

"What are you doing home?" Jameson asked. She looked at Candace, who was shaking. "Hey…What's wrong?"

"What the hell were you doing?" Candace asked nervously.

"In the tree?"

"Yes, Jameson, in the tree," Candace answered.

Jameson looked at Candace with curious concern. Candace was afraid. Jameson had only seen the look in the senator's eyes once in over a year. "Candace," Jameson said softly. She took Candace into her arms. "What's going on? I'm fine, honey." Jameson could feel Candace trembling. "Hey. I was perfectly safe. I promise."

Candace stepped back and gathered herself. "I'm sorry, Jameson."

"Why? For worrying?"

"For overreacting. I just…I didn't expect to see you in a tree."

Jameson chuckled and finally felt Candace relax. "Well, I didn't expect to see you home. What are you doing home so early? Not that I am not happy to see you."

"Sometimes, you just have to hit pause," Candace said.

"Needed the break, huh?"

"Needed to be home," Candace answered.

"We were close to finishing for the day. Give me about an hour to get this mess cleaned up," Jameson offered.

"The yard doesn't look too bad," Candace replied.

"I meant me," Jameson said with a kiss to Candace's cheek.

"You don't look so bad either—now that you are on the ground."

Jameson laughed. "Go get settled. Pearl will be glad to see you," she said before kissing Candace softly. "I'm happy that you are home."

"Me too," Candace agreed. She waved to Duncan and headed for the house. Jameson watched as Candace walked through the door.

"Everything okay?" Duncan asked as he approached his daughter. Jameson just shook her head. "J.D.?"

"No, everything is definitely not okay."

"She mad?"

"No. It's not that. She's home early. She's on edge. Something is on her mind," Jameson observed. She turned and looked at her father.

"J.D., you were pretty high up in that tree. I have to say if I didn't expect to see that, it might have knocked a couple of years off my life too."

Jameson sighed. "Yeah, I know. It's not just that, though. I could hear it in her voice last night on the phone."

"Work?" Duncan guessed.

"Partly."

"The kids?"

Jameson laughed. For once, all seemed quiet on the family front. "No. Everything has been pretty quiet with the three of them for a bit, which I am thankful for." Duncan looked at his daughter curiously. "It's this governor thing. I'm sure of it."

"Think she is going to do it?" he asked.

"I don't know."

"Does she want to?" he wondered.

"I don't know," Jameson answered honestly. "I think

sometimes she does and sometimes she doesn't. Something keeps holding her back."

"Any idea?"

"Yeah, I have a pretty good idea," Jameson admitted. "I just haven't figured out what to do about it yet.

"Why do I get the feeling that is not entirely true?" her father asked knowingly.

Jameson huffed. "All right, maybe I do have an idea. I just hope I'm not left hanging in that tree when I share it with her."

Duncan grasped his daughter's shoulder. "Based on the look I saw on her face? I'd say your tree swinging days are over."

Jameson laughed. "I hope you are right, Dad."

"Well, look what the cat dragged in!" Pearl greeted Candace. Candace sighed and plopped into a kitchen chair. "You feeling okay?" Pearl asked. "You look a little pale."

"Mm. I think I just lost five years off of my life."

"You lost me."

Candace raised a brow. "Jameson missed her calling."

"Still lost."

"She should have joined the circus or maybe taken up residence in a zoo," Candace said. Pearl waited for the explanation. "She was up in that damned oak tree when I pulled in the driveway."

"You know her, she can't help herself," Pearl laughed. "She's careful, and besides, Duncan would never let anything happen to her."

"I know. It still makes me nervous," Candace confessed. Pearl studied Candace closely. Candace looked tired. Pearl couldn't help but chuckle when the senator bent over and lifted the small black cat at her feet into her lap. "I thought you were going to keep an eye on her for me," Candace scolded Jinx.

"You should be thankful he isn't," Pearl said. "Last time Jinx got in the mix of Jameson's climbing she ended up bleeding on the floor."

Candace looked at the cat. "That is true, you know?" She put Jinx back on the floor and looked at Pearl. "It's just—it's so risky."

"Are we still talking about Jameson's climbing?" Pearl asked. Candace groaned. "That's what I thought," Pearl said. "All right, Candy, let's have it."

"I promised to make a decision by the first of the month."

"About whether or not you'll launch a campaign?" Pearl guessed.

"Yes."

Pearl took a deep breath and considered her response. "I think you should do it, if that matters."

Candace was stunned. Pearl seldom offered an opinion about Candace's career choices, wisdom yes, motherly guidance yes, a point blank assessment? No. "You do?"

"Yes. I do."

"Why?" Candace asked.

"You want to," Pearl said bluntly. She saw Candace opening her mouth to speak. "Oh, I've heard it all. I know you, Candy. Better than anyone, except maybe Jameson," Pearl added. Candace smiled. "You spent your life listening to your Granddad. You loved it— all the people, all the debate. You loved it when you were ten and you have never outgrown it."

"Things aren't like they were when I was ten," Candace noted.

"Nope. Sure aren't."

"It could get…Pearl, it could get ugly at points. You know how the press can be. You know how the trail can be. I haven't had a target on my back for a while in an election.

Believing I will win will only make them come at me harder this time."

"I'm sure that's true. What exactly do you think the target will be or should I guess?" Pearl asked. Candace shook her head. "I've heard them chatting away too. So, let them chat, Candy. The kids are with you. Jameson will be all right. She's tougher than you give her credit for."

"It's not just that," Candace said. She watched as Pearl waited patiently for her to continue. "It's different, Pearl. I will have more security, less autonomy. That will directly impact Jameson's life. I don't want her to…"

"If it doesn't feel right to you then don't do it. Just make sure you can live with that decision."

Candace could sense Pearl had more to say. "Say what you're thinking, Pearl," Candace said.

"I think you are scared of losing Jameson," Pearl said bluntly. Candace sighed. "I think you are more likely to lose her by selling her short. She's not going anywhere. If you asked her to buy a one-way ticket so that you could run hell, she'd buy it just to be with you."

"Maybe so, but hell is different for different people."

Pearl put her hands on Candace's shoulders. "Candace," she said softly. Candace looked up in surprise. "You need to decide if you can give Jameson what she deserves."

"What does that mean?"

"It means exactly what I said. It's been a year, Candy. Give her all of you, or you will lose her."

"I…"

Pearl smiled. "You know exactly what I am talking about. Sooner or later you are going to have to trust her completely or you are going to have to let her go."

"I do trust her."

"Then trust yourself," Pearl said. She kissed Candace on

the forehead and smiled. "Now, I am going to leave you kids to your weekend."

"Pearl?" Candace called. Pearl stopped and turned back. "Thanks."

Pearl smiled. "You're welcome."

"Hey there," Jameson greeted Candace from the doorway to the kitchen.

Candace turned to find Jameson holding up a large paper bag. "What is that?"

"Dinner," Jameson said. "I had my Dad run and grab it while I showered."

"Is he joining us?" Candace wondered.

"No. This is a private affair," Jameson answered as she placed the bag of Chinese food on the table. "Well, we do have Jinx to contend with, but I will slip him a chicken finger to keep him quiet."

Candace laughed and walked over to Jameson. "I missed you this week."

Jameson smiled at her lover. "I missed you too."

"Chinese food?" Candace inquired.

"You love Chinese food. Sometimes I think you love it more than you love me," Jameson joked.

"Not a chance," Candace promised. Jameson sat down across from Candace and started pulling out the various containers.

"So, tell me…What prompted you to come home so early?" Jameson asked.

"I had a conference call late yesterday."

"And?" Jameson urged. "Is that why you sounded so stressed out last night on the phone?"

"That was part of it. I promised to have a decision by the first about running for governor."

Jameson nodded. "Okay. What's the other part of it?" Candace was toying with her food. "Candace?"

"It will change things," Candace said quietly.

Jameson took a deep breath. "In my experience things tend to change whether you want them to or not."

Candace looked across at Jameson. She was often amazed by Jameson's candor and her view of life. Many times, it had been Candace to reassure Jameson. Their roles had now reversed. "I know. I just," Candace chuckled. "Maybe I just wish I had a fortune cookie that could actually predict the future."

"Predict the future, huh? What would you want it to say?" Jameson asked. Candace smiled but did not answer. "Well," Jameson said with a deep breath. She fished in her pocket under the table and pushed a fortune cookie across the table to Candace. "Maybe you should try that one."

Candace looked at Jameson quizzically. "What are you up to?" Candace asked suspiciously. Jameson just shrugged. Candace looked back at the cookie and opened the package. She took her time and broke it open to retrieve the message. She studied it carefully for a moment.

A ship in the harbor is safe, but that's not what ships are built for.

Candace was lost in her contemplation of the message. She looked up and was startled to find Jameson kneeling in front of her. "Jameson?"

"It's true. You can build a strong, majestic ship, Candace. It isn't worth its weight nor its grandeur if you never sail it. You can't ever hope to see the world if you are too afraid it will sink."

"Jameson, I…"

"Would you be quiet and let me do this, please?" Jameson asked lightly. Candace smiled. "I know you are afraid of what this will mean for us. I think we've built a strong ship. I trust it to sail across some rocky waters and still find its way," Jameson said. "I love you. I trust you to navigate, if you'll trust me to keep the ship safe and cared for."

"I trust you with my life," Candace said.

"Then share it with me," Jameson responded. "Marry me, Candace."

"Jameson, I…Did you just ask me to marry you?" Candace asked.

"I think those were my words," Jameson said nervously. Candace could not find her voice and the silence began to unnerve Jameson. "Maybe I…"

Jameson's words were silenced by a kiss. "Yes."

"Yes, you will marry me?" Jameson asked in disbelief.

Candace laughed. "Of course, I will marry you, you lunatic."

"Really?"

Candace laughed harder. "Are you actually surprised?"

"I don't know! I never asked anyone before and I… Wait!" Jameson exclaimed. Candace jumped. Jameson reached back in her pocket and pulled out a stunning sapphire and diamond ring. "I have to do this right."

Candace took a breath and watched as Jameson took her hand. It was the most endearing thing she had ever experienced. Jameson's expression was priceless. Candace found herself wishing she could record the moment, although she was certain she would never forget it. Jameson took another deep breath and then looked at Candace.

"Candace, will you marry me?"

Candace was ready to remind Jameson that she had already answered, but the earnestness in Jameson's eyes stopped her. "Yes, Jameson. I would love to be married to you." As Candace spoke the words, she realized the truth in them. She'd been proposed to before, more than once. She'd been married. She'd never once in her life felt the way she did at this moment.

This was not a proposal formulated in the dreams of a young girl about fairytale weddings. It was not the proposal that came as a business arrangement. Candace did not only want to marry Jameson, she wanted to be married to Jameson. Looking at Jameson, she was certain her emotional sentiment was shared equally by her lover.

Jameson slipped the ring onto Candace's finger. She was shaking so much that Candace reached out to steady her. "I'm sorry," Jameson whispered. "I'm just so nervous."

Candace smiled. "I love you, Jameson."

Jameson looked at Candace, who was smiling compassionately at her. "I don't know what lies ahead. I do know I don't ever want to be without you again, no matter what."

Candace closed the distance between them and kissed Jameson lovingly. "I don't want to be without you either." Jameson placed her head on Candace's shoulder. "Are you all right?" Candace asked.

Jameson chuckled. "One more thing I never thought I would do," she admitted. "And, one more thing I can't wait to do."

Candace closed her eyes and held onto Jameson. She understood that sentiment perfectly. Life had changed dramatically for them both in just over a year's time. Candace had never been happier in her life. That was one of the reasons she was reluctant to change anything. Jameson was right. She knew that too. Change was inevitable whether they invited it or not. That was clear. Candace didn't need a marriage proposal to trust in Jameson's commitment. What frightened Candace was the possibility of her life causing Jameson or anyone she loved pain. She needed a reminder that nothing could cause either Jameson or her more pain than being apart. Candace felt Jameson pull back and opened her eyes.

"Whatever you decide," Jameson said. "I will be beside you, ring or no ring."

"I know," Candace assured Jameson. "Just one favor?"

"Anything."

"Limit the tree climbing. I already have twenty years on you. I can't afford to lose any more off my life."

"If I can reach them without the roof?"

Candace laughed. "Lunatic."

Candace woke up and looked over at Jameson. Jameson was sleeping peacefully. Candace reached over and brushed the hair out of Jameson's eyes. Instinctively, she looked down at the ring on her finger. "Oh, Jameson."

"Hum?" Jameson grumbled.

Candace smiled. "Nothing. Go back to sleep," she whispered.

Jameson pried one eye open. "Why are you awake?"

"Go back to sleep," Candace said again.

Jameson forced her eyes completely open and looked at her lover. "Second thoughts?"

"What?" Candace asked.

"Are you having second thoughts about us getting married?"

Candace kissed Jameson in reply. "Not in the slightest, no."

"What is it then?"

Candace kissed Jameson again. Her kiss was filled with passion and Jameson gave over immediately. Candace's hands dropped to Jameson's back and pulled her closer. Jameson was astonished by the intensity of Candace's touch. They had made love for hours before falling asleep contentedly. She wondered when and why this emotional tide had resurfaced in Candace. She was happy to surrender to it. Candace's hands were mapping out Jameson's body methodically. Her kiss continued just as unhurriedly. For a moment, Candace would pull back and gentle her exploration, just grazing Jameson's lips with hers. Then, in another instant she would trace Jameson's lips with her tongue and her searching would begin all over again. The dance went on and on while Candace's hands caressed Jameson lovingly.

Jameson found Candace's tenderness incredibly arousing. Candace had not ventured to touch her in any way that was overtly sexual. She allowed her hands to roam over Jameson's hips, her back, stomach, shoulders, thighs, and neck, lovingly exploring every curve and dip of Jameson's body. When Candace's kiss finally strayed to Jameson's neck, Jameson gasped. "Jesus," Jameson whispered hoarsely.

Candace's mouth continued a slow assault down one side of Jameson's neck and then up the other. She stopped and placed a kiss on Jameson's lips before running her tongue leisurely down Jameson's throat until she reached Jameson's breasts. Jameson closed her eyes and sucked in a ragged breath. Her heart skipped wildly when Candace's fingertips barely brushed over Jameson's nipples. Jameson wanted to call out to Candace, but she could not seem to make the words come. It was as if she were suddenly drowning, drowning in a sea of passion and promise. She reached out for Candace and Candace stopped to kiss the palm of Jameson's hand without words.

The sensation of Candace's tongue beginning to circle her nipple forced a sigh to escape Jameson's lips. Candace looked up and watched as Jameson's expression changed from startled to hopeless surrender. She smiled and dropped her kisses lower. Jameson thought her body might have caught fire. Every nerve was pulsing in anticipation. She opened her eyes to see Candace above her. Her hands grasped onto Candace's as Candace's hips began to sensually rotate against her. Jameson traced Candace's lips with her finger and arched her back to meet Candace's movements. Her heart was pounding with pleasure.

"God," Jameson breathed. "You are so beautiful," she said with wonderment coloring her voice.

"Jameson," Candace called through a moan. Jameson's body moved rhythmically against hers. She held onto Jameson's hands as if they were her anchor. Jameson was her safe harbor. She looked into Jameson's eyes as their bodies melded together in an erotic dance.

Jameson moved her hands to hold Candace's hips, guiding her impossibly closer. She felt a stirring in her center and held on more tightly. Candace dropped her hands back to Jameson's breasts and gently tugged at her nipples. Jameson was softly being transported, much like a leaf is carried by a faint breeze. Jameson was drifting upward, dipping and gliding, helpless to resist the tumbling. She felt no inclination to control the flight. Instead, she let go. Candace was the wind, the air in her lungs, the breath that had given Jameson's existence new life. There was never a need to pretend, to fear or to hold back with Candace. Whether Candace carried her gently or sent her soaring in a violent swirl of energy, Jameson would always land safely, quietly, and lovingly in Candace's embrace. As much as Candace could lift Jameson in what often seemed an endless whirling spiral of emotion and desire, she was also the earth—the rock that grounded Jameson.

Jameson's body rose at the same instant that Candace sank into her. "Jameson," Candace whispered just before her body erupted in a multitude of sensations. Jameson followed, her body climbing and trembling. Candace kissed Jameson urgently as her body shuddered against an onslaught of uncontrollable physical pleasure. Her muscles clenched and her heart thrummed violently in her chest. Jameson returned her kiss with fervor and held on to her hips firmly. Jameson wasn't sure that she would ever reach the ground. Each time she felt herself begin to settle, another gentle breeze would lift her and she would find herself gripping Candace in an attempt to remain grounded.

Finally, Jameson pulled Candace down to her firmly. "Jameson?" Candace's voice called gently. Jameson's only reply came in the form of a tender kiss. She sighed and held Candace close.

"Thank you," Jameson said. Candace was puzzled. "Yes, thank you," Jameson said again. "For letting me love you."

Candace smiled. "Sweetheart, I think it's me who should be thanking you."

"No. It isn't," Jameson said. Candace propped herself up to look at Jameson. "I've never told you this."

"Told me what?"

"Why it's so hard for me sometimes…To let go, I mean," Jameson said. Candace listened attentively. "It was a long time ago. I thought I knew who I was. I didn't have a clue, you know?" Jameson said. "I don't know why I have never told you this."

Candace took a deep breath. She wasn't sure what Jameson was about to reveal, but she was positive it was a painful memory. "You can tell me anything. You don't have to tell me unless you want to."

"I do want to," Jameson said assuredly. She kissed Candace gently. "I was sixteen. He was nineteen," Jameson said. Candace took another deep breath. "I suppose I knew, I mean…I did know that I liked girls. Of course, I did. I just…Well, that wasn't really an option. I didn't think so, you know?"

"I think I understand."

"Anyway…People suspected. I know they did. A couple of my friends hinted about my sexuality—my crushes on girls. It scared me," Jameson admitted. "I don't know what scared me more, to be honest, the idea that it was true or the possibility that people would realize it was true," she said. Candace listened silently and tenderly caressed Jameson's abdomen as Jameson continued. "Jed…He was popular. Older, handsome…Not cute, handsome. He paid a lot of attention to me. Not like he was the only guy to, but…"

Candace smiled. It was not hard to imagine Jameson garnering the attention of either gender. Jameson was a beautiful woman. She was athletic and feminine, all curves and softness, even when she tried to wear a rugged exterior. She had a natural charisma and charm that she was not aware of. It was endearing and one of the many things that Candace cherished in Jameson. "Go on," Candace encouraged her lover.

"It just happened. I guess I should have expected it. I didn't," Jameson said softly.

"Expected what?" Candace asked, expecting she already knew the answer.

"Why else would he want to be with a sixteen-year-old high school girl? It's not like we hadn't made out before. I just…I didn't expect it to continue. And, I didn't know what to do…I just…Candace….I asked him to stop. He said the rumors must have been true," Jameson sighed deeply. Candace let out a nervous breath. Her heart ached for Jameson, for Jameson's innocence. "I didn't kick him. I didn't scream. I cried. I just cried, but even when I was crying…I still…he touched me and it…"

"Jameson," Candace said softly. "He had no right to take that from you. And, you can't always control what your body does, love."

"I should have. How could he have? How could I have? I just…"

Candace kissed Jameson's forehead. "I'm sorry, sweetheart. I am so sorry that anyone hurt you that way."

Jameson nodded as a tear rolled over her cheek. "It's easier for me to make love to…"

"I know that," Candace said.

"But, with you…I want you to take me there. I know that you will…"

"Sweetheart, you don't ever have to be or feel anything with me that is not honest. You know that, don't you?'

"Yes, I do," Jameson promised.

"Good. I'm not perfect. I know there are times that something I say or something I do will hurt you."

"Candace."

"Listen. It's true. We both know that. The last thing I ever want is to see you hurt."

Jameson smiled. "I know. I feel the same way."

"I want you to feel safe."

"I do," Jameson said. "That's the point. I've never felt safer. Not ever."

Candace kissed Jameson and pulled her closer. "Thank you for sharing that with me."

"There isn't anything I don't want to share with you."

"Sometimes, Jameson, I can't remember what it was like without you here. I don't want to imagine what it would be like now."

"Well, there would be no cats and your roof would probably be leaking by now."

Candace chuckled as Jameson snuggled into her embrace. "You really are a lunatic sometimes."

"You love lunatics."

"Yes, I guess I do."

Chapter Fifteen

Candace wandered into the kitchen and stopped to watch Jameson talking to Jinx.

"Your mommy said yes, you know?" Jameson said to the cat at her feet. "That means you are both stuck with me now. So, now you really get two mommies, just like every other kid, or well, kitty in your case."

Candace leaned in the doorway and smiled. "Should I call the lawyer and draw up the adoption papers?" Candace asked.

Jameson stood up and turned to her lover. "You would let me adopt Jinx? Really?" Candace shook her head and closed the distance between them. She kissed Jameson on the cheek and headed for the coffee pot. "So? What are your plans for the day?" Jameson asked.

"Actually, I was going to ask you that."

"Hadn't really thought about it. I told my dad I'd call him later. Things sort of took an unexpected turn last night," Jameson said.

"Oh?" Candace asked. "What things might those be?"

"Well, I woke up thinking about trimming tree branches and I fell asleep thinking about weddings."

Candace sat down at the table and sipped her coffee. "Jameson, out of curiosity, when did you decide to propose?"

Jameson shrugged. "Truthfully?" she asked. Candace nodded. "Uh…well…"

"Jameson?"

"Okay. I bought the ring when you went back to Washington after New Year's."

Candace was stunned. "New Year's this year?" she asked. Jameson shook her head sheepishly. "Jameson, are you telling me you have been keeping that ring since our first month together?" Candace asked. Jameson shrugged. "You're serious."

Jameson sat down across from Candace and sighed. "I

don't know. I just knew someday I would need it. I just didn't know when that someday would be."

Candace laughed. "You are a hopeless romantic, Jameson Reid."

"Not really. I knew it would be a while. I thought about asking you on the Fourth of July. That's when I had the fortune cookie made."

Candace grinned. "Really?"

"Yeah. I chickened out."

"Why?"

"Why? What would you have said?" Jameson wondered.

"I would have said the same thing I said last night."

"Really?" Jameson was surprised. "We'd only been together six months."

"This from the woman who buys an engagement ring the week after she sleeps with someone for the first time," Candace laughed.

"Good point. Remind me never to debate you."

Candace laughed again. "Does anyone know?"

"That I bought the ring?" Jameson asked. "No. What do you think the kids will say?"

"I doubt they will be surprised. What about your family?"

Jameson rolled her eyes. "My mother will be delirious. Not only is her daughter getting married but she's marrying a Democrat, who happens to be a senator. She'll probably want a red, white, and blue themed wedding," she laughed.

"What about you?" Candace wondered. "You said you fell asleep thinking about weddings. What were you thinking?"

"Me? That's your department. You handle my mother, and Dana and the kids," Jameson said. "As long as you show up, it doesn't matter to me. Whatever you want is fine. I just want to marry you. It could be us at City Hall for all I care."

"No wedding fantasies?"

"I didn't say that," Jameson winked.

"You're impossible," Candace laughed.

"What do you want to do? When do you want to? Not that I am pushing. I don't want you to think…"

"Jameson, relax. I would marry you today," Candace said. She sighed thoughtfully.

"But?"

"There's no but," Candace said.

"Uh-huh."

"There's not. There are realities. Some that I don't like," Candace explained. "The press will grab onto this. We have to decide how we want to handle that. Do we try and do it quietly or do we just put it out there?" she continued. "If I decide to run…Well, they will want to make it a publicity plus," she said with a groan.

Jameson shrugged. "Will it help you? If you run, I mean."

"Probably," Candace admitted.

"Okay."

"Okay?" Candace questioned.

"Yeah. God knows I have no other way to help you."

"That's not true," Candace said flatly. "This is *our* life, Jameson. I don't want you to think our marriage is a publicity stunt."

"You worry too much about me," Jameson said. "I don't care what people think, Candace. They can all still believe you hate cats. I know the truth."

Candace rolled her eyes. "I still don't know what I want to do," she said honestly.

"About running or about a wedding?"

Candace smiled. "I would like to do that here," Candace said.

"The wedding?" Candace nodded. "And?" Jameson asked.

"And, I would like it simple and small. You, me, the kids, your family…Maybe a few close friends. No Politicos, no press, no dignitaries," Candace said. "As far as when, I guess I would say when it is a little warmer. And, when Marianne and Rick can be here with Spencer."

"So much for all is quiet on the home front. When do you want to tell them?" Jameson asked.

"How about now?" Candace suggested.

"Now?" Jameson coughed.

"No time like the present," Candace said. Jameson turned pale. "I thought you didn't care what people thought."

"Your kids aren't people," Jameson said. Candace raised an eyebrow. "You know what I mean!"

"Okay. How about we start with the easy ones. Why don't we see if Shell and your parents are available for dinner tomorrow?"

Jameson took a deep breath. "They're going to think something is up."

"Something is up," Candace laughed. "Second thoughts?"

"No. Can't we just go to Vegas and then tell them? It worked for Kelly Ripa and Bette Midler."

Candace shook her head. "Kelly Ripa and Bette Midler? Do I want to know how you know that?"

"I don't need tabloids. Melanie is like E! on steroids."

"I see. Well, I don't think those are the best models for us."

"I was afraid you would say that."

"Would you feel better if Pearl came tomorrow?" Candace asked knowingly. Jameson nodded. "Your protector," she chuckled.

"Pearl is everyone's protector," Jameson said.

"That she is," Candace agreed before making her way to the sink.

"Candace?" Jameson began. Candace turned and raised her brow. "Would you really let me adopt Jinx?"

"Lunatic."

"That will make you Mrs. Lunatic," Jameson quipped.

Candace picked up a dishtowel and tossed it at Jameson. "I guess they call it committed for a reason," she said.

"So? What is going on?" Michelle asked pointedly.

"What makes you think anything is going on?" Candace asked as straight faced as she could manage.

"Umm…Besides the fact that J.D. keeps finding reasons to leave the room, there is the fact that you have casually kept your hand hidden this whole time. Nice ring, Mom," Michelle laughed.

"Shell," Candace whispered.

"Oh, I know. Mum is the word until J.D.'s folks and Grandma Pearl get here. You do know that you can't walk around with your hand in your pocket all afternoon," she laughed.

"Sometimes, Shell, if I didn't know better, I would swear you and Jameson were related," Candace commented.

"Will be soon enough!" Michelle responded.

"Will be what soon enough?" Maureen Reid asked as she entered the living room with Jameson, Duncan, and Pearl.

Jameson looked at Candace curiously and Candace shrugged. Michelle was trying not to laugh. Jameson rolled her eyes. "Why don't you guys have a seat?" she suggested. "I'll go grab a bottle of wine and we can relax before dinner."

Pearl looked at Jameson and crossed her arms. "You'll go get the wine?"

"Well, yeah. You are guests…"

"Sit down, Jameson," Pearl ordered. Jameson sighed and took a seat between Candace and Michelle. Michelle could no longer hold back her amusement and feebly attempted to conceal her growing smirk with her hand.

Jameson looked at Candace and then at Michelle. "Busted?" she whispered to Michelle.

Michelle nodded "Nice ring, though," she whispered back just as Candace lightly smacked Jameson's knee.

"What was that for?" Jameson asked Candace.

"All right, you two," Pearl interceded before Candace could respond. "First off, I have not been a guest in this house in more than forty years. Impromptu family dinners. Jameson wants Candace drinking wine at three in the afternoon. Shell is giggling like a school girl. Quit whispering. Who died? Who is pregnant or who is getting married?"

"Shell! You're pregnant?" Jameson asked excitedly.

"Yeah, and the Pope is a Jewish lesbian," Michelle quipped.

Candace looked a Jameson. "Face it, honey, we are…"

"Busted," Michelle said.

"Am I the only one who is lost here?" Maureen asked.

Jameson took a deep breath and then took Candace's hand. "Sorry, Mom. Okay…The thing is, I asked Candace to marry me."

"And she said yes?" Maureen responded.

"Yes, she said yes!" Jameson answered. Candace laughed.

"About time," Pearl said. Her smile belied the firmness in her voice. Candace looked at Pearl and shook her head.

"J.D., when?" Maureen asked.

"When what?"

"When are you getting married?" her mother inquired.

"We haven't decided that yet," Candace answered honestly.

"Yeah. We still have to tell Marianne and Jonah," Jameson said quietly. She felt Candace squeeze her hand in reassurance.

"Don't sweat it, J.D.," Michelle said. "Marianne will be

fine. It's not like you got Mom pregnant or anything. Although, I'm sure you tried," she whispered not so softly in Jameson's ear.

Jameson rolled her eyes. "I'm never going to live that down, am I?"

"Well, at least it will be legal now," Maureen said.

"Mom!" Jameson scolded her mother.

"You mentioned wine?" Candace asked. "I think I could use a glass now."

Pearl chuckled and followed Candace into the kitchen. She watched as Candace grabbed a bottle of white wine and began opening it. "So, let's see it."

Candace smiled and made her way to Pearl. She held out her hand so Pearl could see the ring Jameson had given her. Pearl was markedly quiet. "Pearl?"

"She is really something," Pearl said emotionally.

"Yes, she is."

"Candy, you don't recognize that ring, do you?" Pearl asked.

"What are you talking about?" Candace asked.

"Come with me." Pearl led Candace into the study and retrieved an old photo album. "I wondered why she asked me about that."

"Asked you about what?" Candace wondered.

Pearl pointed to a picture in the album. Candace squinted without her glasses of bring the picture into focus. It was a photo of her Granddad and her Grandma when they were first married. "I don't…" Pearl sighed and flipped another few pages forward. She pointed to another photo. "Oh my God," Candace gasped. She looked at her ring. "This is almost exactly the same as Grandma's ring."

Pearl nodded. "You can't really tell what kind of stone it is. I wondered why Jameson asked me that. But, you know Jameson. She's curious about everything. She'd asked about the color of the wallpaper, what type of cigars your granddad smoked, every detail she could think of. I told her the story about the time you dressed up in your grandma's wedding dress. How she found you and told you that one day you would find someone just as special as she did. You swore you'd marry someone just like your granddad," Pearl laughed. "She loves hearing those stories about you, you know? I should have known," Pearl mused. Candace's eyes had drifted to her ring.

"Hey," Jameson's voice called from the door. "I wondered what happened to you two. What are you doing in here? I thought you went to get some wine." Candace walked to Jameson and put her arms around Jameson's neck. "What did I do?" Jameson asked curiously. "And, was it a good thing?"

"I love you," Candace answered. Jameson looked at Pearl in confusion. "What? You don't believe me?" Candace asked. "I'm an idiot," she said.

"What are you talking about?" Jameson wondered.

"The ring, Jameson. I'm so sorry. I didn't even notice it was…"

Jameson kissed Candace sweetly. "Well, it isn't exactly the same. Pearl told me that your grandmother always wanted you to have it, but your mother and father gave it to David to give to Carol. I know it's not the same."

"No, it's even better," Candace said with a kiss.

"I'm going to go get that wine," Pearl said. "I trust you will be right behind me?" Jameson nodded. "Good. As fascinating as I find Shell's tale of the fireworks on the Fourth of July, I would prefer you wait until after I leave for a repeat performance," she said as she walked out the door.

Candace collapsed her head on Jameson's shoulder. "Why doesn't she just rent a billboard?"

"Well, look at the bright side. If you run for governor you could save a lot of money and just hire Shell for your campaign," Jameson suggested. "She certainly knows how to get a message out."

"Campaign for what? Madame Candace of the Jameson Reid House of Ill Repute?" Candace asked.

Jameson laughed. "Eh, no one looks for honest politicians anyway."

"Jameson!" Candace swatted her lover.

"Just kidding. Come on, or there will be a whole new campaign running through this family before we know it," Jameson said.

"Jameson? Thanks."

Jameson smiled. "Don't thank me until you hear all of my mother's ideas," she laughed.

"Oh, no."

"Oh, yes," Jameson laughed.

"Red, white, and blue?" Candace asked. Jameson just smiled. "Oh, boy," Candace chuckled. She let Jameson lead her back to their family. "Why do I suddenly think running a campaign might be less stressful?" she thought silently.

🫏 🫏 🫏

"No," Candace said firmly. "I said no. There are only two letters in the word, Daniel. It shouldn't be that difficult to understand—even for you."

Dana walked into Candace's office and flinched at the tone of the senator's voice. Candace was annoyed and on the threshold of angry. Dana took a seat on the sofa and listened to Candace's end of the phone call.

"What would possess you to even ask me to co-sponsor this bill?" Candace barked into the phone. She played with the glasses on the bridge of her nose and tapped the pen in her hands repeatedly on her desk. "Of course, I understand the issue, Daniel. I am not putting my name on something that has the potential to empower the wrong people."

Candace could feel her head beginning to pound. Two weeks back in Washington and she was ready to go home. The climate in the nation's capital was contentious at best. Candace had one policy that she never compromised on. If she felt in her gut that a bill would do more harm than good, she would not sponsor it nor would she vote for it. Compromise was necessary to get things done. Compromising her morals was not something she was willing to do. It had become an increasingly difficult policy to adhere to. Lobbyists and donors and worse still, lobbyists for donors, were always knocking at her door. She often wondered who the authors of the majority of legislation that rolled across her desk were. Were they congressional staffers or corporate and special interest lobbyists? Candace groaned inwardly as she listened to the senator on the line. Everything these days seemed it was special interest and little of it served the interests of the people she represented.

"No. Flat out, unequivocal no. That's it, Daniel," she repeated her answer. "That's nice. I'm sure that President Wallace will appreciate your efforts," Candace said. "My answer is still no." Dana looked over at Candace and Candace shook her head in disbelief. "Yes, well, I have not made a decision about that yet. That has no bearing at all on my answer. Yes. You as well, Senator." Candace hung up the phone and rolled her eyes. "Nitwit."

"Senator Barker?" Dana guessed.

"Senator Nitwit," Candace corrected. "What is it with these men? Do they not understand when a woman says no, she means no?"

"Are we still talking about legislation here?" Dana asked.

"Yes…and no. I'm tired of it, Dana, the lack of respect. Half these guys couldn't pass a fifth-grade history test and they treat the handful of us women as if we are their wives or worse still, daughters. I am not Senator Barker's wife. Talking to me like I am a teenager who hasn't learned about the birds and the bees! He'd better watch himself before he gets stung on the ass. I could teach him a thing or two about birds and bees."

Dana couldn't help herself. She erupted in a fit of laughter. Candace tossed her glasses on the desk and chuckled. "Birds and bees, Senator?" Dana was laughing so hard she began to cry.

"Senator Fletcher," the office intercom beckoned.

"Yes, Susan?" Candace replied through a few giggles.

"There is a delivery here for you," Susan said.

"That's fine, Susan. Bring it in," Candace said. She looked back at Dana and they started laughing again.

"Whose office did you two toilet paper?" an amused voice inquired from the doorway. Candace and Dana both turned in surprise.

"Jameson?" Candace asked in disbelief. Jameson just smiled. "What are you doing here?"

"Nice to see you too, Senator Fletcher," Jameson responded.

"Well, get in here," Candace said.

"Dana," Jameson greeted her friend. "Sorry, if I am interrupting something important," Jameson said playfully.

"No, your fiancée was just explaining the birds and the bees," Dana replied.

Jameson looked at Candace suspiciously. ""Environmental legislation?" she asked.

"Cute," Candace laughed. "Not exactly." Candace stood and greeted Jameson with a hug. "Now, really…What are you doing in Washington?"

"I have a meeting in Baltimore at three. Thought I might be able to lobby you for dinner?"

"No lobbying necessary. When did this all happen?" Candace asked.

"Just this morning. Bryan was supposed to make the trip. I figured we could save on the hotel expense if I came instead."

"I see," Candace said.

"So…Dinner in Georgetown? Dana, would you like to join us?" Jameson asked.

"Davey has his first T-Ball game," Dana said.

"That will probably be more exciting than dinner in Georgetown," Candace commented.

"Maybe. You think Senator Barker is bad? You should see some of these parents," Dana groaned.

Candace laughed. "I have every confidence you will put them all in line if necessary."

"True. It's what I do," Dana agreed.

"All right," Jameson began, "sorry to pop in and out. I need to get going. Have to catch a train." She leaned in and kissed Candace on the cheek. "Meet you here later?"

"Actually, how about we meet at Martin's? Say around six-thirty?" Candace suggested.

"See you then. Wish Davey luck for me," Jameson said to Dana.

Dana waited until Jameson had closed the door and then turned to Candace. "What was that all about?"

Candace sighed. "I don't know. Something is on her mind."

"Maybe she just missed you," Dana suggested.

"Oh, I am sure she misses me. That's not why she came down here. She's up to something."

"Well, at least you know it isn't for a proposal," Dana offered.

"At least not marriage," Candace laughed.

"Come on, Candy. You know J.D. She hates being away from you. What could she possibly have up her sleeve?"

"Dana, in the last year Jameson has convinced me to take a lover twenty years my junior. I have gotten engaged when I swore I would never marry again and remodel my entire home. And, even more unbelievably, I have allowed a cat to keep residence in that home. What does she have up her sleeve? God only knows," Candace said.

"She's good for you," Dana said flatly.

"Yes, I know," Candace admitted. "I just hope I am as good for her."

Dana smiled. "Still twirling this governor race around in your head? Stop worrying, Candy. I've known J.D. since we were barely twenty. She's never been happier. And, J.D. is tough. I've always admired that in her, the way things roll off her."

Candace offered Dana a weak smile. She believed that Jameson was happy. She also knew Jameson was a determined person. Jameson was hardly tough. Jameson was the most sensitive person Candace had ever known. Candace was aware that most people saw the humorous Jameson, the professional Jameson. They knew J.D. Reid. Candace loved J.D. but she was in love with Jameson. Jameson was the person underneath the exterior, much like Candace was the woman behind Senator Fletcher. Jameson's appearance in Washington meant something was on her mind. Candace was eager to find out exactly what that might be. She sighed and looked at Dana. "Let's get down to business. Seems we both have important dates tonight."

🐎 🐎 🐎

"How was your meeting?" Candace asked Jameson.

"Fine," Jameson responded. "Typical. Nothing out of the ordinary."

"Uh-huh. You flew down here for a typical meeting to save money on a hotel?"

"I flew down here to see you," Jameson said taking a sip of her wine. "I missed you." Candace looked across at Jameson doubtfully. "What? I did miss you."

"I know. That isn't why you are here. What's going on?" Candace asked.

"Candy?" a voice startled Candace from behind her.

Candace saw Jameson's expression fall and turned to the sound of the voice. "Jessica?"

Jessica Stearns smiled at her former partner. "It's been a while," she said softly as she made her way to stand beside Candace and Jameson's table.

"What are you doing in Washington?" Candace asked.

"I do still have friends here, Candy," Jessica chuckled.

Candace sighed. "I didn't mean it the way..."

"I know," Jessica said a bit sadly. She extended her hand to Jameson.

"Oh, God, I'm sorry. Jameson Reid meet Jessica Stearns," Candace made the formal introduction.

"Nice to meet you," Jameson said cordially.

"I hear congratulations are in order," Jessica offered. Candace smiled a bit uncomfortably. She had not seen her former lover in over two years, not even in passing.

Jameson watched the exchange between Candace and Jessica with interest. She had heard stories and opinions about the infamous Jessica Stearns from all of Candace's children, Dana, and even Pearl. Candace never spoke ill of Jessica in spite of the scandal Jessica's affair had caused. That was not Candace's way. She had moved on. Jessica had been part of her life, an important part. Jameson often wondered about the woman who had shared Candace's life before her. She wondered how anyone could be foolish enough to let Candace go.

Jessica was every bit as attractive and polished as Jameson would have expected. She also noted the genuine affection in Jessica's eyes as she looked at Candace. Jameson had never given any thought to the likelihood that she would eventually confront this part of Candace's past. She'd met Candace's ex-husband a handful of times. That had been inevitable. They shared three children. To her surprise, she had been relaxed in his presence. He and Candace had been apart for many years. Their divorce was amicable. While Jameson was certain there was no animosity between them, she also recognized there was also little emotion at all. Jessica was different. Candace had loved her once. Jameson understood that. Jessica had hurt Candace deeply. Jameson knew that as well. She smiled at Candace when Candace grasped her hand.

"Yes," Candace said to Jessica. She smiled at Jameson and turned back to her former lover. "Thank you."

Jessica nodded. "I hear you might be spending less time here shortly," she said to Candace. Candace sighed. "You are going to run, aren't you?"

"I'm not sure yet," Candace answered.

Jessica looked at her curiously then looked at Jameson and nodded. "How are the kids?" she asked with genuine interest.

"Good," Candace beamed. "How about you?"

"The same," Jessica said. "Work, work and more work."

Candace laughed lightly. "Comforting to know some things don't ever change," she teased.

Jessica looked at Jameson. "And, some things do," she said. "I've taken enough of your time," she said.

Jameson surprised herself with her words. "Why don't you at least join us for a drink while you wait for your table?" Candace looked at Jameson in disbelief.

"I would love to, but I have someone waiting for me," Jessica said with a gesture to the far corner of the restaurant where an attractive woman was watching their table curiously.

Candace smiled. "How is Monica?"

"She's Monica," Jessica laughed. Jameson noted the mischievous glint that mingled with remorse in Jessica's eye. "It was good to see you, Candy. And, to meet you, Jameson," she said sincerely. She leaned in and placed a friendly kiss on Candace's cheek. "I'm happy for you, Candy," she whispered. Candace nodded and watched Jessica make her way across the restaurant.

"You okay?" Jameson asked.

Candace turned back to Jameson and smiled. "Sorry about that."

"Don't be," Jameson said sincerely. "Are you sure you are all right? We can go if…"

"I'm all right," Candace promised. "It was a little awkward, but in a way I'm glad it's over."

"You mean seeing Jessica again or her seeing you with me?"

"Both," Candace replied honestly.

"She seems very nice," Jameson said quietly.

"She's a good person, Jameson. She just isn't good for me."

Jameson sipped her wine and let her gaze drift back across the room to where Jessica was seated with her partner. This was not how she had planned the evening. She didn't feel any jealousy, which surprised her a bit. She did wonder what was going through Candace's mind. Jameson was not one to push. She resigned herself to letting her questions lie at least for the moment. She smiled when she saw Jessica glance her way. "Your loss, my gain," she thought silently.

"What are you grinning about?" Candace asked.

"Nothing," Jameson said. "Just enjoying my wine."

"Mm…You are terrible at hiding things, you know?"

"Not true. I hid that ring for over a year," Jameson reminded her lover.

"I guess you did. Anything I else I should go snooping for?" Candace asked. Jameson just shrugged. "Just so long as it's not another cat," Candace said.

"No. No new additions without prior notice," Jameson replied with a wink.

"I'll remember you said that."

Candace had been quiet all evening. The dinner conversation had taken an abrupt turn to discussing Jameson's project, the kids' lives, and some legislation that Candace was battling with. Now, Candace was lying in Jameson's arms while Jameson combed her fingers through Candace's hair. "Candace?"

"Hum?" Candace moaned in contentment.

"Why don't you want to run for governor?"

Candace sighed heavily. "That's why you came down, isn't it?"

"You have to decide this week," Jameson noted. "I guess I just want to understand why when everyone seems to think you should, you don't seem to want to."

"I do want to," Candace said tacitly.

Jameson brushed her lips over Candace's head. "Talk to me."

"Oh, Jameson, the past has a way of coming back to haunt you sometimes. Politics has a way of making that happen."

"Is this about what happened tonight?" Jameson asked.

Candace shifted to look at her lover. "No."

"I don't understand," Jameson confessed.

"It's not only my past that can resurface," Candace said.

"You lost me," Jameson said. Candace sat up and took a deep breath. Jameson noted that she was twirling her engagement ring thoughtfully. "What is it?"

Candace sucked in a nervous breath and released it slowly. "I don't know how to…"

"You can tell me anything."

"I know."

"Candace, nothing you could tell me would change us. It doesn't matter to me if you run for governor, stay in the Senate or want to come home altogether. I just want you to be happy."

"I am happy," Candace said. "My choices affect other people. I know that too."

"What is it?"

Candace kissed Jameson gently and spun the ring on her finger again. "My grandfather was the best person I ever knew. I mean, he was kind but strong," she said. "I always wanted to be like him."

"From what Pearl says you are a lot like him."

"Yeah."

"You are a lot like her too," Jameson laughed.

Candace nodded. "I know," she said. "There's reason for that, Jameson," Candace said. Jameson frowned at the pained expression on Candace's face. "My grandfather was not perfect."

"No one is perfect."

"No. They aren't. He loved my grandmother. She loved him. I always envied that. I mean, my parents' marriage was more of an arrangement. Granddad, he was always so attentive to my grandmother. It's hard for me to believe he ever strayed."

"You mean he had an affair?"

"Yes. A lengthy one, actually," Candace said. "Back then, you could conceal those things publicly. There were barriers that the press did not cross when it came to public officials. That was one."

"Did your grandmother know?"

"Yes. She knew. He had to tell her after," Candace's thought trailed off.

"Candace?"

Candace sighed. "After Pearl was born." Jameson's jaw fell open. Candace nodded with an uncomfortable grin. "Pearl is technically my aunt."

"I...Does she know?" Jameson wondered.

"She knows. She doesn't know that I know."

"How do you know? I mean, if Pearl didn't tell you...Why wouldn't Pearl tell you that?"

"Pearl would never shatter my image of him—not ever. As for how I know, my grandmother told me just before she died.

Funny, she loved Pearl, just like Pearl was her own," Candace reminisced.

"Like Pearl loves you," Jameson commented.

"Yes."

"Wow. Are you worried about someone unearthing that skeleton? Candace, no one has ever even mentioned that Pearl…"

"Things are different now, Jameson. People delight in unearthing old drama. They don't consider the people involved. They just like the sensationalism. My Granddad, he was a popular figure, a successful governor. I don't ever want to see that tainted. I don't want Pearl to endure that either."

"How would anyone even find out?" Jameson asked.

"I don't know that they would. I don't know if it's worth that risk to me."

Jameson leaned in and kissed Candace gently. "I think you should talk to Pearl."

"I can't," Candace's eyes began to grow teary. "How can I…."

"Yes, you can," Jameson said. "Pearl loves you. I mean…Candace, I think you are the most important person in her life in most ways. I never really understood that, but…"

"Pearl is my mother in every way that matters," Candace said. "My grandmother, when she told me, she was so calm. It was as if she believed it was just meant to be that way. She told me that Pearl's mother…Well, she was absentee. She took off when Pearl was barely eight. Pearl actually lived with my great grandmother for seven years before she moved into my grandparent's house as their 'housekeeper'. I knew that, but I never knew why. No one talked about it." Jameson was stunned. It was the type of story she envisioned as the makings of a T.V. movie. Candace continued. "But, Grandma felt about Pearl the way Pearl does about me. Truthfully, Pearl is just like Granddad. If anyone bothered to pay attention they would see how much she even looks like him—like me."

Jameson chuckled. It was true. She had always found it uncanny, but Jameson chalked up the likeness she saw in Pearl and Candace to all the mannerisms they shared more than anything. That, she accepted came from so many years of being around each other. "I can't tell you what to do," Jameson said. "I think you owe it to yourself to talk to Pearl. She's wondering what is holding you back too."

"I know. I feel like I am betraying a confidence. It's her past. It's their past. I don't want my future to bring up painful memories for Pearl or to taint who my Granddad was."

"Well, I don't see how what you told me taints anyone. It was a different time. Your grandparents never walked away from Pearl. I would say that is a testament to who people thought they were. That they were right," Jameson said. Candace closed her eyes and listened. "Plus, Candace, couldn't this come up some time anyway? I understand he was governor and maybe you think someone will reach, but sooner or later it might come out anyway. And, I think you and Pearl deserve to be honest with each other. You've both been keeping this secret to protect the other. I know it feels earth-shattering. It really isn't. It just feels that way. Sometimes, you have to face the past before you can confront the future."

"When did you get so insightful?" Candace asked playfully, but lovingly.

"I'm not. I've learned a lot this year about that. Letting go of the past, I mean. It's the past. You can't change it. I think it hurts you more if you try and avoid it. You're hanging on to something you can't change when you need to let it go."

"What about you?" Candace asked.

"Me?"

"Yes. You just moved to open an office here in D.C. for one thing," Candace said.

"I would have done that no matter what happened

eventually," Jameson said. "And, who knows? That might prove a very wise decision in another five or six years," she said.

"You really are okay with this?"

"I wouldn't have asked you to marry me if I wasn't," Jameson said. "Look, I know I joke a lot. I know…Well, I know we still have a lot to learn about each other. I think as long as we are honest, we will be fine no matter what happens. I don't think the ghosts of the past should dictate our future, whether that's here or New York or anywhere else."

"You just want to live in that Governor's Mansion," Candace poked.

"It's a bonus," Jameson said. "When will you announce your campaign, Governor Fletcher?"

"After I talk to Pearl," Candace said. "Jameson, this will impact our plans."

"You mean the wedding?" Jameson asked. Candace nodded. "I've been thinking about that, actually."

"Really? What have you been thinking?"

"What if we do it the Fourth of July?"

"You mean at the barbecue?" Candace asked.

"I was thinking before that. Simple. Just my parents, Pearl, the kids and us," Jameson said.

"Jameson, what about your brothers and…"

"They can all come for the barbecue the next day. You can invite as many people as you need to for that. That will be our celebration. I don't care how public it is. If I thought we could get away with it just being the two of us…We both know my mother and Pearl would kill us both."

"That is a safe bet."

"And, I want the kids there," Jameson said.

"You do?" Candace was a bit surprised.

"They're not my kids, Candace. They are my family. It's strange sometimes, but I feel sort of…Well…"

"Protective?" Candace guessed. She'd seen Jameson's protective streak around both Michelle and Jonah.

"Yeah, I guess so. Is that strange?"

Candace kissed Jameson soundly. "Not at all." She laid back in Jameson's arms. "Thank you for coming down here and making me talk," Candace said.

"Thanks for saving me money on the hotel bill."

"You are impossible," Candace chuckled.

"Good night, Governor."

"Not yet," Candace chuckled.

"Eh, gotta get used to it somehow."

"You don't even know if I will win," Candace said.

"Yes, I do. It was in my fortune cookie the other day."

"Uh-huh."

"It was! It said: *Men play the game, but women know the score.*"

"And that somehow managed to convince you that I would become governor?" Candace laughed.

"Fortune cookies don't lie," Jameson said.

Candace kissed the skin beneath her lips. "I love you, Jameson, even if you are a lunatic."

Chapter Sixteen

Jameson was spinning the straw in her soda continuously. Michelle reached out and grabbed her hand. "What is up with you J.D.?" Michelle asked.

"What do you mean?"

"I mean, you call and invite me to dinner like there is something important you need to tell me. Now that we are here, you seem more interested in the contents of that glass than me," Michelle observed.

"I'm sorry."

"What's wrong J.D.? You and Mom have a fight or something?"

Jameson snickered. "No, not this week anyway."

"Do you guys ever fight?" Michelle asked, curious to know the answer.

"Sometimes. Not actually fight, I guess—disagree. Usually, she is right," Jameson admitted.

"Okay, so love conquers all is still the theme of the day then."

"You are such a wise ass," Jameson laughed. "There is something I want to talk to you about."

"You are starting to freak me out here," Michelle said. Jameson had been acting odd all evening. She had barely eaten her dinner. She was distracted even when there were no visible distractions. Michelle could not recall seeing Jameson so scattered.

"I'm sorry. I was just thinking about your mom."

"She seemed all right when I talked to her yesterday. What's going on J.D.?"

Jameson smiled. "Nothing, Shell. Nothing you need to worry about," she said. Candace had headed home from Washington and had planned to spend the next day with Pearl.

Jameson's mind had been preoccupied with the conversation she knew Candace intended to have. That was not why she had called Michelle. Michelle looked at Jameson skeptically. "Honest," Jameson promised. "Everything is good. I guess maybe I'm not sure how to ask you this."

"Ask me what? Oh, God, you don't want to set me up with someone, do you? Because, J.D. I can find my own dates…I mean…"

"Shell! God! No."

"Okay? So, what gives?" Michelle asked.

Jameson took a sip from her straw. "I should've ordered beer."

"J.D.!"

"Oh, all right. The thing is…Your mom and I…Well, I have this…You know…Well, I thought we might make things official in July."

Michelle laughed. "You mean get married? It's not a four letter word, J.D. Geez, I thought you were about to tell me you have an STD or something."

"Shell!" Jameson scolded and then started laughing.

"What do you want me to address envelopes or something? Get the lesbian daughter to do all the licking."

Jameson threw an ice cube at Michelle. "If your mother heard the things that come out of your mouth…"

"Ha! She's marrying you for God's sake," Michelle said. "My mouth shouldn't be a shock."

"God! I'm not even going to respond to that."

"No? Guess my mother isn't the only Fletcher woman who can render you speechless," Michelle quipped.

Jameson tried to respond, but words failed her. Michelle loved to tease Jameson mercilessly. In truth, Jameson loved it too. She understood it was part of Michelle's acceptance of her. Michelle was gloating at her perceived victory. Jameson shook her head and laughed.

"Well…Maybe so, Shell," Jameson confessed. "You Fletcher women certainly are a unique breed," she said. "So, would you be willing then to stand up for me when I officially become part of this Fletcher insanity?" Jameson asked. Michelle stared blankly at Jameson. "Shell?" Jameson was shocked when she noticed that Michele had become teary eyed. "Hey, listen…I'm sorry. You don't have to feel like…"

"I would love to, J.D."

"Really?" Jameson asked. "Are you sure? Because if…"

"I'm just surprised you would ask me," Michelle admitted.

"It's going to sound weird, but I kind of think of you like a little sister. I mean, I know you are Candace's…"

Michelle chuckled. "I get it. For the record? I feel the same way. It means a lot that you would ask me. I guess I just figured you would ask Toby or Steve…or maybe even Dana."

"No. It's not that I don't love them, I do. I feel like this is something I really want you to be a part of."

"What does Mom think?" Michelle wondered.

"I haven't told her who I planned to ask. She'll understand," Jameson said.

"She probably thinks you will ask Toby or Dana."

"I doubt that. They won't be there," Jameson replied.

"What?" Michelle asked.

"Just you and your brother and sister…Well, Rick and Spencer, my mom and dad and Pearl."

"That small?"

"Yeah," Jameson said.

"That's what Mom wanted, huh?" Michelle guessed.

"No. She wanted small. I wanted even smaller," Jameson laughed.

"Better get used to those crowds, J.D. If Mom runs a big campaign you'll be in them a lot."

"I know. I just would rather one of them not be on the most important day of my life," Jameson said honestly. "I'd kind of like to keep that one personal."

Michelle nodded. "Well, just don't lose your voice that day. I can handle holding a ring, even holding you up, but I am not speaking your vows to my mom. That's just too weird, even for me."

"No worries," Jameson said.

"So? When is the big day?" Michelle asked.

"July 3rd. Party to follow on July 4th. Then you get the crowd."

"You're good at this," Michelle complimented. "Covered all the bases. Maybe you should quit architecture and run Mom's campaign."

"I don't think so," Jameson answered.

"So, she is going to run…"

"Shell…"

"J.D.…"

"Your mom…"

"Oh, I get it. It's like Mom hiding her engagement ring from me until Grandma Pearl and your folks got there that day. I get it. Mum's the word."

Jameson rolled her eyes. "Maybe it's you who should consider politics."

"I don't think the world is ready for two of us," Michelle said.

Jameson laughed. "Ready or not, I have a feeling the apple is not that far from the tree."

"Maybe someday," Michelle said. "After I am old and married like you."

"Laugh it up. Your time will come."

"Maybe," Michelle said with a wink.

"Shell? What aren't you telling me?"

"Mum's the word," Michelle said. "Now, come on. I could use an adult beverage after all this bonding…and you are buying!"

"Why am I buying?"

"You're the parent. It's your job to provide," Michelle said as she pushed the check for their dinner to Jameson and left the table.

"Kids," Jameson grumbled.

Pearl sat on the couch watching Candace as she sipped her wine. "Careful there. Jameson isn't home yet and I can't carry you up those stairs," she warned Candace. They had enjoyed a day together shopping, talking, and teasing each other. It had been longer than either had realized since they had spent any quality alone time. Pearl could tell that Candace's thoughts had drifted to someplace troubling in the last few moments. She reached over and removed the glass of wine from Candace's hand. "Let's have it," she said.

"What do you mean?"

"Candy, you can fool almost anyone. You have never been able to put one over on me. Your face is a roadmap to the truth."

"Must be hard to follow with all those added lines," Candace joked. Pearl crossed her arms and waited. "I don't really know how to start," Candace admitted.

"The beginning is usually a good place."

Candace chuckled. "I'm not even sure I know where that would be," she said.

"I know this is not about Jameson. So, what is it? One of the kids?"

"I ran into Jessica last week."

"And?" Pearl urged.

"It got me thinking about the past," Candace said.

"In what way?"

"Just how it has a way of popping up when you thought it was behind you," Candace replied.

"It is behind you," Pearl said.

"Yes, but it can get drudged up. That can be painful."

"Did it upset you to see Jessica?" Pearl asked.

"No, not really. It was a little awkward when she came up to our table. Jameson was so gracious."

Pearl smiled. "I've no doubt. Did it upset Jameson?"

"No," Candace said happily. "I think she was curious about Jessica."

"Yeah, she's curious how she could have blown her life with you," Pearl said.

"I don't think…"

"Oh, she is. She told me so more than once," Pearl laughed. "So, if it's not Jessica that upset you, what is it?"

Candace took a moment and then sighed. "You remember when Grandma got sick?" she asked softly. Pearl nodded sadly. "I used to sit with her for hours. I think I felt guilty. I mean, I loved her, but I was always with Granddad. I guess I felt like maybe I'd missed something."

"Your Grandma was the sweetest person I ever knew," Pearl said. "She was like my mama."

Candace wiped a tear from the corner of her eye. "You know she felt that way about you, don't you?"

"Candy, what is this about?"

"Pearl, Grandma…She told me a story."

Pearl nodded and smiled. "She told you that your Granddad was my father," Pearl guessed. Candace nodded. Pearl smiled more broadly. Candace could transform into a little girl in less than an instant with Pearl. "He was. For all the lies and all the secrets, he was my father."

"I'm sorry, Pearl."

"Sorry? Whatever are you sorry for?"

"For how that must have made you feel," Candace said.

Pearl could see the curl in Candace's lip that always appeared when she was battling her anger. "It made me feel like a second class citizen, to be honest," Pearl admitted. Candace grimaced. "Thing is, I still loved the old phony. And, I loved your Grandma."

"I know. I can't believe that he…"

"This is why I never told you," Pearl said. "You see? That thing you said about the past? You're getting upset over a memory that isn't even yours."

"Pearl, there is no one on this earth outside of my kids and Jameson that I love more than you."

"I know that, Hellion. I know that. But, you can't be angry at your granddad. That was a different time. You know that. He loved me. He did. Your grandma, she wanted him to acknowledge it. I think he was just too afraid."

"Of what? His reputation?" Candace snapped.

"No, Candy. He was too afraid for hers. Too scared for your father's—for yours. He did the best he could."

"Bullshit!"

Pearl moved beside Candace and took her into an embrace. "Is this what you've been so worried about? You think some young twerp might dig out the skeletons in the Stratton closet?"

"It's not as crazy as you make it sound," Candace said. "You know how it works. People are already comparing me to him. Look at my family. Untraditional. It's ammunition, even if it's stupid. And, I won't hurt you like that."

Pearl laughed. "Hurt me? Candy, I don't much care who knows or who doesn't know who my parents were. I know who I am. I know who I was to him. No one can change that. And, no one can change the past now. It's over. All this is just memories. It might surprise you, but my memories of my parents are not so sad. When I lived with your great grandma, I had the best life. Your grandma and granddad were always kind to me, always there for me as much as they could be. When I moved in with them? Hell…I hardly lifted a finger. You know that. Certainly no more than your daddy and his brothers did," Pearl laughed.

"Why did you stay? I mean after they passed?"

"Because it's my family," Pearl said. "Families are what they are. I wouldn't change mine. I like my life. I wouldn't have it if I'd had another family. You don't need to worry about me. I just don't want those ghosts to hurt you."

"I wish you knew how many times I laid awake wishing you were my mother," Candace said softly.

"I do know," Pearl said. Candace had begun to cry in her arms. "Your mama is who she is, Candy. She loved you the best she could. If you ask me, she never had anyone love her, not even really your father. Like my own mama, she just didn't know how to be one. Families aren't always what you are born into. You make them as you go."

"I know, but…"

"There is no but," Pearl said. "Your granddad, my father…He thought you hung the moon. Turns out, we are very much alike—so do I." Candace began to sob and Pearl rocked her gently. "You need to let this all go. Let it go, all of it. You have too much to let the weight of these old hurts jeopardize everything you have to look forward to."

"That's what Jameson said," Candace chuckled through her tears.

"Smart kid, that one."

"She is. Smart, I mean."

Pearl laughed. "You need to let go of that too."

"What do you mean?" Candace asked.

"Well, to me you are still a kid. Jameson is a woman, a grown woman who loves you. She's your equal."

"I know. People are going to talk. You know that as well as I do," Candace said.

"Yeah, but in my experience most of the time no one is really listening. They forget what they heard five minutes before, just as soon as something else strikes their fancy. Ghosts, Candy. All these things you are worried about, that's what they are, just ghosts. They're not real. Just passing images, memories and snapshots of other people's imagination. You know what's real. Don't let those ghosts haunt you."

Candace snuggled against Pearl. "Thanks, Mama."

"That's what mamas are for," Pearl said. "Now, you stop all this foolishness and go remind folks what it was like to have a Stratton in the Governor's Mansion."

"One more thing," Candace said.

"What's that?"

"Well, Jameson and I decided to do a small ceremony here the day before the Fourth of July barbecue."

"Smart idea," Pearl said.

"It was Jameson's."

"I'm sure it was. So, how many people am I cooking for?"

Candace laughed. "None. You are not cooking anything. Not this year. I'm having everything catered. Period."

"I know I'm supposed to know where this is going..."

"I want you to stand with me when Jameson and I get married. It's only going to be the kids, Maureen, and Duncan. That's it. I'm past having anyone give me away," Candace laughed. "It would mean the world..."

"Candy, I would love to be there with you—this time," Pearl chuckled.

"I think you might just love Jameson even more than me."

Pearl kissed the top of Candace's head. "No. I love Jameson because she loves you so much. And, I know that when I am gone someone will be there to protect you."

Candace closed her eyes and let Pearl hold her as if she were still a child. She found herself pondering a conversation she had with Marianne. Sometimes, it was nice to be needed. Candace hated to see her children disappointed or in pain, but she was grateful when they still felt inclined to slip into her embrace for comfort. Sometimes, it was nice to be a child that needed her mother. Pearl had always been Candace's haven. She had been the person who always made Candace feel safe, loved, and protected. Pearl was right. For the first time in Candace's life, she had two places to find refuge. One with the woman who had protected her since childhood, the other in the arms of the person who would hold her for a lifetime. Candace sighed in contentment.

"Don't you get any ideas about going anywhere anytime soon," she warned Pearl.

Pearl laughed. "And miss this show? It's cheaper than cable. No way."

"I'm not stumping here. It's my wedding, not a campaign stop," Candace reminded the group seated before her.

"I'm not suggesting that it should be," a voice responded.

Candace looked at the voice's owner. She'd known Jason Singleton for fifteen years. He was an up and comer in the Democratic Party when Candace first arrived in Washington. He was bright, intuitive, imaginative and driven. Those were all the qualities that made someone an effective campaign manager. Candace admired all of those qualities. Jason could also be aggressive. The line that stood between determined and aggressive was often extremely fine. There were times in a political campaign when an aggressive posture was beneficial. This was not one of them. Candace could see Dana and several of her staffers flinching in the background as she stared down her campaign manager.

"That is exactly what you are proposing. Jameson and I will decide what photographs to release and when we will release them. I'm not restricting guests at the barbecue from playing on their little phones and posting their little sentiments. The day before is for our family."

"Candy, be reasonable," Jason implored her.

Candace looked out at the rest of the room from over her glasses. "Would you please excuse us? Jason and I need to have a discussion."

Dana motioned to the small group that was gathered in Candace's office. She stopped in the doorway and grinned at Candace from behind Jason's back. He was about to get a lesson in Who's The Boss 101. "I'll see you in a bit," she said. Candace nodded her agreement to Dana as the door closed and promptly returned her attention to the man seated in front of her.

"Candy, this is a golden opportunity. I am sure that Jameson understands that."

Candace nodded thoughtfully. She removed her glasses, set them down gently, and rubbed her eyes. She deliberately moved from behind her desk to lean against the front of it and shook her head at the younger man. "This is not about what Jameson understands."

"What is it about?" he asked her pointedly. "You have a chance here, one that not many people get I might remind you."

"What kind of chance might that be?"

"You know exactly what I am referring to. How many people launch a campaign at the same time they are getting married? On the Fourth of July no less!"

"Actually, we are getting married on the third of July," Candace reminded him.

"Cute, Candy. You are trying to tell me that this is just happenstance? You didn't plan this timing deliberately?"

"I didn't plan this timing at all," Candace said flatly. "It was Jameson's idea to get married that weekend, not mine."

"Smart woman. I like her more and more," he said.

"Glad you approve, and yes, she is," Candace agreed.

"Even your partner sees the low hanging fruit here," he said.

Candace chuckled. That was true. Jameson had excellent instincts about many things. Candace had no doubt that Jameson saw the political gain in the timing of their wedding. That was where the compromise of the weekend had been born. Candace recognized that. Jameson did not need to say anything specific for Candace to realize that their plans were, in fact, one of many compromises they would make in their relationship. Jameson was a private person marrying a public figure. She had engineered a plan that would respect both their private world and Candace's public persona. Candace had no intention of breaching that unspoken agreement. She folded her arms across her chest and raised an eyebrow at the man before her.

"I think we need to establish some ground rules, Jason. First, I will accept your advice at face value. I accept that it is based on what you see in my best interest regarding this election," she said. Jason smiled. "With that said," Candace continued, "you will respect that the decisions ultimately lie with me. When I say no, it means no. When I close the debate, it is closed."

"You aren't even open to debate," he said.

"Oh, you will find that I am open to debate on many things. You want to rearrange the campaign schedule? We'll talk. You want me to address one issue over another? I am all ears. You want to align this campaign with a certain group or issue? We'll discuss it. You want me to appear beside someone at an event? The conversation is open. What is not ever open to debate is my family. Any decisions that affect my children, my marriage, or the people I care for will rest with me and me alone."

Jason groaned. "You know as well as I do that family can

be either an asset or liability. Nothing in a campaign is off the table for the press. You of all people know that."

Candace nodded. "I certainly do know that. That is precisely why those decisions rest with me."

"Candy, this could go either way in the courtroom of public opinion. It all depends on how it is spun."

"Jason, I want you to listen to me."

"I am listening to you! You are not listening to yourself!"

Candace laughed. Jason was still young. He was energetic and she genuinely liked him. He still had a great deal to learn. She had spent her entire life around politicians and campaigns. The courtroom of public opinion was a playground. It moved back and forth, up and down just like a swing. You could kick as hard as you wanted, inevitably you would fall back down again. Sometimes it was best to just stretch out your legs and coast for a bit.

"You are going to do well," she complimented him. Jason was confused by the praise. Candace laughed at the peculiar look on his face. "You're not married yet," she observed. "No children running amok."

"No. What does that have to do…"

"It has everything to do with everything," Candace said. "For you, this is life itself. Am I right?" she asked knowingly. "There is more to life than campaigns and elections, Jason."

"I understand that."

"Do you?" she questioned him.

"Why run if you aren't willing to put everything into it?" he asked.

Candace took a deep breath and let it out slowly. "Everything? I've spent my entire life in this world. I do mean my entire life. As early as I can remember I followed my grandfather at campaign stops. I watched him press the flesh. I learned how to work a crowd. He was a master."

"Yes, he was," Jason agreed. "Most people think that he

could have been president if he'd wanted," Jason said. Candace smiled. "So could you, Candy. It's not only me who believes that."

"Maybe he could have been. He never wanted to. Maybe I could be. I'm not at all sure that is what I want either."

"Why on earth not?"

"Because…There are more important things in life than elections, Jason. At least, there is for some of us. There are two kinds of people in this business," she said. He listened. "There are those who are in it to win it. It's a competition. It's a challenge to be the best and come out the victor, to climb the ladder as high as it can take them."

"And the other?" he wondered.

"The other is a different breed. They enjoy the competition and they love to win. There is exhilaration in the game of an election. There is also gravity at its end. They fight for the right to serve. They are gratified by their victories. They are even prideful. That is a necessity for survival in this business," she told him. "But, they are not arrogant. They understand their power is derived from the flesh they press. At the end of the day, they are humbled more than inflated by that fact. People matter more than positions, Jason. When you lose sight of that, you lose everything," she said.

"No one is questioning your integrity," he said.

"Wrong. Everyone will question my integrity at some point, even you. Everyone that is, except the people who love me. Me. Not Senator Fletcher. Not potential Governor Fletcher. Not Governor Stratton's granddaughter. Not the woman on the magazine cover or the morning talk show. Me. Those are the people who matter the most. My grandfather never lost sight of that. His decision to wage a campaign or to quietly retire was steeped in that understanding. So is mine."

Jason groaned. "I understand, Candy. I don't see how this compromises that."

"I know you don't. You don't need to. That's not your job. Your job is to advise me on how to maneuver in this campaign. It's to keep the wheels lubricated. It's to coordinate and create positive momentum around my candidacy," she said. She watched as he began to speak and stopped him. "You will have to trust me on some things. Someday, there will be no more elections for Candace Fletcher. When that day comes, there will still be three children who need their mother. God willing, there will be Jameson beside me. That day might come in a year. It might happen in ten or twenty. It will come. All this will be a memory that is left in the past. This is part of my life. It's not my life's foundation. That lies elsewhere. Whether or not you believe that, I assure you it is the reason I have made it this far. It is the reason I will win this election. It is the reason I even have the courage to try."

Jason shook his head and smiled ruefully. "I can't say I agree with your decision, but I hear you."

"Good. Now, go find Dana and send her in here. You have a campaign launch to plan."

Jason nodded and marched off dutifully. Candace took a deep breath when he closed the door. "It's going to be a long year," she mused.

Dana was leaning on the corner of Susan's desk when Jason exited Candace's office. "I see you are still in one piece."

"I feel like I just got grounded," he said. Dana and Susan laughed. "It's not funny. She's scarier than my mother."

Dana patted him on the shoulder. "You'll find there are a lot of us who wish we had a mother like Candace Fletcher," Dana said honestly.

Jason nodded. He had just been lectured and effectively put in time-out. In some ways, he felt like a chastised child.

Usually, that would have infuriated him. Somehow, he had emerged from the experience more determined than ever to please Candace Fletcher. "How does she do that?"

"What's that?" Dana asked.

"Reduce you to a two-year-old and make you want her approval at the same time," he said.

Dana and Susan shared an understanding glance. "She's the real deal, Jason. I've met a lot of people in this town, worked for a few, and with many more. Candy is a rarity. People love her. People loathe her. Either way, they tend to respect her. Take my advice, listen at least as much as you advise. You'll learn a lot more than how to run a campaign." she told him. Dana hopped from her perch and headed for Candace's door.

"She wanted you to…"

"I know," Dana said. "Go nurse your wounds," she laughed. "I'll check on the beast that lies within."

Jason laughed. "I'll come back after feeding time," he said.

"Just remember, Jason, never mess with mama bear's cubs or her mate. You'll learn quickly how sharp her claws can be." Jason nodded his understanding and left.

"Think he'll make it?" Susan asked.

"Possibly," Dana said. "If he's smart he'll win over Jameson and Pearl. If he does that? He's learned."

"If he doesn't?"

"He better just not piss them off. I learned about Pearl my first month on the job. He's got double the trouble," she laughed heartily.

"You are enjoying this, aren't you?" Susan asked.

"Every, single, solitary second," Dana admitted. "This is going to be an awesome year."

Dana disappeared through Candace's office door and Susan shook her head. "It's going to be a year all right. I just wonder how we'll all survive it."

Jameson collapsed her head into her hands on her desk. There simply were not enough hours in the day. She had four projects that she needed to oversee. She had three meetings that had run long and put her behind. Now, she was supposed to go shopping, of all things, with Michelle and her mother. She pounded her desk lightly in silent defeat.

"See you for dinner?" she heard a familiar voice outside her office.

"Wouldn't miss it. Seven still good?" she heard Michelle's voice answer.

"Seven is perfect," Melanie responded. Jameson picked her head up slowly and strained to listen. She could hear the faint sound of their voices, but they had dropped to a whisper and she could not make out the words.

Jameson shook her head. "What are those two up to?" she wondered.

"Hey," Michelle called as she opened the door slightly. "You okay?"

Jameson forced a smile. "Great."

"Uh-oh. Bad time? I thought we were supposed to meet here?"

"No...I mean, yes. We were supposed to meet here. Lately, there is no good time," Jameson said.

"J.D. you look like shit. What is wrong?" Michelle asked.

"Just tired. I really need to wrap two of these projects before next week. I just have no idea how I am going to do it. Probably going to have to inconvenience you and crash at your place all weekend. Sorry."

Michelle laughed. "J.D., my place is actually your place. Remember?"

"Nah. You pay rent," Jameson said.

"Uh-huh. Like half what the place is worth. Don't worry about me. I probably won't be home this weekend anyway."

"Really? Why's that?"

Michelle grinned. "Actually, celebrating the end of the school year with friends," she said.

"What kind of friends?" Jameson asked suspiciously. "Oh, I see," Jameson smirked. "This is that mum's the word thing of yours. When do we meet her?"

"Friends, J.D. Just friends."

"Yeah…You have that look," Jameson said.

"What look?"

"The one your mother gets when she's about to…"

"Stop! I don't want to know!" Michelle shuddered.

"I was going to say open her fortune cookie. But, thank you for confirming where your mind is."

"All right, so maybe there is someone that I might be interested in. We're just friends. That's all."

Jameson nodded. "Well, I hope it works out, Shell. By the look on your face, you like this woman almost as much as your mom likes her fortune cookies, and that's saying something."

"So? You ready to go shopping or what?"

"Or what," Jameson responded. "Is there a what? If this is a multiple choice question, I will take answer B, please."

"I might let you off the hook, but your mom is another story," Michelle said. Jameson mumbled something under her breath. "What was that?"

"Nothing. Let's go. Your mom is going to kill me for not coming home this weekend."

"I doubt it, but why don't you just have her come here?"

"To the condo?" Jameson asked.

"Yeah. Why not?"

"Maybe. She's been on a tear with Pearl for this barbecue." Jameson said.

"This barbecue is your wedding reception," Michelle reminded Jameson.

"I know."

"J.D.?"

"I'm okay. Just too much to do and not enough time to do it. That, and I don't know how to deal with Gollum."

"Who?"

"You know, Gollum," Jameson repeated.

"Like the creature in Lord of the Rings?" Michelle asked. "I'm afraid to ask."

"That little ankle biter that's following your mom around the last month."

Michelle erupted in laughter. "Jason?"

"Yeah, him. The ankle biter."

"Ankle biter?" Michelle kept laughing.

"Yeah. He's always on her heels and when he's not he's on mine or Pearl's. Ankle biter—slithering around all the time. He's Gollum," Jameson said.

"Well, maybe when we pick up your rings later you will be able to banish him," Michelle offered through her laughter.

"What are you talking about?" Jameson asked.

"The One Ring. J.D. You're the one who called him Gollum. Don't you get it? Do you even know the story?"

"No! I know he is a slithering little creature who repeats himself constantly."

Michelle covered her face and shook her head. "He's just trying to get a feel for you," she said.

"It's annoying," Jameson replied.

"I'd get used to it. You're going to have gnaw marks on your ankles for the next year," Michelle said.

"Great. And, she was worried about Jinx? How can a woman who deals with slimy little creatures all day be opposed to cats?" Jameson wondered aloud.

250

"Well, you seem to have cured her of that aversion. Maybe Jason will grow on you."

"Yeah, like a fungus," Jameson replied.

Michelle laughed harder. "Come on. Look at the bright side."

"There's a bright side?" Jameson asked.

"Sure. At least Gollum isn't going shopping with us."

"Remind me not to call you when I need cheering up," Jameson said.

Michelle pushed Jameson out the door. "Let's go old lady. Slithery creatures are nothing compared to mothers left waiting, and yours is no better than mine on that count."

"Ugh. I told her we should have just flown to Vegas," Jameson grumbled. "One more week. Just one more week."

"Until you're an old married lady," Michelle said. "Look at it this way, you get stuck with us for life. Your ankles will only need bandages for about a year unless Mom runs for president or something crazy like that."

"Oh, God, I'll need a body cast. Let's go. Explain this ring theory of yours to me on the way."

Michelle rolled her eyes. She waved to Melanie on the way out. Melanie mouthed her question to Michelle silently. "Ring theory?"

"Later," Michelle mouthed back.

"Did you say something?" Jameson asked.

"Nope. Come on. I'll explain on the way."

"Where is J.D. going?" Bryan Mills asked Melanie.

"Something about rings and theories. Don't ask me," Melanie shrugged.

"You're awfully chipper. What gives?" he asked.

"You know…When the boss is away, the architects play," Melanie said as she skipped off.

"This place has gone crazy," he laughed as Melanie skipped off in one direction and J.D.'s arms flailed in protest of something as she walked out the door with Michelle. "Completely insane."

"I'm glad you came up here for the day," Jameson said.

"So am I," Candace agreed.

"Did you talk to Marianne yet?" Jameson wondered.

Candace smiled. They had made no plans for any kind of honeymoon. Candace had commitments that would occupy her time only a week after their wedding. They had agreed to spend their downtime with family. Rick had to be back in Austin right after the weekend for a meeting. Jameson had suggested that they offer to take Spencer for the week. It would give Marianne and Rick some time alone. And, it would be one of the last opportunities they would have to make the offer before Candace's campaign revved up into high gear. That was Jameson's reasoning. Candace was all too aware that Jameson loved it when Spencer visited. And, Jameson understood completely that one of the many things Candace struggled with was the lack of time she had to spend with Spencer. For most couples, the idea of celebrating their nuptials with a toddling nearly two-year-old would seem insane. For Candace and Jameson, it seemed the perfect plan.

"I did," Candace said. She watched as Jameson's eyes mirrored hopefulness and apprehension. Marianne had embraced Jameson as much as anyone in the family. It always took Candace's eldest a bit longer to warm to change and to new people. Once she did, she became a stalwart supporter. Jameson, however, still worried about Marianne's opinion the most. "She was concerned about intruding on our time," Candace explained.

Jameson frowned. "Spence isn't an intrusion."

"I know," Candace said. "I think she is excited about some time alone with Rick. If you are sure that you don't mind entertaining Spencer by yourself for a few days when I have to be in Washington. And, you will be on your own with Marianne when she comes back the following weekend." Jameson's eyes grew wide. "Are you okay with that?" Candace asked.

"She said yes?" Jameson was surprised.

"She did, although she said she thinks we have both lost our minds."

"Nah, we can do all sorts of fun things with him. And, who knows when we will get that chance again," Jameson said.

"You sure you want to play grandma for a week?" Candace chided.

"Ha-ha. I get to play Jay Jay. You are the nana. You and you alone."

"Not exactly true after next weekend. You will, in point of fact, be a grandma by default," Candace grinned.

"A cool, hip, young grandma."

"Are you insinuating something?" Candace asked.

"Me? Of course, not," Jameson feigned innocence.

"Uh-huh."

"You are the coolest Nana I know," Jameson said.

"I am the only Nana you know."

"No, you're just the only Nana I am sleeping with," Jameson replied without missing a beat.

Candace attempted her best grimace. It was quickly eclipsed by her laughter. She had been so busy with plans for the barbecue, with the campaign gearing up, and with her responsibilities in Washington that she had not spent much time relaxing. She had initially balked at Jameson's request for her to spend the weekend in Albany. After all, Jameson had work to do. She still had a million irons in the fire to contend with before taking a week and a half away from the normal chaos of her career. Jameson had become and adept negotiator. She promised Candace to step away from all things work related after noon on Saturday until noon on Sunday. It was only twenty-four hours. It was twenty-four hours that Candace now realized she desperately needed.

"Thank you," Candace said.

"For sleeping with you?" Jameson chided.

Candace rolled her eyes. "That too, I suppose," she conceded. Jameson wiggled her eyebrows. "You really are a bit touched."

"We can test that theory, you know?"

"What has gotten into you?" Candace laughed.

"I don't know," Jameson admitted. "I'm just happy. Right now, I'm just relaxed. Not thinking about anything, if you know what I mean."

"I think I do."

"Remember that time right after we met when you called the house for me and came home with Chinese food?" Jameson asked.

"I remember that you had one of your kooky notions that Roman statuary would be a beautiful addition to our home," Candace said.

Jameson chuckled. "It might have worked. Did you have any idea then?"

"About?"

"That one day it would be 'our' home," Jameson asked curiously.

Candace smiled. "I don't know. I do know that I came home because I wanted to see you."

"You did?"

"Um-hum. Somehow, Jameson you have always been able to make me laugh. You were never intimidated by me," Candace said.

Jameson laughed. "Are you kidding?"

"What?"

"Maybe not intimidated, but I've never cared what another person thought of me so much," Jameson confessed.

Candace kissed her gently. "I think you are amazing, Jameson. I always have."

"Really? Always? Even when I tortured you with birds?"

Candace laughed. "Even then. Why did you ask if I remembered that day?" Candace wondered. Jameson's face flushed with embarrassment. "What?"

"I," Jameson started to answer and stopped to take a deep breath. "When you were telling me about Pearl and your mother…"

"Go on."

Jameson looked up at Candace. "I took your hand. Do you remember that?" she asked. Candace nodded. "I never told you this, I think I knew right at that second that I was falling in love with you."

"Jameson…"

Jameson smiled. "That's how I feel right now," she said. Candace was confused. "Like I did at the moment. Sitting here with you, just talking. The difference is that I know you will be here tomorrow when I wake up."

"You may be a lunatic, but you are certainly a romantic one," Candace said as she placed a kiss on Jameson's cheek. Jameson blushed. "You do know that things are going to get crazy soon," Candace said.

"Good thing I'm already a lunatic then, huh?"

Candace smacked Jameson playfully. "You sure you are ready for all of this? Permanently, I mean?"

"Never been more sure of anything in my life."

"Good. Jameson, what about this place?"

"My condo?"

"Yeah."

Jameson nodded. "I was thinking when Shell's lease is up, I would let her buy me out for the remainder of the mortgage."

"What?"

"Why not?" Jameson said.

"Jameson, Shell will never accept that from you. You know that. It's almost paid off."

"Well, the she can negotiate," Jameson laughed. "Look, she won't ask you for help, Candace."

"Why? Does she need help?" Candace asked with concern.

"No. She can afford the rent I charge her. She's not exactly making a killer salary teaching, honey. It's tight for her. And, you know, she had to buy the car and buy her way out of her lease in Massachusetts. It sort of put her behind a little, I think."

"She told you that?" Candace asked.

"She's let a few things slip when we are together. You know Shell, she's got some serious bravado. I've been there. I can just tell when I'm here."

"Why wouldn't she just come to me?" Candace sighed.

"Because she is just like you. She's proud. She wants you to be proud of her. She would never go to you, Candace, not for money."

"She could come to me for anything."

"She knows that. That's why she won't."

"So, you want to help her and make it as if she is helping you. Am I right?" Candace asked.

"Shell is like my little sister," Jameson said. "But, she's also your daughter. I would do anything for her. I would do anything for any of your kids."

Candace kissed Jameson tenderly. "They are lucky to have you, you know?" Candace said. Candace was continually moved by Jameson's interactions with her children. Jameson and Michelle had grown close. To most people looking in, they appeared to be buddies. They were. But, underneath that Candace saw clearly how much Michelle looked up to Jameson, and how protective Jameson was of Michelle.

Candace never intruded. She never eavesdropped. Living

with someone made it impossible not to hear things. She had recently come home and overheard the tail end of a phone conversation Jameson was having. She had assumed by the tone that Jameson was talking to Michelle.

"Things have a way of working out," Jameson said. "No one said you have to keep going in the same direction. Look at me. Look at your mom."

Jameson never mentioned the conversation. Candace kept the brief comments she heard to herself. It wasn't until a few days later when Jonah called home to ask her what she thought of an unexpected research opportunity he had, that Candace put the pieces together. Jonah had told her, "Jameson said everything happens for reason."

Candace looked at Jameson as Jameson shook her head uncomfortably. "They are lucky to have you," Candace assured her. "You have a lot to offer, Jameson and not just to me. Don't think I don't recognize that." Jameson nodded. Candace sensed a need to lighten the conversation. They were both relaxed. That sometimes opened up intense conversations. Right now, they both needed to escape a bit. "What do you say to a date night?" Candace suggested.

"What did you have in mind?" Jameson wondered. "Wait! Let me guess! Chinese food at Blue Orchid. Am I right?"

"Good start," Candace agreed.

"Start? Okay, so what about after dinner?" Jameson asked flirtatiously.

"I don't know. I guess you will have to consult your fortune cookie," Candace winked.

"I hope I get the one that says: *You will soon get unexpected kisses in unexpected places.*"

"They do not make a fortune cookie that says that!" Candace laughed.

"Don't be so sure," Jameson warned her fiancée. "Let's go. I'm hoping you get the one that says: *A thrilling time is in your immediate future.*"

"I have no doubt," Candace laughed.

Jameson held the door for Candace as she walked through. "*In bed,*" Jameson snickered. "I wonder if anyone ever told her to add that to her fortune."

"What are you mumbling about?" Candace called back.

"Nothing. Let's go! I think I might teach you an old tradition after dinner."

"Do I want to know?"

"I guess that will depend on what your fortune says," Jameson answered.

"Oh, God. With my luck it will say: *It is better to be alone sometimes.*"

Jameson laughed. "It has potential," she muttered.

Chapter Seventeen

Marianne walked into the kitchen and found her mother staring out the back door. "Mom?"

Candace turned to her daughter and smiled. "When did you get here? I didn't even hear the door."

"Just now. Rick is taking the bags upstairs."

"Where's Spencer?" Candace asked.

"J.D. commandeered him the minute we pulled in," Marianne said. "Actually, I was kind of hoping that Rick and I could talk to the two of you before everyone gets here."

Candace frowned slightly. Marianne had traveled miles in her acceptance of Jameson. Candace had thought that she was actually happy to have Jameson in their family. She couldn't imagine what Marianne would want to discuss with them. She took a deep breath and held it for a moment.

"It's not what you are thinking," Marianne said.

"What's not what you're thinking?" Jameson asked as she entered the room carrying Spencer.

Candace's face immediately lit up at the sight of her grandson sleeping on Jameson's shoulder. "Marianne and Rick have something they want to talk to us about," Candace said.

Jameson looked at Marianne hesitantly. Marianne sighed. "It's not what you two are thinking. Honestly. Can we just go sit in the other room and wait for Rick?"

"You sure don't waste time," Jameson said with a nervous chuckle.

"I just want to talk to you before Shell or Jonah get here later," Marianne explained.

"Okay. Should I be opening wine or pouring coffee?" Candace asked.

"Neither," Marianne responded. She grabbed her mother's hand and led her toward the living room.

Jameson whispered in Spencer's ear. "What is your momma up to, buddy?" she asked the sleeping toddler. He nestled into her neck. "Yeah. I'm with you there, bud. Hold me. I'm afraid," she giggled as she made her way into the living room. Rick followed her in and took a seat next to his wife. Jameson sat beside Candace.

"You have our full attention," Candace said. "What's on your minds?"

Rick smiled and Marianne took his hand. "You know that Rick lost his mom when he was only eleven," Marianne said. Candace and Jameson acknowledged the statement silently. "Well, it's something we've both talked a lot about. When we had Spencer, we talked about it. What each of us would do if one of us passed unexpectedly or got sick."

Candace felt the breath leave her body. "Marianne?"

Marianne saw the fear that washed over her mother's features. "It's okay Mom, no one is sick." Candace let out her breath and felt Jameson squeeze her hand. "In fact, we are all well. All of us," Marianne grinned.

"Marianne?" Candace asked again.

"I'm pregnant."

Candace smiled widely. "That's what this was about?"

"Partly," Rick said. "We wanted to tell you both first. That's because we also wanted to ask you something," he said.

"What?" Candace asked.

Marianne looked at Jameson, then at her mother, and then back to Jameson. "J.D., we've talked about this a lot. I know you and Mom don't want to have children," she said. Jameson looked at her curiously. "We both think it's important that we have a plan, God forbid anything happened to us. I hope that never happens, but if it ever did…"

Jameson nodded. "What are you asking?"

"We would like you two to raise them. It won't happen,

but it would give us peace of mind if we knew you would agree," Marianne said.

Candace looked at Marianne in disbelief and then at Jameson. Jameson instinctively held Spencer a little tighter and looked directly at Marianne. "You never have to worry about that, either of you. I shouldn't speak for your mom. In this case, I'm fairly sure we are on the same page. If that's what you would want, then put your mind to rest. You always have a home here. Spencer does and so does anyone else that might come along."

Candace tightened her grip on Jameson's hand. "Jameson is right. I have to tell you that I am a little surprised. What about Rick's brother and sister, or your own?" she asked.

Rick nodded. "They are all wonderful. We also know you would make certain that our children know that, that they know their family."

"Of course," Candace agreed.

Rick cleared his throat. "The truth is," he stopped and looked at Candace. "You are the only mom I've ever really known. My mom was sick for a long time. My dad was lost when she died. Spencer....Well, look at him," Rick pointed to his son who was sleeping contentedly on Jameson. "We don't want to impose on your life. We just…"

"Spencer could never be an imposition," Jameson said. "It's true. I told you," she looked at the pair seated across from her. "I told you once that your mother and I didn't have any plans to have children. That's the truth. We don't have plans. Things happen. I hope it never happens that your kids have to spend more than a weekend or a summer vacation here because that's what they want to do. If it ever happened, and it won't—I can promise you they would be raised to know who their parents were. We would do our best for them in every way we could. Not just your mom, me too."

Marianne nodded. "I know, J.D."

Candace smiled at her daughter. "Enough with the heavy drama. When do I get another grandchild?"

Marianne laughed. "Sometime right after the first of the year," she said.

"I think you just gave your mom the best wedding present she could get," Jameson commented. She watched as Candace made her way to Marianne and enveloped her in her arms.

"Thank you," Candace whispered to her daughter.

"Thank you, Mom," Marianne said.

"You really don't know how much what you both said means to me," Candace replied.

Marianne smiled. "Yes, I do."

"What is going on in here?" Michelle said as she threw her bag on the floor. "I thought I was coming home for a wedding," she said. Candace turned and Michelle saw the tears running over her cheek. "What the hell? You made her cry on her wedding weekend?" she barked at her sister. Candace started laughing and shook her head. "Okay? What am I missing?" Michelle asked.

"I'm pregnant," Marianne said.

Michelle nodded and looked at Rick. "You the father of this one too?" she asked seriously.

Rick jumped slightly as the rest of the room fell into a fit of laughter. "Understand our choice now?" Marianne whispered to her mother. Candace just laughed.

"Better be a girl this time. One named Shell. That sounds about right," Michelle said.

"You birth it and you can name it," Marianne shot back.

"The only thing I am birthing right now is a beer. Once I find it," Michelle said as she wandered off to the kitchen. "Come on preggo," she called back to her sister. "I'll pour you a nice glass of milk."

"Little shit," Marianne griped as she made her way toward the kitchen.

"Grab me a cold one too!" Rick called out.

"He meant milk!" Marianne's voice carried.

Candace shook her head and flopped back onto the couch beside Jameson. "You do know what you are getting into tomorrow?" she asked.

Jameson leaned in and captured Candace's lips in a tender kiss. "I knew a long time ago you had a thing for lunatics."

Candace chuckled. "That in a fortune cookie too?"

"Nah, but you fell in love with me. Something must have paved my way."

Candace placed her head on Jameson's shoulder and her hand on Spencer's back and closed her eyes. Jameson leaned back and closed hers. Marianne stopped in the doorway and smiled. She turned and beckoned her husband and sister to the doorway.

"They look good like that," Rick said.

"Yeah, don't get any ideas," Michelle whispered. "Jameson has an aversion to ankle biters. I think you two will have to provide the new additions."

Marianne looked at Michelle. "Now, you know, you are telling us *that* story."

"Okay, but let's wait for Jonah."

"That good?" Marianne asked and pointed toward the kitchen.

"I went shopping with Jameson. Trust me. It's good. Like fireside, beer drinking kind of good. J.D. hates shopping, has deemed Mom's campaign manager Gollum, and actually asked mom if they could get married in Vegas," Michelle said as the trio slowly walked down the hallway.

Marianne shook her head. "Why do I always have to be pregnant when there is an occasion for beer?"

"Don't look at me!" Michelle laughed. "No itty bitties for me. I practice safe sex."

"Shell, you are a lesbian," Marianne said more loudly than she had planned.

"Where there is a will, there is a way," Michelle chimed. She took a long pull from her beer.

"I don't want to know what that means. Backyard now," Marianne ordered.

"God, you're bossy," Michelle complained.

"And you are annoying. Go!"

Jameson felt Candace shaking with laughter against her. "Gollum?" Candace asked.

Jameson groaned. "She really should just rent billboards to embarrass me. It would be easier."

"Don't give her any ideas," Candace said. "Now, really? Gollum?"

Jameson groaned. "It's like this…"

"You ready?" Candace called. Jameson turned and nodded. Candace smiled and approached Jameson slowly. "Still have time," she said.

Jameson shook her head. "I might be a lunatic. I'm not stupid," she said. She took Candace's hand and led her through the back door.

Jameson looked out at their family. There was no fanfare, no music, no tuxedos, not even an expensive dress, only some simple flowers. Candace walked hand in hand with Jameson to stand under a large oak tree in the back yard. She had purchased an elegant, ivory pantsuit that complimented the navy suit that Jameson had chosen. Pearl stepped beside Candace and Michelle to stand with Jameson. Candace could sense the photographer behind her. Life was full of compromises, even on this day. Jameson had a close friend who agreed to photograph the wedding. Candace had asked one of her dearest friends to officiate. Justice Bevins had been appointed to the Supreme Court just three years earlier. Candace had known the colorful judge in law school. Jameson was more than happy with the arrangement. It had quieted Gollum's concerns. Candace chuckled as they stood before the judge recalling Jameson's explanation as to Candace's campaign manager's nickname. She took a deep breath when Jameson turned to her to speak her vows.

"We said simple," Jameson said. "I have been trying to think of a way to explain how I feel right now, today. You are the one who delivers speeches. I design buildings. I have even built them. That got me thinking. Anything that lasts starts with a strong foundation. It is simple. I love you. It's that simple. I don't want to think about my life without you in it. It's that simple. No one has ever made me laugh more. No one has ever understood me better. No one has ever accepted me so completely. No one has ever made me feel safer. No one. I've never been as honest with anyone in my life as I am every day with you. You were my friend before you were my lover. You've become the foundation of my life. There is no more—my future. There is only our future. I don't want a future without you in it. You are the rock that is my foundation. The strongest person I know. The most loving. It's that simple, Candace. I promise you that no matter what, I will remember the simple things. The fact that I love you. The fact that I miss you when we are apart, that you make me laugh, that you accept me, that you trust me. I'll do my best to build this marriage into the strongest part of both of our lives. That is what I do. Nothing has ever meant more to me than building our relationship, our marriage. Not one thing. It really is that simple. I love you."

Candace smiled. "Jameson…For many years I thought I understood life and love. I learned many things raising my children, working, losing people that I cared for. I seem to learn something new from you each day. I look forward to coming home, not because this is a house filled with sentimental memories, but because you are here. It isn't the house. It isn't the state. It's you. I've spent too many years dwelling in the past. I forgot that the past is really just the memories we make today. I want a life full of colorful memories with you. I want to look back one day and know that I lived every second of our life together loving you and letting you love me. It makes me know that I am alive. You remind me in every moment why I fell in love with you. The truth is, Jameson, I fall in love with you every day. Each time I see you talking to Jinx. When you are mulling over a problem at your desk. I fall in love with you when I see you holding Spencer or laughing with Shell. I watch you and sometimes I have to remember to breathe. When you hold me, everything in the world fades away. I'm home, exactly where I am meant to be. I promise you I will never forget what comes first in our life. You and me, our family. That's what you've given me, a whole family. I promise that I will cherish that for the rest of our lives. You are right. It is that simple."

Michelle handed Jameson her mother's ring and kissed Jameson on the cheek. "I'm glad she found you, J.D."

Jameson smiled. She was startled to see that Michelle was crying. Pearl was crying. Why was everyone crying? She looked at Candace and Candace chuckled. Jameson was deliriously happy. She had thought she would choke up. She and Candace had both cried the night before. They had been talking about the next day. Their conversation wound its way around Rick and Marianne's request. It had taken them both back several paces. It was all the proof either needed that they were creating a family. It might have been different from what many people would envision, but it was their family. In many ways, Jameson felt she had spoken these vows to Candace a million times. She slipped the ring on Candace's finger with a smile.

Candace accepted Jameson's ring from Pearl and slipped

it onto Jameson's finger. She held it in place for a moment and looked into Jameson's eyes. "I love you, Jameson."

Jameson brushed her lips against Candace's forehead. "I love you too."

"It seems the senator and her wife are determined to lead this ceremony," Justice Bevins joked.

"Is she?" Jameson asked.

"What?" Justice Bevins responded with a chuckle.

"My wife? Is she my wife now?" Jameson asked to the sound of laughter.

"Yes, Jameson. She most certainly is, so I suggest you kiss her and make it official."

Jameson ignored the laughter surrounding them. She took Candace's face in her hands. "Thank you for marrying me," she said before kissing Candace tenderly. Jameson pulled back and Candace wiped some lipstick off of Jameson's lip.

"You're welcome," Candace said. She leaned into Jameson's ear. "I will thank you later."

Jameson beamed. She hugged her parents and Pearl, then each of Candace's kids. "What do you all say we go enjoy a glass of champagne?" she suggested. "Except you, Marianne. You and Spencer get apple juice." She took Candace's hand and walked off with her mother and Pearl beside them.

"Jonah?" Michelle asked her brother.

"Yeah?"

"Is your tent still in the barn?" she asked.

"I think so. Why?" he responded.

"I think we might want to camp outside tonight," she suggested.

"You can camp outside. It's hot and besides, Mom has people coming to set up at six in the morning. I need my sleep," he replied.

"Oh? You think getting up at six will be more traumatic than sleeping in your old room?" she asked him.

"Yeah."

"Well, then I hope you have earphones. Because, Jonah – some things you just can't 'un' hear," she said with a smirk and scurried off to catch up with Marianne and Rick.

Jonah stood still for a moment until his sister's meaning took root. "Wait!" he yelled after her. "Shell! Wait up! You are helping set it up!" Michelle turned and stuck out her tongue at her brother. "And, you better find Mom's bug spray!" he called.

"What on earth are those kids yelling about out there?" Pearl asked.

Jameson peeked out the back door and motioned for Candace to join her. Jonah was racing Michelle toward the barn and Spencer was trying with all his might to toddle behind them. "Tent," Jameson said.

"What?" Candace asked.

"Bet you a back rub they are getting Jonah's tent."

"Why would they do that?" Candace asked.

"Oh, Candace," Maureen Reid said a bit dramatically.

"Oh, God," Candace groaned.

"I think I might recall hearing that too. Was he visiting last July?" Maureen joked. "Duncan?" she turned to her husband.

"I think I'll go help the kids," he said.

"Chicken," Maureen called.

"Mom!" Jameson swatted her mother. "Watch it or you'll be out there with them," she warned.

Candace laughed. "How exactly do they think they got into this world?"

"It wasn't me," Jameson held up her hands.

Candace rolled her eyes. "Lunatics. All of you."

"Yeah, well…Get out the straitjackets, Mrs. L. You are the head of this asylum," Jameson said.

"Can't be worse than Washington," Candace laughed. She kissed Jameson and let her lips linger. "Don't look now but your ward is on its way in."

"Mm. Can we put them to bed without dinner?" Jameson whispered.

"No, but we can send them outside to play afterward," Candace promised with a playful kiss. She walked away and joined Pearl at the kitchen table.

Jameson waited a moment and followed. "I don't care if Shell goes on CNN," she laughed. "Hope that tent is sound proof."

Jameson moved behind Candace, who was looking out the window and caressed her shoulders. "Watching the kids?"

"Mm," Candace answered. She leaned back into Jameson and closed her eyes.

"Did you have a good day?" Jameson asked as she nipped lightly at Candace's neck. Candace reached for Jameson's hands and held them around her. "Candace?"

"I had a dream like this once, a long time ago."

"A dream like what? That we got married?" Jameson asked. She moved Candace's hair aside and kissed her neck gently.

Candace sighed. "No, a dream that you came up behind me, wrapped your arms around me, and told me that you loved me. I realized when I felt you there, in that dream that I was in love with you."

Jameson pulled Candace closer. "I do love you."

"I know," Candace said. She brushed her fingers lightly up and down Jameson's arms as Jameson's hands drifted upward and cupped Candace's breasts. "I think you might have done that too."

"Oh?" Jameson asked. She nibbled softly on Candace's earlobe and grazed over Candace's nipples with her thumbs.

"You definitely did that," Candace moaned.

"Tell me more," Jameson said.

"Mm. I wish I could. Something woke me up right after I said that I loved you."

Jameson turned Candace in her arms. "When did you have this dream?"

"The day you first kissed me," Candace confessed.

Jameson stroked Candace's cheek. "You were so beautiful that night. I remember walking in and thinking I would pass out. I wanted to tell you the moment you walked up to me that I was in love with you."

"I knew," Candace said. "And, I knew that I loved you…so much, Jameson. So much, it hurt. Like right now."

Jameson kissed Candace softly. She felt Candace melt into her. There was no urgency in their kiss. It was longing, a desperate, penetrating need that went far beyond physical attraction. Jameson could feel the light trembling in Candace's body and she held her close. "Shh," Jameson whispered. "Why are you crying?"

"I don't know," Candace admitted. "It just hit me, just feeling you behind me."

"What? That we're married?"

"No. The truth is, I've felt more married to you since the first night you slept beside me than I ever did to Jonathan," Candace said. She reached up and kissed Jameson tenderly. "Maybe it's just that I know where I will be for the rest of my life, where I was always supposed to be."

Jameson kissed Candace and led her to their bed. She began unbuttoning the ivory blouse that Candace was wearing, taking the time to trace along the sides of Candace's breasts. Her kiss moved gently over Candace's throat as her hands pushed the soft material off of Candace's shoulders. Candace held on to Jameson's head, her fingers combing through Jameson's hair as Jameson lowered her to the bed. Jameson hovered above

Candace, looking down at her in admiration. "You have no idea how beautiful you are," Jameson said.

Candace smiled up at Jameson and touched her cheek. "That is just how you see me," she said.

"No," Jameson replied. Her fingers skimmed the softness of Candace's cleavage and she bent down to capture Candace's lips in an ardent kiss.

Candace moved her hands over Jameson's back tenderly. She was overcome by the intensity and honesty of both Jameson's words and her touch. There was a unique exhilaration in feeling completely safe even as every hidden vulnerability they each possessed surfaced against their will. Candace felt Jameson remove her bra and the softness of Jameson's lips fall over her breast. She struggled to inhale a full breath against the familiar ripples that traveled over and through her. She closed her eyes and allowed herself to float on the wave of desire that she knew would continue to surge until it finally crested and pulled her under.

Jameson was lost in her exploration of Candace. She never tired of the woman beneath her. Making love to Candace was intoxicating. Jameson felt transported into a foreign world that existed only for them. The sound of Candace's sensual sighs, the feel of Candace's fingers as they tugged gently at Jameson's curls, the warmth that emanated from the body beneath her overwhelmed her. Candace encompassed Jameson's senses, banishing everything that surrounded them. She closed her lips around Candace's nipple and circled it slowly. Candace moaned. Jameson continued teasing Candace. The way Candace was moving in time with her stoked the embers of a simmering fire in Jameson. Jameson had been intent on letting the warmth between them smolder. Now, she felt familiar sparks igniting. She raised a hand to brush over Candace's throat just as Candace threw her head back in submission.

Candace could feel her entire body tingling with

anticipation when Jameson began raining faint kisses across her abdomen. Amid the fire burning between them, it felt a great deal like cold raindrops. She shivered slightly. Jameson pulled her closer, her kisses continuing their path lower. Jameson pulled off Candace's pants swiftly and moved still lower. Her fingertips grazed the tips of Candace's nipples. Candace trembled. Jameson's lips reached Candace's center. The cool caress of Jameson's kiss was swiftly replaced with the blazing heat of her tongue and Candace cried out.

Jameson was instantly on fire. She had lost an inclination to maintain a slow burn. She tasted every inch of Candace. Candace began to writhe beneath her. Jameson tugged gently at one of Candace nipples while her tongue danced over Candace and dipped inside of her. She was startled when Candace pushed away and then pulled Jameson up to her. Jameson looked at Candace in concern. She was met with a hungry gaze. "I need to feel you," Candace told her. Jameson was still puzzled. She searched Candace for her meaning. Candace grabbed the bottom of Jameson's blouse and pulled it over Jameson's head. It was the only explanation Jameson required. She closed her eyes as the rest of her clothing was stripped away and Candace's mouth enclosed over a straining nipple.

"Jesus," Jameson cried out. Candace could feel the warmth of Jameson's arousal on her stomach. It stirred her passion further and she arched her back in response. She was reeling from the steady pulse that throbbed in her core. She needed Jameson. She needed to feel her, to taste her, to lose herself in Jameson. Jameson sensed the urgency in Candace and pulled back slightly from her touch. She kissed Candace deeply, a searing kiss that swallowed both their cries. She deliberately shifted their positions, placing Candace above her.

Candace smiled and arched a fair brow at her wife. Jameson's eyes had glazed over and darkened into a lustful haze.

"What do you want?" Candace asked seductively. "Tell me, Jameson."

Jameson was often quiet when they made love. She sensed that Candace needed to hear her voice her need. "I want you while you take me," she confessed.

Candace leaned in and kissed Jameson urgently. She licked along Jameson's neck and stopped at her ear to whisper. "Do you have any idea how much I want you?" she breathed. Jameson moaned throatily. "I'm going to take you someplace you've never been until you beg me to stop," she promised.

Candace's declaration fanned the flames of Jameson's need higher. Jameson slid down on the bed and gripped Candace's hips, guiding her to where she wanted her. Candace followed the unspoken direction. She turned and slowly lowered herself closer to Jameson's mouth. Without warning, Jameson's tongue had begun lavishing its attention over the length of Candace's center. Candace lifted in response, but Jameson grabbed her hips and pulled her still lower. Candace could feel the reverberations of Jameson's quiet moaning against her and it set off a series of small tremors in her core. She took a deep breath and bent over Jameson, gripping Jameson's thighs and flicking her tongue faintly over Jameson's need. Jameson lost her breath for a moment. "So good," Candace sighed.

"Oh, God," Jameson whispered against Candace as she resumed her searching and probing. Jameson felt Candace's hips begin to rotate and slipped a finger inside her. Candace's response was to suck Jameson's clit between her lips for a second. Jameson pressed deeper into Candace, feeling Candace meet her thrusts. She struggled to keep pace with her tongue when Candace entered her.

Candace tried to steady herself and concentrate on making love to Jameson. Jameson was bringing her higher by the second. Her muscles had grown rigid. Her heart was pounding. Her head was swimming in an array of sensation. She could feel

Jameson's muscles clenching, and her legs beginning to tremble. Candace gripped Jameson tighter, her breasts fell against Jameson's stomach while Jameson's nipples rubbed against hers. They fit together perfectly, in every way. Candace's body erupted in a blast of violent shuddering without warning. She strained to maintain her attention to Jameson's need. Jameson lifted up to her and Candace felt Jameson's hips buck uncontrollably. It produced another incredible swell of pleasure within her. Candace tried to pull away, but Jameson pulled her down and thrust into her again, gently but forcefully. "Jameson!" Candace cried out before finally collapsing in exhaustion.

Jameson guided Candace back up and into her arms. She brushed a strand of blonde hair away from Candace's eyes and kissed her tenderly. She pulled back slowly and looked into Candace's eyes. "I would give you the world if I could," she said earnestly.

Candace smiled. "You already have, Jameson. You already have," Candace promised before snuggling into Jameson's embrace.

Jameson breathed in the woman beside her. She chuckled at the realization that Candace had immediately fallen asleep. "I love you, Candace," she said with a kiss. "More than you will ever know."

"God, there are so many people here," Jameson said.

"Yeah…Well, your wife is a popular lady," Dana said. Jameson beamed and Dana giggled. "You really are like a teenager in love, J.D."

Jameson shrugged and took a sip from her beer. "I guess. I was never in love as a teenager, so I have nothing to compare it to."

"Where is the missus?" Dana asked.

"Candace is with Gollum and that guy from that magazine," Jameson said. Her gaze had drifted across the back yard to Michelle.

"Gollum?" Dana asked.

"Huh?"

"Who is Gollum?" Dana asked in amusement.

"Jason," Jameson replied evenly. Her attention had landed on a familiar pair of faces in the distance.

"Hello? J.D.?"

"Sorry," Jameson turned back to Dana.

"You okay? You just went from school girl to serious in less than sixty seconds. What gives?" Dana wondered.

"Just putting the pieces of a certain puzzle together," Jameson said. She looked back over toward Michelle, who waved. Jameson held up her beer and smiled. She watched and sighed heavily as Michelle turned her attention to a cute little redheaded architect.

"Why are you looking at Melanie like you want to kill her?" Dana asked.

"I am not."

"You so are. I always thought Melanie was your favorite at work, the way you talk. I mean, you talk like you love the girl to pieces," Dana observed.

"I do, just not more than I love Shell."

"What does that have to do with anything?" Dana wondered.

Jameson sighed and put her arm around Dana. "Everything," she said.

"You've done a great deal to the house," Don Burgess commented.

"Me? No," Candace laughed. "This was all Jameson," she said proudly.

"That's how you two met?" Don asked.

Candace smiled at him. "It is. My press secretary and Jameson have known each other for years. Her husband Steve and Jameson have been best friends since college."

"And, you had never met before?" he asked.

"No. It's actually strange that we hadn't in some ways. Dana is one of my closest friends." Candace led the reporter and Jason down the hallway.

"It's a beautiful home. It was your grandfather's, wasn't it?" Don asked.

"It was, and his father's, and my great-great grandfather's as well," Candace explained. "I spent most of my free time as a child here with my grandparents. I love this house. You should have seen it before Jameson got her hands on it," she laughed. "It was a shadow of what it looks like now."

"It doesn't look new," he commented.

Candace nodded. "No, it doesn't, does it? That was a neat trick. She's very talented and very thorough," Candace said. She pointed to a light fixture that hung in the living room. "That, for instance," she said. "That chandelier is actually a period piece from the early 1800s. It's wired for modern convenience. The lights come through the hollowed candles. Those are real."

"Clever," he said. "Must have cost a fortune for all those details."

"Not really. It took Jameson a while to find the pieces that fit the style of each room. The detail work took time. She wired that in a weekend," Candace said proudly.

"You mean she did it herself?" the reporter asked in disbelief.

"Yes," Candace beamed. "Originally, I had thought that I would just have some cosmetics done and the addition to the kitchen built. Jameson loves a challenge," she chuckled. "And, she just threw herself into it. Found a lot of hidden treasures in the process in the attic. And, a few hidden issues too. So, the entire house was in upheaval for a year. She and her father did as much as they could themselves. But, work takes precedence sometimes and we couldn't live in the rubble. So, contractors handled most of the structural work, even the painting. Not the details though. She didn't trust them for that," Candace laughed. She led the pair into her grandfather's study. "This is my favorite room. Always has been. This one, Jameson did herself."

"I feel like I just stepped back in time," Jason commented. "I thought Jameson was an architect?"

Candace laughed. She wanted to respond. *Well, she thinks your Gollum.* She didn't. "She is an architect. Quite successful, although she could tell you more about that. I find it fascinating, but I can't begin to comprehend the plans she lays out on our kitchen table sometimes," she said. "Her father owns a small construction company in Ithaca. Jameson grew up building things. She loves it. This was Granddad's study. It's almost exactly as I remember it, only in even better condition."

Don Burgess turned to Candace. "Must be a lot of memories here."

"There are," she responded.

"What do you think he would say?" Don asked. "If he were here now?"

"About his study?" Candace quipped. "He'd probably never leave it and Grandma would never forgive me."

"No, I mean about you. Your life, your decision to run for the office he once held. How do you think he would see his granddaughter as the first lesbian governor? Do you think he would approve?"

Candace took a moment. She noticed that the color had drained from Jason's cheeks slightly. She had expected these questions to arise. She was not anticipating them so soon. "I think," she began, "that he would see his granddaughter."

"Yes, but by all accounts your grandfather was a steadfast family man, and a faithful man in his religious convictions. Do you think he would approve? His reputation and legacy are impacted by your entrance into public life, more so now than ever."

"That's true, I suppose. My grandfather lived in a different time, Mr. Burgess. I don't know what he would say about my relationship although I am reasonably sure he would adore Jameson," she answered.

"Don't you worry at all? Surely, you know there will be comments and questions now. Not everyone supports marriage equality. You've taken a huge step in that regard. It may polarize more people than you think, even here in New York. How the press depicts you to the public and how people react. You've often said that Governor Stratton is your role model. What do you think your grandfather would advise you? Do you think he would be glad that you are pursuing his old office?"

"That's not really," Jason began.

Candace held up her hand. "It's a fair question," she said. "My grandfather was an interesting man, Mr. Burgess. You mentioned his focus on family. You are quite right. He was a people politician. Do you know what I mean by that?" she asked him. Burgess shook his head. "I mean that his desire to serve was about people. He loved people. People first, politics second, press last. Those were his priorities. Things have changed in many ways. You are asking me several things. Do I think my grandfather would approve of me as a lesbian? Do I think he would approve of my marriage? I think my grandfather might surprise you. Family was always first, even on the campaign trail, even when he was in office. He was not a perfect man, Mr. Burgess. He was a man who chose to try to lead. Did you know that he employed more women in his administration than anyone before him? He valued people. So, I don't know what he would say. That was a different time. I do know that he loved me. I do know that Jameson loves me. I think he would see that. I don't dwell on those questions. There's no point."

"But others will raise them."

"True. They will. And, they will believe whatever they choose. Most never knew my grandfather, and even those who did, Mr. Burgess, they knew Governor Stratton, not Granddad. He was part of a greater person. I am not running for governor to reclaim the past. I am running to make an impact on the future. History teaches us, but it is past. None of us can go backward. And, why would we want to when there is so much living still to do?" she asked him.

Jameson sidled up next to Melanie. "Having fun?"

Melanie jumped and then smiled. "I am, J.D. This is great. By the way, I am really happy for you."

"Thanks. What about you?" Jameson asked.

"Me?"

"Anyone interesting in your life these days?" she asked.

Melanie blushed. "Maybe. Not sure yet."

"Oh?" Jameson inquired. She watched Melanie's gaze fall on Michelle and sighed. "Mel," she said.

"Yeah?"

"Be careful," Jameson said bluntly. Melanie turned to Jameson and flushed immediately in embarrassment. "Shell's been hurt once, pretty badly."

"J.D., I..."

"Just listen. She's a big girl. This might sound weird to you. Shell's not just my friend. She's only nine years younger than me. I get that. To me, she is like a little sister, but in reality she is my step-daughter now. I love her."

Melanie smiled weakly. "The thing is J.D., I love her too." Jameson was surprised at Melanie's revelation. As far as she knew, Melanie was straight. That worried her. Her hackles were raised protectively. She adored Melanie, but she loved Shell. It was almost unsettling how protective she felt. Melanie watched Jameson's jaw tense. "J.D....I really do. I didn't plan it. I didn't see it coming. The thing is, she's become like my best friend. I don't even know how she feels. I don't want to lose her, so you don't need to get all mama bear on me. I haven't even said a word to her."

Jameson took a deep breath and scanned the crowd for Michelle. Michelle's forehead creased in worry when she caught sight of Jameson looking at her and standing beside Melanie. Jameson chuckled uncomfortably and turned back to her friend. This was an awkward situation. Melanie was a friend but also Jameson's employee. Michelle was Jameson's friend but also Jameson's step-daughter. Melanie's words had stuck a personal chord with Jameson. No one could predict when they would fall in love. She looked at the ring on her finger and back to Melanie with a shake of her head.

"You do know how she feels," Jameson said. Melanie swallowed hard. "Look, I can't tell you this doesn't worry me. It does. If you really love Shell, you owe it to her to tell her that. I just hope you are prepared for what that means."

"J.D., Shell is not some experiment if that's what you are thinking. I miss her when she's not with me, you know? Like...I just want to talk to her. It's kind of scary for me too, you know? I've known for a long time I guess, about me. I just ignored it. My parents, they won't be like your parents are, J.D. With Shell, I just...I don't want to lose her."

"I can see that. I do understand. Just be sure this is what you want. Shell, she talks a good game. She's really very sensitive and I do know when she falls, she falls hard," Jameson said.

"Yeah, I know. If she hasn't fallen for me, I lose her altogether."

Jameson saw Michelle beginning to make her way over. "Somehow, Mel, I don't think you need to worry about that," she said. "Just know…You break her heart, I'll kick your ass. And, I'm a lot less intimidating than Candace," Jameson said just as Michelle reached them.

"What are you two whispering about over here?" Michelle asked. Melanie looked at the ground nervously.

Jameson shrugged. "We weren't whispering. You just weren't here to hear us," she said. "I need to go find my wife," she said with a smirk.

"That's so weird to hear," Michelle said.

"Yeah, not really. One day you'll get to practice it too, I'm sure," Jameson said. Melanie coughed. "You okay there, Mel? Something go down the wrong way?" Jameson asked with a pa to Melanie's back. Michelle looked at Jameson suspiciously and instinctively put her arm around Melanie. Jameson shook her head. "Don't do anything I wouldn't do," she said.

"Based on Mom's scream last night, I'd say we are screwed then," Michelle quipped.

Jameson shrugged. "Jealousy doesn't become you, Shell." She winked at the pair and took her leave.

🐴 🐴 🐴

Candace searched the crowd for Jameson. "She's over there," Pearl said as she pointed to the pool. "How'd the tour go?" she asked Candace.

"Oh, you know…Fine. What would Granddad think of his married, lesbian granddaughter running for his old office?"

"He'd be very proud," Pearl said. "And, he would love Jameson, just in case you wondered at all."

"No," Candace said. "I know he would."

"You do?"

"Sure. You love her. You're just like him," Candace said.

Pearl smiled. "I guess I am, except that I am a far better cook."

"Agreed," Candace chuckled. She smiled as Jameson caught sight of her and began heading over.

"Speaking of just like someone," Pearl gestured to Michelle.

"What is going on there?" Candace asked. Michelle was sitting next to Melanie with her head on the architect's shoulder.

"Young love," Jameson answered. She kissed Candace on the cheek.

"What?" Candace asked. "Shell is in love with Mel?"

"Yep. Think so," Jameson said. "And, Mel is in love with Shell. Oh, God, that rhymes. Mel and Shell? That's just…"

Candace whacked Jameson gently. "Leave them alone," she said. Jameson moved behind Candace and wrapped her in an embrace. Candace leaned back happily.

"They're cute," Pearl said.

"Mm," Jameson groaned.

Candace gently stroked the hands holding her. "You don't approve?" she asked Jameson as the trio watched Michelle and Melanie in the distance.

"It's not that," Jameson said.

"What is it then?" Pearl asked curiously.

"Like I told Mel, if she breaks Shell's heart I'll have to kick her ass. Good architects are hard to find, you know."

Candace laughed. "A little protective, are we?"

Jameson huffed. "Maybe, I am," she admitted.

Candace leaned back farther and let Jameson support her weight. "How do you know it won't be Shell to break Melanie's heart?"

Pearl laughed. "You two. Why do you think anyone's going to get their heart broken?" Candace and Jameson both turned to Pearl. "Peas in a pod. See that? I seem to remember a similar pair sitting in my kitchen all goo-goo eyed and too afraid to say anything about it."

"What are you talking about?" Candace asked.

"Uh-huh. Nice try, Candy. Just like looking in the mirror, isn't it?" she chuckled.

"We were never like that," Jameson said indignantly.

Pearl looked at the pair and shook her head. "Kids," she muttered before walking away.

"What do you think?" Candace asked.

"About them?" Jameson replied. She felt Candace's nod against her. "Well, I hope they are as lucky as us."

"Me too."

"Hey? Where'd Perez Hilton go? Is he snooping around here somewhere still?" Jameson asked.

"Do you have a nickname for everyone?" Candace wondered.

"I'll never tell," Jameson said.

Candace laughed. "No worries about snooping. I left him in the company of Gollum."

"Ooo. You must not like him much. His ankles are gonna be sore tomorrow." Candace laughed harder as Jameson's lips brushed over the top of her head. "You are a complete lunatic."

"Careful how loud you say that. Perez will be calling you Governor Gazoo."

"Maybe he should call me Governor Reid."

Jameson pulled back and spun Candace to face her. "What?"

Candace grinned. "What?" she repeated the question back to Jameson.

"I asked you first."

"You don't think it sounds good?" Candace asked.

"I didn't say that. Everybody knows you as Senator Fletcher. That's your name."

"Actually, *my* name is Candace Stratton. It was until I married Jonathan. I don't think it's appropriate for me to keep my ex-husband's name. That's not fair to my wife."

Jameson smiled. "I appreciate that. It doesn't bother me. You do what you think is best."

"I will," Candace said flatly.

"Good."

"Senator Candace Fletcher might just be a thing of the past. Need to make way for Governor Candace Reid," Candace said. She kissed Jameson and then leaned back in her arms again.

"Gollum is gonna freak," Jameson laughed with delight.

"Well, he'll get used to it. It'll give him something else to gnaw on."

Jameson chuckled. "Good, I like my ankles."

"I do too," Candace said. "Don't worry, honey. He'll have plenty of little Perez Hiltons' heels to nip at. Should keep him off of yours," Candace said.

"Oh, man…You are Mrs. Reid! I married my mother!" Jameson cracked.

Candace laughed loudly. "Complete lunatic."

"Who happens to love you," Jameson said.

Candace sighed. "I love you too, Jameson. Just remember that tomorrow and the day after that."

"Don't worry. I will."

"I'm counting on it."

About the Author

J.A. Armstrong is a woman, a mother, a wife, an author, and an explorer. From a young age she told tall tales and created make-believe worlds full of adventure and romance. The difference between J.A.'s tales and those that she spent most of her young life reading, was that she never had much interest in those gleaming knights in shining armor that her friends seemed to dream about. She always wondered why the princess required a prince. What if the princess fell in love with one of her ladies in waiting? What if the princess was the hero rescuing a damsel in distress and sweeping her off of her feet?

Those stories were nowhere to be found, so she created them in her imagination, and played them like episodes of a television show secretly in her mind. In one tale she would be the hero, sweeping in to save the day and capture the heart of her true love. In another, she would be patiently waiting until a beautiful woman appeared and carried her away into a new and exciting world. Sometimes she was a famous artist, other times a lonely princess, and once in a while she was a pirate or even a space traveler. Every so often she was a simple farm girl, a doctor, the president, or even a rock-star. No matter what J.A. became in her fantasies, the outcome was always the same, she found her one true love. And that is where all of these stories were born.

Series by JA Armstrong Available on Kindle

www.jaarmstrongbooks.com

OFF SCREEN

Off Screen

The Red Carpet

Dim All the Lights

Writer's Block

COMING SOON

Casting Call

Intermission

BY DESIGN

By Design

Under Construction

Solid Foundation

COMING SOON

Rough Drafts

New Additions

SUMMER 2015

Special Delivery

Printed in Great Britain
by Amazon

Zukünfte des Computers

IIquIIIII

Herausgegeben von
Claus Pias und Joseph Vogl